"Check My Six"

So You Want to Be a Navy Pilot

By
John Schleter

PublishAmerica
Baltimore

ISBN: 1-4241-2829-3
PUBLISHED BY PUBLISHAMERICA, LLLP
www.publishamerica.com
Baltimore

Printed in the United States of America

Dedication

To all of the Naval Aviation Cadets who went through flight training in the SNJ, and especially to class 33-54.

Acknowledgements

I wish to thank my family and especially my wife Faye, for their encouragement and support. A special thanks to Louise B. Wyly, my writing instructor.

Contents

1

"West tower, Whiskey Charlie 414 turning base, request touch and go, gear down and locked," transmits NavCad Bob Bossman.

"Roger, Whiskey Charlie 414," answers the air traffic controller, "Cleared for a touch and go, call downwind."

The Angel of Death streaks over the Pensacola, Florida countryside. Its senses aroused, the horrific apparition in anticipation of a panoramic scene of terror and tragedy, excitedly seeks a distant sound, a rumbling sound that echoes through the air.

The roar of Naval aircraft reverberates across the landscape, as planes claw into the sky, their engines strained to mechanical limits. The Angel of Death bursts upon them, spreads its wings, hovers, and waits.

Bossman lowers his left wing to commence his landing, but due to a crosswind, has started his approach too close to the runway. He knows he should wave-off, but wants to be known as an aggressive Navy fighter pilot, and decides to press on.

The Angel of Death swoops lower.

Vacationers, and local populace, flock to Florida's northwest panhandle near the Alabama border to enjoy the pleasures of this tranquil peaceful paradise drenched in dazzling sunlight with high thin wispy white clouds and brilliant blue skies, unaware of the carnage about to take place.

In this area lay the cradle of Naval Aviation, with its Basic flight-training program at Naval Air Station Pensacola along with its outlying airfields.

Superlative young men volunteered for flight training at NAS Pensacola, to protect our nations freedom, compete to be awarded the coveted Navy Wings of Gold, and to join the ranks of the most elite military pilots in the world, Naval aviators. These young men are Naval Aviation Cadets, known as NavCads.

College educated, two years was the minimum, and most had been athletes and leaders in high school and/or college. Combined with an above average IQ rating, exhaustive physical and academic tests were required. Only three percent of all applicants passed the Navy's flight physical. They were the cream of America's youth.

The armistice in Korea, which ended several years of bloody combat, was tenuous at best. War could erupt again at any time simply by miscalculations on either side. In 1954, America still needed military combat pilots. These cadets hoped to fill that need.

It was 1000 (10 O' Clock A.M.) at Navy West Airfield, an outlying landing practice airfield; temperature was in the mid sixties. An open, square shaped large grass covered field with dual concrete parallel runways, it was the primary field to practice take-off and landings. Those landings that did not end in a full stop were known as-touch and go's.

Bossman continued the approach. His aircraft, silhouetted against the blue sky, was the big yellow colored, 600 horsepower, low wing, tandem cockpit, North American "Texan" Navy SNJ training aircraft. He entered the final approach for landing in a left turn, thirty-degree angle of bank at a low speed and low altitude.

Suddenly the SNJ increased the bank to a steep ninety degrees, its wing pointed directly to the ground. Bossman had overshot the centerline and attempted to get back on line to the center of the runway. He jammed on full power to avoid a stall, and pulled back hard on the control stick.

The ground crew and cadet spectators watching the plane heard the roar of the engine, and with the extreme wing angle and screaming engine, they knew Whiskey Charlie 414 had entered the danger zone.

"Level your wings Whiskey Charlie 414," shouted the landing signal officer (LSO) into his radio. The LSO was stationed at the side of the runway to observe and assist the pilots. "Level your wings or you'll stall; wave-off, wave-off." he screamed as he shot out red flares into the sky from his flare pistol. A wave-off from an LSO is a mandatory order to any Navy pilot to add power and discontinue the landing.

"I can cut it," radioed back Bossman as he continued the tight turn, "Negative on a wave off."

Within the blink of an eye, the wings of the big SNJ wobbled quickly for a brief second, the entrance into a classic stall. Nose first, the SNJ plunged toward the ground, Whiskey Charlie 44's violent impact with mother earth was ordained. A collective gasp was heard from those on the ground as they knew in an instant they were witness to a horrible event, and helpless to do anything about it.

The SNJ smashed violently into the ground and cart wheeled down the airfield. It began to disintegrate, first the left wing, then the engine, the right wing, and finally the tail section. Only the fuselage remained intact after several hundred feet of disintegration. It finally came to a stop, its shattered canopy upright toward the sky. The pilot's helmeted head rested against canopy without any movement. Blood streamed from his face, mouth, and legs, his legs gently twitched.

NavCad Chuck Capp squinted at the wreckage, his jaw clenched so tight that it hurt. Sweat beaded on his forehead. He was with a group of Pre-flight cadets to observe take off and landings, a requirement before they could begin to fly.

"What a mess," growled Capp through clamped teeth to Jim Quirt, his best friend standing next to him. "My guts in a knot, that's not what we came here to see. But that's what happens when ego gets in the way of common sense, and the laws of physics."

Capp was a natural leader. An athlete in college, he was tall, dark haired with a square jaw and a broad forehead topped by heavy dark eyebrows. Optimistic, gregarious, one of the guys, he loved practical jokes, and girls. He had bright blue eyes that turned ice blue when angry, and twinkled when happy. Women said his gaze penetrated right through them. Combined with a dazzling wide smile backed by gleaming white teeth, he was the epitome of what a Navy pilot should look like. Rugged looking, with an air of danger like a tiger at rest, confident to the point of being arrogant, he had all the potential to be an Ace. His goal was to win the award for top student pilot at each stage of flight training.

"It's nice to see your empathy toward one of our comrades," answered Jim Quirt sarcastically. "I don't think he planned on being a statistic in an accident report. He was trying his best."

Quirt was about the same height as Capp and slightly heavier. He possessed a withering command of the English language, which enabled him in any verbal confrontation to filet an opponent to the bone. Everyone who met him commented that he was an Elvis Presley look-alike.

"Don't give me that crap," said Capp. "We've known each other too long. The pilot blew it. He screwed up. He didn't follow procedure. You try to be a hot-dog at this stage of the game, and you die, simple as that."

From behind them came a raspy, insolent voice. It belonged to Pete Pervis, a NavCad who hated Capp, and told everyone that he, not Capp, was to be the number one student pilot regardless of what it took. Pervis was thin, argumentative, and aggressive, with a smile that always seemed to be a sneer. A psychology major in college, he enjoyed talking about death. There was something scary about him, nothing a person could put a finger on, but it was there.

"I heard you two heroes babbling. See that wreckage out there," sneered Pervis. "That's going to be you Capp. You don't have what it takes to be number one."

"Pervis, you skinny, pockmarked psycho," snarled Capp. His teeth were bared, fists clenched, and veins pulsated on his neck and forehead with every beat of his heart. Capp leaned forward, thrust a finger at Pervis's face and spat out words that were meant to penetrate flesh.

"No body, and I mean no body, wants anyone to crash. You're a mental case. Why you haven't been kicked out of the flight program, I don't know. You're a loser and an embarrassment to everyone. Look at what's left of that airplane. Look at it! There's a real person in that cockpit who's hurt, maybe dead. Don't ever say that in front of me again or I'll jam your delusions of being number one where the sun doesn't shine."

Pervis glared at Capp, but didn't answer. He knew he had crossed the line of camaraderie and teamwork. Plus Capp's eyes had turned to an ice blue color.

"May Day, May Day!" the international aircraft call sign of distress, radioed the West Field tower air controller on the emergency 'Guard' radio channel, which was transmitted to the Warner Field tower located at the airfield where the pilot was based, and to all aircraft in the area. "Whiskey Charlie 414 crashed on landing at West Field. Condition of pilot unknown but probably has severe injuries. Send the Medivac chopper. We need a flight surgeon. All aircraft depart the West Field area. West Field is closed."

Captain Ron Smith, the Officer in Charge of the NavCads, a tough Marine pilot, crew cut red hair, a neck like a tree trunk, and a physique like a professional wrestler, turned to the cadets,

"No one move toward the wreckage. I know you want to help, but leave that to the emergency personnel. Let's board the bus; your day here is over. Until then, think about what you've just witnessed. The SNJ is a solid safe airplane, but it's unforgiving of extreme carelessness."

One by one, the NavCads boarded the long, gray colored bus. Slowly it pulled away, blue smoke emitted from its exhaust pipe, back toward NAS Pensacola. It was their last day in Pre-Flight ground school.

"I hope he makes it," said Capp to no one in particular as he looked back toward the wreckage. "They've got to get him out before it starts on fire."

The cadets glanced at each other, each deep in their own thoughts at what they had just witnessed.

The eerie wail of the crash sirens penetrated and overwhelmed the drone of aircraft departing the traffic pattern, as the ambulance and fire truck roared toward the mangled wreckage. It was a race to extract the pilot before a fire started.

Three firemen from the fire truck tried to open the canopy but it was jammed shut from the impact. The pilot was still unconscious, his head rested against the side of the canopy. Two firemen stood on the port side of the cockpit and one on the starboard.

"Pull the red emergency release handles on each side of the canopy," shouted First Class Ray Anderson, a tall lanky muscular veteran from Indiana. "That should release it."

"It's not moving," answered Third Class Kaloski. Kaloski was shorter, built like a weight lifter, blonde and sunburned with a crew cut.

"Get the big rubber mallet and pound on it," ordered Chief Sam Bowman, a brawny square jawed take-charge type, who had experience with many aircraft crashes. "If that doesn't work, smash out the rest of the Plexiglas to make an exit area. We've got to get him out of there. I smell gas fumes. He waved to the fire truck personnel and shouted, "Get some foam on the gasoline by the cockpit."

"The canopy's moving," yelled Koloski, "but it's not releasing. Wait a minute; here it comes. Everybody pull hard."

The canopy released with a jerk.

"O.K., good work," said Bowman, "Throw it on the ground away from the cockpit."

Anderson reached into the cockpit and unlocked the pilots lap and shoulder harness. The unconscious pilot slumped forward.

"Anderson," said Bowman, "You're on the other side, help me lift him out. Gently! His back may be broken. I hope we can get him out before he comes to."

The pilot woke and screamed in pain as they tried to extract him.

The firemen, their jaws clenched, faces creased with sweat, eyes reduced to a slit from their intensity of effort, reacted to the scream by releasing their hold.

Bossman looked into their faces. A look of pain and terror on his bloody face, his eyebrows furrowed, he moaned through bloody lips,

"Help me, I won't scream again."

His body quivered from shock and pain, and he again passed out.

"I can't budge him, his legs are jammed in the rudder pedals," shouted Anderson. "What do we do? I still smell gas fumes."

"Keep pulling," shouted Bowman. "We've got to get him out of here, even if we pull his leg off. I've got a crowbar. Let me reach in there. I'll try to bend the metal that's holding him. Anderson, tell the fire truck to get more foam on the gasoline."

"Roger," answered Anderson as he raced over to the fire truck to pass on the Chief's order, and then raced back to the wreckage.

The Chief leaned into the cockpit with the crowbar, placed it between some bent metal, and grunted with extreme effort. Sweat ran down his forehead and his forearms bulged. He was able to move some metal, which trapped the pilot's foot.

"Pull!" shouted the chief as he levered the metal to the side.

Anderson and Koloski pulled, ignoring the pilot's moans of pain.

"He's coming," Bowman shouted. "Keep pulling, keep pulling. He's almost out. He's free. Get him away from the plane."

They lay the limp bloody pilot on a stretcher.

Two corpsman, First Class Roberts and Third Class Bartok took over and carried him to the ambulance where they commenced emergency medical procedures.

"I'll remove his helmet and cut off his flight gloves," said Bartok, a skinny kid with thick glasses. "Look at his helmet, it's split open. He'd be dead without it."

"Let's try to stop the bleeding," said Roberts quietly. Roberts was tall, experienced in trauma injuries, with a look of intelligence, and eyes that seemed to notice everything. "He's going into shock. His leg is really bad. I hope he doesn't lose it, but it's mangled down to his foot. Most of the blood is coming from his leg, but his hands, arms and face are also bleeding. Looks like his nose is broken, and he may have internal bleeding which we can't stop. Hope he gets to the hospital, quick."

"Roger," answered Bartok ominously.

"Relax, Sir," Roberts said gently to the pilot, not knowing if the pilot could hear him. "We'll give you something for your pain. The flight surgeon should be here soon, and he'll get you to the NAS Pensacola hospital."

A muffled explosion rippled through the air behind them. The gasoline on the ground that surrounded the SNJ's cockpit burst into flames. Heat from the fire could be felt by the corpsmen even at their distance. Luckily, no one was near the plane. As the plane burned furiously, the fire truck moved in to extinguish the flames.

"Look at that," said Bartok. "A few minutes more..." he paused, looked at the bleeding unconscious cadet, and then at the blazing inferno. "I'm going to throw up."

The Angel of Death swooped lower, and lower. Its mission was almost complete.

2

Chuck Capp's big powerful Pontiac convertible turned off Alabama highway 97, on to the road to Naval Air Station Warner Airfield, toward the main gate guarded by Marines. Scrub brush and grass that looked like weeds lined the side of the road, typical for this area of Florida. Bright sunshine, blue skies, and a temperature of seventy degrees, made for a perfect afternoon.

Capp's car was a dark blue Pontiac convertible with a white top, broad white sidewall tires, white mud flaps, enough chrome to make a blind man blink, white leather seats, blue metal dashboard, ivory colored radio buttons, and a steering wheel of ivory and chrome. It was a beautiful car that caught the eye of many a woman, which was one of its intended purposes.

As Capp approached the main gate, he shouted with glee,

"Look at that gate you guys. Through that gate pass the best pilots in the world. And those pilots are right in this car. Get your ID's and orders out, we're about to start flying. Yeahh!"

"First we have to get past those hard-ass Marine gate guards," answered a worried Dwight Munson. "I don't think they like cadets."

Munson was round faced, dark crew cut hair, straight nose, and had a reddish complexion. He was jovial and a friend to everyone. He wasn't out of shape, but food was his joy, girls and flying were close behind. About average height, a constant smile on his face, very intelligent as he had majored in Physics and no one ever saw him lose his temper. Somewhat immature in the ways of the world, not too aggressive, more of a follower than a leader, everyone knew Munson as a great guy who'd give you the shirt off his back.

"Don't worry about it," said Cy Curtin. "They're taught to intimidate, and they carry guns, so don't irritate them." Curtin was thin, serious, and blue eyed, with prematurely balding fair hair. A college graduate who majored in accounting, he liked everything in exact order. He was intelligent, not very athletic, but competitive, as were most pilots.

"These marines really look sharp," said Capp to his mates. "You could cut a finger on their trouser crease."

Capp stopped his car at the gate, a small rectangular glass enclosed building with sliding doors on each side, so the guard could step out to control personnel entering or departing the airbase.

"Good morning, Corporal. We just checked out of Pensacola pre-flight and are here to check into the Warner Cadet Barracks."

"Good morning," answered the corporal sternly. The corporal was lanky but appeared to be in excellent physical condition, no fat on that body. His immaculate uniform was a tan color, shoes that had a shine in which you could see your face, and a fore and aft cap in which the front and rear were perfectly aligned on the center of his head.

"Pull over to the parking area. Go into the security office and register your car." He motioned to Capp where to park.

Capp pulled into a parking area next to a small red brick building, parked, entered, walked up to the long counter top where several marine guards stood, and announced who he was and what he needed.

"Good morning," said Capp. "I'm here to register my car and get a base sticker."

The guard, a short bulldog looking red faced private, looked at Capp as if he was dirt, and said, "Let's see your insurance and proof of ownership."

"Roger," answered Capp and handed him the papers.

The guard grunted, checked the insurance and title papers, opened a drawer, pulled out a light blue colored sticker with a date embossed and said, "Follow me."

Capp followed him outside. The guard walked around the car, inspecting it as if he knew what he was doing, glared at the cadet passengers, verified the vehicle identification number, license plate number, stood for a minute, turned and handed the sticker to Capp.

"Put this on the outside of the driver's lower left windshield. Remove it if you sell this car."

"Thank you," answered Capp. "Can you direct me to the cadet barracks?" Capp knew where it was, he just wanted the marine guard to have to do something for him.

The guards face got redder and he answered, "Follow me inside and I'll get you a base map."

Capp followed him in; the guard went behind the counter, opened a drawer, handed the map to Capp and demanded, "Anything else?

"That should do it, you've been quite helpful," answered Capp. He was going to kill him with kindness and wanted to let the guard know that he wasn't intimidated. "Good bye," said Capp as he turned and walked to his car.

"We're past the first hurdle," said Capp. "No one shot us. I wonder why gate guards dislike us; I don't think it's an act? Don't they realize that in the next war, they could be stuck in a foxhole with bad guys all around them, and we're going to save their butts by wiping out the bad guys with lots of airborne ordnance? Maybe that's too much to expect. Anyway, let's find the Waldorf Astoria, or any reasonable facsimile thereof."

"The Waldorf Astoria; you're a dreamer," said Munson.

"There it is," said Capp after a few minutes of driving, "Splinterville USA; a two-story World War II relic that should have been torn down years ago. Painted a brilliant white, hot water heated radiators that clank all night in the winter, squeaky floors, four cadets to a room, a complete lack of privacy, and one fan with no air conditioning. During the summer nights, you'll lie on your cot with your legs spread apart, sweat rolling off your body, and try to ignore your room-mates snoring. But, it's home, right? And we're here to fly, right?"

"You know," said Munson, "There's nothing worse than a dyed in the wool optimist. At least in Pre-Flight, we had beautiful brick buildings with two fans in each room. This is a step down."

"This makes you tough," answered Capp. "C'mon, let's check in."

They walked in to the OOD's office (Officer of the Day), and stood at attention. The office was spotless. Behind a polished wood countertop was the OOD's desk, with an American flag on a tall pole beside it.

"Cadets' Capp, Munson, and Curtin reporting aboard, Sir," said Capp, holding a salute.

A sharp looking slim, tall, Marine officer dressed in a tan uniform with a tan tie, Naval officers wore black ties, brown hair with a crew cut, flat stomach, obviously in superb physical condition, looked up at Capp from behind the desk, swung around, stood up and walked to the counter.

"At ease. Welcome aboard. My name is Captain Johnson, OINC (Officer in Charge) of Battalion Two. Here are your room assignments which have been selected at random. Evening chow is 1700 in the galley, right down the street. Morning chow is at 0600, and morning formation is 0700. You'll be busy. Get your shoes shined. See you tomorrow, dismissed."

They each saluted, turned on their heels and left to find their rooms, all of which were on the second floor.

Capp walked up the squeaky ladder (stairway), down the white passageways (hallways), the wooden deck (floor) squeaked as he walked, and strolled into his room.

"Good afternoon gents, I'm Chuck Capp. Which bunk is open?"

"Hi y'all," said a large red-faced person with a southern twang. "My name is Moose Redmond."

"Hi, I'm Sam Sibley," said another large person with a huge smile, also with a southern twang, "The hottest race car driver in the south."

"Hi, I'm Bob Marino," answered the third cadet. "And the last bunk is reserved for you, above me." Marino was about the same size as Capp. No southern accent, but a trace of a Boston or East Coast accent was evident.

"I don't suppose anyone would care to roll some dice at the ACRAC (Aviation cadets recreation activity center), for a lower bunk," said Capp.

"Haw, haw," laughed Redmond. "You damn Yankees are all alike, Carpetbaggers to the end. Tell you what, I'll roll for a beer, I'll roll for a woman, but I'll fight you to death to keep my lower bunk."

"I give up." said Capp as he raised his hands above his head in mock surrender. "That upper bunk looks pretty good."

Capp unpacked and neatly placed his clothes into the closet, and wood dressers. Four dressers were pushed together in the middle of the room, one for each cadet. They had a drop down drawer in the middle to be used as a desk. There were two windows on the outboard (outside) wall, opposite the hatch (doorway). A large black colored fan was above the doorway, and one sink below the fan off to the side. Obviously, the first cadet up in the morning got the sink; the rest had to go to the common head (bathroom) where there were many showers and sinks.

"We'll see you guys later," said Capp, "maybe at the ACRAC?"

"You bet," answered Redmond. "Always like to roll the dice and take some free beer from you Yankees. Haw, Haw, you'll get used to it."

"Right," said Capp sarcastically.

He turned and left to see how Munson and Curtin made out in their rooms. Both were in Curtin's room. Jim Quirt walked in; he had driven by himself and just checked in. All had upper bunks because they checked in so late.

"You can't win them all," said Capp. "Next time we go to the beach, after we check in. I'm hungry, anyone else ready for some chow?"

"Now you're talking," said Munson. "I can eat any sorrow away with food."

As they walked to the galley, down neatly mowed grass boulevard streets that could be in any house beautiful magazine, Capp asked,

"Any of you have southern boys in your room?"

"I do," answered Quirt. "Why?"

"Back home, up North, I never heard the words "Yankees" or

"Rebels" used in normal conversation. Strange, are they still living the damned Civil War?"

"You bet," answered Quirt. "They stay together, like a cult, constantly play their god-awful country music, and have a reputation of being aggressive pilots. Most of them grew up with guns and fast cars. They love to hunt, fight, and drink."

"Thanks for the update", answered Capp. "I'll remember that if I ever need some backup in a fight at a Pensacola bar. I still think they're a strange group of people." He laughed, "However, here we are, four Yankees, no Rebels, a Northern cult? Maybe they aren't so weird. Haw, Haw."

The galley was typical for the Navy; clean, white painted walls, floors that shined, and rows of tables in front of a buffet type food setup. Several sailors assigned to the galley, were servers, and stood behind the steam tables from one end to the other.

Capp picked up a metal tray with hollowed out sections for different foods.

"Pre-Flight chow was pretty good," said Capp. "Let's see what Warner offers. I've never heard of bad Navy chow, and there's always plenty of it."

The server, Airman Conrad, slopped a large pile of hamburger on Capp's plate.

"I can't eat that much hamburger and I didn't ask for it. It looks like overcooked meat loaf. Take it off."

"Sorry," said Conrad, a tall thin seaman with a wry smile. "We have orders to serve up all of the hamburger in the Navy's inventory. There's too much on hand. I don't care if you eat it or not, but until it's gone, you're going to get extra hamburger for breakfast, lunch, and dinner."

"Why don't you just throw it out instead of us throwing it out?"

"The orders said to serve it," answered Conrad. "I guess that sounds better than throwing it away, probably a political thing."

"How long is this going to go on?" asked Capp.

"We estimate about a month or two." answered Conrad. "There's lots of hamburger assigned to Warner. You can have two servings if you want."

"Are you kidding?" answered Capp. "I like my hamburger on a bun with onions, pickle, and mustard, not a large gloppy lump."

"Bon Appetit," said Conrad cheerily. "Be sure to come back for seconds."

Capp shook his head in disbelief, filled up the rest of his tray with mashed potatoes, vegetables, and fried chicken, turned and left the serving line, walked down the aisle and grunted as he sat down with everyone at the table.

"Jeez, makes you wonder how we ever won wars with logic like that."

"Bon Appétit," laughed Quirt. "Today hasn't been so good. Tomorrow will be better. "We're scheduled for our first flight on Thursday. Until then, they can pile hamburger on my tray until hell freezes over. We're here to fly, not eat, right Munson?"

"Well," answered Munson, "After today, let me think about that."

After they finished, Capp said,

"Looks like we're done here, let's motor on down the road and check out the ACRAC. It's too early to hit the sack. Maybe we can get a hamburger. By the way, the food here's not bad. What does our local food expert Munson, think?"

"Four-O." answered Munson. "I may survive after all."

"Remember the ACRAC parties in Pre-Flight?" said Capp. "Nothing will ever be as good as that. Remember those co-eds from the Mississippi girl's colleges that were invited to formal cadet Balls? One of them told me, we were their knights in shining armor, future warriors of the air, and some of the best potential husbands in the world, that's why they all showed up. I liked the warrior part, but not the husband. Fortunately, the Navy requires all cadets to be single, or some guys may have bit the dust. They were some beautiful women. Too bad the chaperones were so uptight. Some of the girls really wanted it, but we couldn't get away by ourselves. I got some good phone numbers though, so all isn't lost."

"You've got the world's greatest imagination," said Quirt. "They really wanted me. But I've got to agree, they were beautiful in their evening gowns and perfumed hair. Those are great memories we won't forget, the live music, the dancing, and every cadet trying to figure out a way to, as it is called, have intimate relations. Those crummy chaperones probably could read our minds."

The ACRAC was a bright spot for all NavCads on the base, a social gathering place after working hours and weekends, with tables, booths, a bar, and a grill. A jukebox that was always too loud, along with beer, hamburgers, and hot dogs. Laughter from the cadets could be heard over the total din. Pool and a ping pong tables were in other rooms. It was the place to go to relieve the tensions and stresses of flying. Rowdy songs and beer contests were common. Females were not invited in from the local towns, which at some bases was the practice, but not at Warner. Female companionship, therefore, was a weekend quest into Pensacola, Mobile, or New Orleans.

They arrived at the ACRAC, Capp opened the door, and the music blared in his face.

"Yeahh, loud music, the smell of beer, and hamburgers, my kind of place, c'mon, let's find a table, the first rounds on me."

"How can you even think of hamburgers?" asked Curtin.

"These are real hamburgers," said Capp. "Not that mess at the galley."

"Look at that," said Capp. "That jerk Pervis is here, I keep hoping he'll quit. Think I'll mosey over and see what's on his corrupt little mind, be right back."

"Careful," said Quirt, "He's a mean drunk. Don't get fouled up on your first night here. Get away from him if he's drunk."

Capp sat down next to Pervis.

"I didn't know the Navy let scumbags in here," said Capp. "Where's your room? Out in some pup tent by the garbage dump?"

Pervis slowly turned and looked at Capp. It wasn't a look of friendship. His eyes narrowed like the slits of a viper.

"You really got some guts coming over here. I don't like you, and you weren't invited."

"I suppose you're still in denial at what you did in Pre-Flight," said Capp.

"You're a creep," answered Pervis. "You cost me the chance to be a class officer. Somehow I'm going to get even, in spades."

"I don't know what you're torqued off about," said Capp. You bought the answers to the aerology final exam and didn't study. The rest of us were busting our hump to get good grades. You didn't. You tried to shortcut the system. You bet I turned you in. You have no morals or ethics. This program isn't for cheats. If I could've found out who sold the answers to you, I'd turn him in, too."

"It was never proven," said Pervis. "You guessed."

"No I didn't," answered Capp. "In a drunken stupor, you told Cadet Sam Anderson, who was also drunk, and he then told me the story. He said, you really thought it was funny that we studied hard, and you didn't have to."

"At the Captains Mast hearing, Anderson wouldn't confirm your charges and I was found not guilty," said Pervis. "But your accusation cost me those bars. I'll get you if it's the last thing I do."

"I think you either threatened Anderson, or bought him off," said Capp. "Anderson isn't the type to make up stories. By the way, the reason you didn't make class officer was that you didn't meet the Navy's standards. You're going to foul up again. It's in your nature. I hope I'm there to see it."

"You won't," said Pervis. "I'm going to be awarded the best cadet and pilot at Warner. That's one way I'm going to kick your butt, and I've got a lot of other ideas. You picked the wrong guy to be your enemy; it's dangerous. Capp, you threw down the gauntlet, and you'll pay."

"People are known by the enemies they make," answered Capp. "I won't lose any sleep."

Capp backed away, turned and went back to his table.

If at that moment, Capp had turned around and saw the hate flowing from Pervis's face, he might have lost some sleep.

3

0700. Monday morning November 1954, Warner Airfield.

The weather was warm and humid. Cadets were lined up in four platoons on the concrete apron in front of the cadet barracks, commonly called "The Grinder." Each barracks was a Battalion, and four barracks were a Company. Capp and Quirt were in the third platoon, second battalion, which was assigned when they had checked in the previous night. Each platoon had a platoon leader who stood in front of each platoon. The Battalion Commander stood out in front of the platoon leaders. Temporarily, the platoon leaders were spit and polish Marine Sergeants.

Capp stood in the Parade Rest position next to Quirt, legs apart, and fingers on their hands spread straight in the small of their backs.

"Looks like our first day is one of confusion," said Capp. "We're not exactly combat ready."

"There are four Marine Sergeants and Captain Anderson trying to get us organized," answered Quirt. "We could walk in circles to really foul them up, but I want to get to flight gear issue. I want that leather jacket."

"Battalion-Attenhut!" ordered Captain Anderson. Platoon 1, 2, 3, 4 "Attenhut!" ordered each of the platoon Sergeants. The cadets snapped their heels together, hands straight down along their legs, thumbs on the trouser seams, backs ramrod stiff, and heads facing forward.

"This sun's hot," said Capp in a whisper. "Let's crank up our engines and fly out of here. I suppose they're going to inspect us."

"That's the Navy way," answered Quirt.

"Prepare for inspection." ordered Captain Anderson.

"Open ranks, March!" shouted the platoon sergeants.

The front row of cadets took one step forward. Each row commenced with the Dress Right drill. The cadets turned their heads to the right. Capp shuffled next to Quirt and held up his left arm to touch the top outside of Quirts right shoulder. Each cadet did the same to the man next to him. The end cadet looked straight ahead. It was a method to make an even line of cadets.

"Ready-Front!" shouted each of the Marine Sergeants. The cadets faced forward and lowered their arms to their sides.

"Ready for inspection." answered each Sergeant.

Capp groaned.

Captain Anderson, followed by each platoon Sergeant, walked in front of each line of cadets, stopping occasionally to straighten a cap or a tie, until everyone was inspected. The cadet's khaki colored fore and aft caps, black ties, khaki shirts and trousers were spotless. Shoes were shined to a mirror-like gloss. No negative comments were noted for any of the cadets.

"Sergeant Franks," ordered Captain Anderson, "Read the plan of the day."

"Aye, Aye, Sir," answered Franks.

Sergeant Franks had a voice like a hoarse bloodhound, and he shouted at his top volume.

"Today you will march in formation to the Flight Aviation Supply Shack, and be assigned your flight gear. When finished, you will then proceed to the Aviation Safety buildings where you will complete the syllabus in the practice Bailout Trainer, and indoctrination in parachutes. You will not be allowed to fly until those are completed to the satisfaction of the instructors. After completion, proceed to the hangar area, Hangar One. You will be assigned a locker to stow your flight gear. At 1300, after noon chow, proceed to ground school in building 101.

Captain Anderson walked to the front, "Battalion-At Ease." The cadets relaxed. "These next few days will be busy. You'll be assigned flight gear, bail out of the Bailout Trainer, get checked out in parachutes, and attend ground school. On Thursday, all of your ground training will focus into why you came here, flying. You'll meet your flight instructor to begin your flight syllabus and fly your first flight.'

'For those of you who want to be class officers, the signup sheet is in my office. You must know how to march a platoon of cadets and conduct morning formation. Not all applicants will be accepted, but don't let that stop you from signing up. You will be tested on your experience level. There will be two cadet officers assigned to a room. You all look very sharp. Good luck. Platoon leaders, take over."

"Two to a room," said Capp. "That almost makes it sound attractive. Damn, I'd like a lower bunk."

"Get your head out of your butt," answered Quirt. "We're here to fly, not be a fake class officer."

"Third Platoon, next stop," shouted Sergeant Rodriguez, "is flight clothing issue. Attenhut. Right face. Forward-hough! hup, hup, hrup, hup; hup, hup, hrup, hup" chanted Rodriguez in his rough, but melodic manner."

The four cadet platoons moved forward in perfect order, arms swung together in unison, heads held high, and all in perfect step.

"I love these Marine Drill Sergeants," said Capp out of the side of his mouth, "Each one has their own way of counting cadence. We're on our way, finally."

"What tough bastards," said Quirt. "I can see why they're first to land on an enemy beach."

"Silent cadence, Hough!" ordered Rodriguez.

The Sergeant stopped counting verbal cadence. Young men all in a perfect line, their heels contacting the pavement together which made coordinated sounds, kept the platoon in perfect step. It was the mark of elite marching units.

Chuck Capp made his heels contact the deck hard to make the cadence sound, glanced at Quirt, "Pretty sharp, huh, we can outmarch most Marine platoons. What a team, sounds great, looks great."

"Screw marching," answered Quirt. If I never march again it'll be too soon. I want to fly from point A to B, not march. It's hot. Screw marching."

The platoons arrived at the Flight Clothing Issue shack; a long white one story building that had an inventory of flight gear and accessories needed to perform mission requirements at Warner Airfield.

"Single file," said Rodriquez. "Flight helmets first."

Capp punched Quirt in the back,

"Damn, my knees are shaking. Did you ever think we'd ever get this far? This is it buddy. We're going to look like those pilots in the movie, 'Bridges of Toki-Ri.'"

"That's the movies," answered Quirt. "This is the real thing. Capp," he laughed, "Your smile is so wide, it's going to break your face. I guess you're ready."

A Storekeeper in charge of helping cadets, Second Class Williams, put a green colored fabric inner liner cap on Capp's head and said,

"Looks like a good fit. Don't want it too tight or headaches will be the order of the day on a long flight. As you can see, the radio cords are attached to the left side, and the earphones need to fit over your ears. How's that feel?"

"So far so good," answered Capp.

"Now let's put on the hardhat," said Williams. "It's kind of ugly, made of a plastic type material, with raised areas on the exterior, but it'll protect your skull in an impact. You have the choice of any color you want, as long as it's gold. That's a joke sir, a joke."

"I'll take gold," laughed Capp.

"Snap the straps from the inner liner onto the outside of the helmet's snaps and tighten the chin strap to make a secure package," said Williams. The radio boom mike slides into metal grooves on the right side and it moves up and down, perfect, right in front of your lips. Now the goggles with the dark lenses, pull them from on top of the helmet, down in front of your eyes, you look ready to go. What do you think?"

"It's great!" answered Capp. "Bring on those SNJ's."

"Better get a flight suit first," said Williams.

Capp moved in a line and tried on a flight suit. It was khaki colored, one piece from the ankles to the neck, with a fold down collar. It zipped from the crotch to the neck, with many pockets on the front of the legs, chest and on the side of each arm for pencils.

"This would be great for working on a car," said Capp.

"I'll pretend I didn't hear that," answered Williams, "but you're right. We've got to keep a close eye on these, in fact on all of the gear."

Capp kept moving.

"Let's try on your gloves," continued Williams. "These are the Navy's finest. Yellow colored soft calfskin and they extend up over your wrist. If you ever have a fire in your cockpit, these will save some skin.'

'Next is your plastic kneeboard for your maps that lays on the top of your thigh with an elastic strap that wraps around your leg and snaps on to its right side. Maps and papers slide under spring loaded plastic holders located at the top and bottom of the kneeboard.'

'For a masterpiece, how about this, a long white silk scarf with blue letters of USN on it, yours may one of the last classes to get scarves, take care of it. When they're gone, they're gone. Some day, they'll be a collector's item."

"It's beautiful, said Capp. "Don't think I'll sweat this up. Maybe some day when I'm flying an open cockpit Stearman, that'll be the time to wear it, Eddie Rickenbacker the second, what do you think?"

"I think the flight boots are next," answered Williams. "Lace them up all the way when you fly, you don't want to walk around in bare feet if you have to bail out.'

'And now what everyone wants, the dark brown leather flight jacket with a fur collar, zippered front, flap pockets, elastic waist band, the classic symbol of a Naval Aviator. Even Air Force pilots want these. Try it on."

"All right!" exclaimed Capp. "Four-Oh. Hey Quirt, even you look like a Navy fighter jock. Clothes make the man, right?"

"This is great," answered Quirt. "The final mark of what the well dressed tiger looks like. Now we have to fly like a tiger to earn the jackets reputation."

"Hey Pervis," yelled Capp across the room. "Even the jacket won't help your cause. You should take it off so you don't embarrass the rest of us real pilots."

Pervis who was standing by the mirror, admiring himself looked at Capp,

"You, should take it off smart-ass. You're going down in flames, mark my word."

Williams looked at Capp and then at Quirt,

"I get the feeling the two of you don't like each other."

"Like, is a generous term," growled Capp as he glanced up at Williams from under his eyebrows, "Anything else in this barn of goodies?"

Williams didn't like the look in Capp's eyes, and had the feeling he'd tread on a hot button. He was smart enough not to ask any more questions about the two of them.

"Right, one last item," answered Williams, "Sunglasses. New models are coming out soon, so take care of these that have metal sides that hook behind the ears. Now all you need is a big wrist watch and you have the look of a classic Navy fighter pilot."

"If I ever have a chance to give someone a ride in an SNJ," laughed Capp. "You'll be the first. Thanks for your help."

"My pleasure," answered Williams. "I'll hold you to that SNJ ride."

"Hey Quirt," shouted Capp, "Let's get our butts over to the Bailout Trainer, and guess what…, we don't have to march." Capp pulled Quirt's cap down over his eyes, "Wipe that stupid grin off your face, you look like a man that hates marching."

"You got that right Ace," answered Quirt re-adjusting his cap, "Let's get out of here before the Sergeant changes his mind. He loves to march, must be a control freak. If we hustle, we can be first in line."

They hurried toward the hangar area where all of the planes were parked. On one side of a hangar was the Bailout Trainer. On the other side was the Parachute shack, a separate long white frame building where parachutes were packed and pilots checked out their chutes before each flight. They entered the front door and walked up to the counter.

"Hi," said Capp to a tall skinny sailor with a crew cut haircut,

"Cadets Capp and Quirt have arrived in perfect formation, and we're here for parachute indoctrination."

"Good morning Gentlemen, "I'm First Class Waring, parachute rigger exceptional, and will indoctrinate you in the finer parts of the parachute. As you look around, you can see parachutes being rigged or stretched out on the long tables to your left, rolled carefully, and packed into the chute bag. We're required to make a monthly jump in a chute, so we're very careful to make sure they are packed correctly. We know the pilot's neck is on the line if he has to jump, so we pack them properly, whether or not we have to jump, professionalism, right?"

"This guy I like." answered Capp as he gave a thumbs up to Quirt.

Waring spent about fifteen minutes explaining the rigging process and announced,

"That completes your indoctrination. Please stop by the shack anytime. Anyone have any questions? None, OK, then proceed to the field where the bailout trainer is located. May you never have to use a chute, but I guarantee, if you do, they'll work. Good luck in your training."

"Thanks," answered Capp. "By the way, if my chute doesn't work, can I bring it back for another one that does?"

"There's one guy like you in every class." laughed Waring. "Better move out before I schedule you for a jump, today."

"Right," laughed Capp. "C'mon Quirt, let's go. The Bailout Trainer is right around the corner."

As they left the parachute shack, Capp blinked and squinted from the sunlight as they hurried down the sidewalk toward the corner of the hangar.

The hangar was a huge gray colored steel building with doors that slid together in several sections at each end, so the hangar could be totally open for aircraft to be towed in and out. The interior walls and the concrete floors were painted gray. On the enclosed sides, there were catwalks and offices with windows, some up on the sides, and others at floor level. The floor level rooms on one side were for the maintenance personnel who worked and maintained the aircraft. On the other side were the cadet's lockers, the briefing and ready rooms. In front of those rooms were the assignment boards on the hangar deck, on which the flights, aircraft, cadets and their instructors were assigned. The upper rooms were non-maintenance, and housed flight administration, flight operations, the Commanding Officer and his staff.

"Wow, said Capp, "The sun is really bright. Luckily we now have our cool looking Mark IV sunglasses," as he took them out of the case and put them on. "What a great day. Hey, here we are, just look at that, a real live SNJ. Low wing, tandem Plexiglas cockpits, and a huge propeller in front of a huge engine, it must be ten feet high and thirty feet long. What a beauty."

"Actually this SNJ is a piece of crap, a Hangar Queen," answered Quirt. "It'll never fly, as it's stripped of all parts except the ones that make it operate here. Let's get this done and then we can get into one that really flies."

"Who cares," said Capp. "It still looks great."

A short stocky sunburned sailor walked up to them, "You both look like candidates for the Bailout Trainer. I can tell by all the flight gear you're lugging around. Stand over here with some of your fellow cadets and I'll brief all of you. I'm Second Class Machinist Mate O'Donnell and will be your ground instructor. In the rear cockpit of the SNJ is Third Class Swenson, who'll control the engine. The Bailout Trainer is a real SNJ that's tied down with the tail raised so it's in a level position. On the port (left) side above the wing is a trampoline that you'll bail out into."

"At my signal the instructor in the rear cockpit adds full power so there's lots of wind blowing over the wing. Watch me, and when I point to the trampoline, release your lap belt, harness and radio cords, crouch on the metal seat so your head is not in the wind stream above the canopy, and bail out of the port side of the cockpit, aiming at a spot on the lower rear part of the wing where the trampoline is located. In the air, if a pilot jumps straight out, or up, he would hit the tail section and be killed. If you don't jump properly, you rate a Down and will have to repeat until it's completed to my satisfaction. Any questions, O.K., let's get started. Who wants to go first?"

Capp and Quirt waved their hands enthusiastically.

"Bring on the slipstream," shouted Capp.

"I like enthusiasm," laughed O'Donnell. "Put on your flight gear just like on a real flight, strap on your chute so the straps are very tight, it's got to go with you, then climb up on the wing, and get into the front cockpit. Strap yourselves in and I'll help you, after which I'll jump down on the deck beside the wing."

Capp put on his flight gear, and parachute.

"Wow," said Capp, "This chute makes it hard to walk, much less climb up on the wing."

"I'll push from behind," answered O'Donnell. "You'll get used to it. Climb up on the wing next to the fuselage. There's a non-slip sandpaper type coating on the surface of the wing."

Capp raised his leg to step onto the lower part of the wing and pull himself on.

"Uggh," grunted O'Donnell. "You've got to lose some weight, Mr. Capp. Put your foot on the metal step on the side of the fuselage, and then step into the cockpit. O.K., now place the chute into the planes metal hollow seat, and there you go. You sit on your chute, which has a cushion for comfort. Your shoulder straps are located above and behind your shoulders, pull them down into your lap where they hook into the lap belt, which has a metal lever that locks them all together. Keep them tight. Hook up the planes radio cords to your helmet cords, there; you're all set to go. Ready?"

"I'm out of breath," said Capp. "This is work. Thanks for your help. The parachute's bulky; hope I can get out of the cockpit."

Capp gave O'Donnell a thumbs-up; O'Donnell jumped down from the wing, looked at Swenson, and twirled his fingers over his head in a rotating motion.

Swenson added full power. The SNJ and the trampoline trembled in the windblast.

This is noisy and windy, thought Capp. Concentrate, look at O'Donnell; he's brought his arm down and is pointing to the trampoline. Here we go. Unhook the radio, c'mon, they won't disconnect-pull harder, there they go. Pull down the goggles, unlock the lap belt disconnect, throw the shoulder straps back over my shoulder, am I free? Stand up in a squat, this really is a small area, turn to the port side, sight at the lower wing, put my hands on the canopy sides, push hard with my legs and pull with my hands. Go! Ooof, that trampoline is hard. Did I pass? Let's get off this trampoline and onto solid ground.

Capp walked over to O'Donnell and smiled.

"That was an experience, hope I don't ever have to do that for real."

"You did fine, but this is really sterile," answered O'Donnell. I've talked to pilots who've actually bailed out. They say the plane is generally out of control, and getting out of the cockpit with all of the "g-forces" is difficult. Some pilots don't make it. But at least this gives you the correct procedures."

"This is great," said Capp. "You know, sitting in a classroom and getting briefed on this gives a person the feeling that this is a piece of cake. It isn't. This is real, and harder than I thought. I'm glad my first bail-out was here. At least if it's ever for real, I'll be more prepared. Thanks."

"O.K. Mr. Quirt," said O'Donnell. "Let's get your chute on."

"Roger," answered Quirt. "At least I won't look like a fat whale being barfed out of a tin can; I'll do it with class, and without a speech. Let's go."

Quirt climbed into the cockpit, and when the time was ready, launched himself out, on to the trampoline, legs flailing in the air.

Capp held his sides in laughter as Quirt was trying to get off the trampoline on to the ground, "Quirt, if that's the vision of class, the world's in trouble."

"Get lost," said Quirt. "My foot slipped and I went out sideways, but who cares, I made it. X marks the spot on the trampoline where I landed, perfection."

"Nice try," answered Capp. "You looked like a glump."

"An O.K. glump," said O'Donnell. "You passed. Both of you have a ball flying.

"Yeahh," shouted Capp as he pounded Quirt on his back, "We're on our way."

"Off we go, into the wild blue yonder, shouted Quirt as he also pounded Capp on his back. "Hey, guess who just showed up," said Quirt, "Pervis the creep."

"Hey Pervis," shouted Capp. "Better late than never, you'll never be number one dragging your tail. By the way, be sure and jump straight up when you bail out, it'll impress the instructors."

Pervis walked over to Capp, put his face close to Capp's and sneered. "Some day you'll need to bail out. Maybe you won't make it. It's in your future."

4

0645 Wednesday morning; temperature 50 degrees, clear and sunny.

Capp walked through the passageways. With each of his steps the polished floors squeaked, as if being abused. He entered Quirt's room.

"Hey Quirt," shouted Capp, "Time to muster, One more day to flight time. This day we do standing on our heads. Get off your duff and out of the rack. You'll wrinkle your uniform, and we certainly want to be spic and span for our new fake officer, Battalion Commander, whoever he is. Let's go below to the recreation room so we can get close to the front door for morning muster."

Quirt was lying on his upper bunk, hands folded behind his head, staring at the white painted ceiling. Rolling over on his side, his head deep in the pillow but one eye able to look at Capp,

"Screw the wrinkles, screw the new fake officers, I came here to fly, not sweat the small things." answered Quirt. "What's with the Gung Ho rush to go below? I was having a great fantasy about beautiful women crawling all over my body. You ruined it!"

"Fantasies are for wimps." laughed Capp. "When we get in town I'll line you up with some real women, real flesh and blood; believe me, it's better. Now back to reality, wrinkled uniforms create demerits, and too many demerits can get you kicked out of flight training. C'mon old wrinkled one, let's go."

Quirt groaned, rolled out of the top bunk, landing on his feet with a large sounding thud.

"O.K., mother hen," answered Quirt. "Someday, I'm never again going to wear form fitting, clean, starched clothes. Baggy pants and a sweatshirt, that's it."

They left the room, walked down the passageway and into the recreation room. It had brown paneling on the walls, with several comfortable leather chairs and couches facing different directions. Photos of airplanes in combat situations along with the Marine Corp and Navy emblem lined the walls. The ever present pool table was at the end of the room. The Navy encouraged pilots to shoot pool as much as possible. It was felt that the angles in pool increased fighter pilots skills who used angles in a dogfight to get an advantage on an opponent. The lighting was bright, with windows that looked out onto the street. It was an attempt to create a masculine, military setting, and it seemed to be effective. It definitely was a masculine room. A television set was blaring from the front of the room, and several cadets were standing, watching the morning news.

"Let's sit in the back," said Capp. "That television drives me nuts with all of its noise and babble. It stifles conversation. Look, no one is talking to each other, just staring blankly at the screen. What a waste."

Quirt exhaled a large breath, slowly and deeply, and rubbed his eyes for a few seconds.

"You know, I could still be in my rack instead of this place. Why do I listen to you? Morning formation is fifteen minutes away. Damn, those women were beautiful."

"Yeah," said Capp. "And you probably would've been late for morning muster. I wonder who volunteered to be class officers? In Pre-Flight, class officers were chosen for their excellent grades, leadership, and ability to march and lead other cadets in marching drills, appearance-in other words, those in the top ten percent of the battalion. A sword was a badge of distinction. We both were class officers, so we know.'

'Here, I'm sure there are some Pre-Flight cadet officers who signed up, but there also will be a bunch of wannabes who never made it in

Pre-Flight, who just want the sword and the chance to have power and control over others. Do you realize they can give demerits? Makes you shudder. They could wreak havoc on cadets they don't like. I hope the Marine officers who selected them asked some tough questions of the candidates, and also review all demerits for fairness."

"C'mon Capp," answered Quirt. "You're paranoid. We'll breeze through this flight program, get our wings of gold and the Ensign bars of an officer. Nothing can get in our way. We're hot, right?"

"Yeah," said Capp rubbing the back of his neck. "But there's this gnawing sensation in the back of my neck, a kind of survival response that makes the hair stand up, just like prehistoric cavemen had when danger was near."

He looked at Quirt and laughed,

"You know, you're right, let's get on with it. There's the bugle call to muster, forward and onward."

Speakers located on walls all over the barracks, blared the trumpet call to muster, and the loud voice of the Master Sergeant shouting,

"Attention on deck, attention on deck. All hands fall out to the grinder for muster; fall out, fall out."

The trumpet again blared, loud enough to shake the walls.

Capp laughed as a multitude of cadets pushed out of the doors, knocking against each other to get to the cement apron in front of the barracks.

"This is like blocking in football," shouted Capp to Quirt who was right behind him, "Except, that door jams don't give, and you've got to knock over the cadet next to you to beat him out. Yeahhh."

"I'm behind you," Quirt yelled back. "You're my lead blocker."

They ran, pushed, and shoved against other cadets as everyone tried to get out the door at the same time, but couldn't, a compressed mass of humanity resembling sand flowing thru a funnel.

"From now on," panted Quirt with exhaustion, "Let's stand outside before the bugle sounds off so we don't have to go through this stupid exercise of pain."

"O.K., we're out with no broken arms," said Capp as he looked over the cement apron where cadets were lining up in their assigned platoons. "It looks like our platoon flag is over there, let's get lined up. Our fake platoon officer is already there, I don't recognize him; let's hope he's not a jerk.

A loud voice shouted, "Battalion, Attenhut!"

"Oh no," said Capp. "It's Pervis! He's the Cadet Battalion Commander. The hairs on the back of my neck are standing straight up. This doesn't look good for your old dad."

"Don't give him any crap," answered Quirt. "Look straight ahead, ignore him."

"Battalion, prepare for inspection," ordered Pervis.

"He can't do that," said Capp. "This is only a muster to check attendance. Only Marine officers can hold inspection."

"Hang on to your butt," answered Quirt. "It's about to happen."

Pervis walked up and down, between the lines of cadets standing at attention. The platoon commander and a marine Sergeant followed him.

"Well, well," said Pervis as he stopped in front of Capp. "What do we have here, a cadet with un-shined shoes?" He turned to the platoon commander, "Give cadet Capp five demerits and one hour of marching, to be completed Saturday at 0800 on the grinder."

Capp's shoes were perfect, and he started to mouth a protest.

"You got a problem mister?" sneered Pervis. "Perhaps a few more demerits for un-officer like conduct would square you away."

"No problem Sir," answered Capp as he regained his composure. His eyes were ice blue.

"Good," said Pervis. "I'll be watching you Saturday. If you're AWOL, your demerits will double." He turned and continued down the line.

The inspection was completed.

Pervis went to the front of the battalion and ordered,

"Battalion-At Ease. Today we'll march to ground school. This will be the last day of marching as a battalion. Starting tomorrow, flight training will commence. Morning muster will be held as usual, but each cadet will be responsible to arrive at the hangar on time for his scheduled flights, and any other scheduled activities. Battalion-

Attenhut. Platoon officers, march your platoon to the ground school building."

"Aye, Aye Sir," answered each class officer platoon leader. "Platoon Three, right face, forward-march." Each platoon commenced marching in formation.

"This is war," said Capp out of the side of his mouth to Quirt while they were marching. "That little Napoleon isn't going to wash me out with his fake demerits. Get your thinking cap on Quirt, there's got to be a solution."

"Pervis doesn't know how bad the two of us can be," answered Quirt. "We'll get him, but just don't give him a real reason for more demerits. We'll get him."

They looked at each other and smiled the sweet smile of revenge.

5

The battalion arrived at the ground school building.

Pervis turned to the battalion and ordered, "Battalion-Halt."

Each platoon leader ordered in unison, "Platoon, 1, 2, 3, 4-Halt."

All of the cadets came to a stop in front of the ground school building.

"Today, each platoon is assigned to their respective classrooms. Ground school is scheduled for the whole day. In the future, you will check the Plan of the Day on the barracks bulletin board to see where your classes are to be held. The plan of the day will be posted by 1800 each day. Gentlemen, you are responsible for your own muster, no one will hold your hand. I will attend classes with platoon One. At the end of classes today, form back here to march to the barracks. This is the last day we will march together, as the flight schedule is different for each cadet. Battalion-dismissed," ordered Pervis.

All of the cadets relaxed and walked toward the ground school building, walking together in various groups.

"Boy is that Pervis a jerk," said Capp. "No one is going to hold your hand," mimicked Capp in a feminine voice. "What a jerk. He probably would like someone to hold his hand; why else would he insult us like that? Do we nickname him Pervert Pervis, or Pervis the male organ? What do you think?

"He is strange," answered Quirt. "All I can think of, is he must have had a really fouled up childhood. I think Pervert Pervis works just fine. This is the last base that has cadet officers. Let's get through Warner, and we'll never have to deal with him again."

"You're right," answered Capp. "We still have to find a way to beat his fake demerits, we'll think of something.'

'Look at that ground school building. Gleaming white, same two stories, wood, built before World War II and it will be our destiny for the next several weeks. It's an artists setting, green grass, blue sky, sidewalks, large blue and white sign on the side of the building, Aviation Ground school, it could be our barracks except for the sign. These buildings all look alike, wonder how long before they fall apart?"

"Depends on how many wars we get involved in," laughed Quirt. "Americans like to fight. Now that we're a world power, stick around for a while, there'll be another war, and these wooden firetraps will have to replaced, probably with brick or concrete. Unless of course, Russia drops a nuclear bomb on Warner, then it won't make a difference.

"If that happens," answered Capp, "Let's hope Pervis is here."

You've got a fixation on Pervis, said Quirt. "Forget him, we'll fix him, you just wait. This is a very tough program, and distractions can cause problems. Again, forget him."

"O.K., O.K., you're a good friend my man," answered Capp. "Let's find our classroom."

They walked up to the building and entered the front door, surrounded by other cadets.

"Let's find the bulletin board," said Quirt.

They walked down the passageway to their left, and located the board. He ran his finger down the listings and said,

"There it is. Our platoon is scheduled for engines, room 103. C'mon, it's over here."

"You know," said Capp, "the Navy really has excellent training. It's amazing how they can take a bunch of glumps like us, most who have never done anything mechanically more complex than change a bicycle tire, and teach us how an airplane is put together. This week it's engines. Then the electrical system, next the fuel system, the hydraulic system, the communication system, the basic body frame, the landing gear, and we do it-hands on. I think that's the secret. We actually touch and work with all those systems. The public schools could take a lesson from the Navy as to how to get a student from A to Z. After that it's navigation, communications and aerology. We've had most of this in Pre-Flight, but repetition is what makes a person a pro, practice, practice, practice. It's going to be a busy few weeks."

"Don't count me in your little un-mechanical pile," said Quirt. "I used to take apart the engine on my car, replace most of the parts, and yes, it still ran, saved me a lot of money."

"I bet you didn't know what you were doing," answered Capp. "Just experimenting until something fit or started to run. You never had a class on auto repair; you were just hit and miss."

"You're right on the hit and miss part," said Quirt. "But that's one way to learn. However we're not going to take a plane apart, that's for the mechanics. But knowing what happens when switches or levers are moved is part of our survival. We've only one engine and therefore only one of everything to know. Can you imagine what a multi-engine pilot with four engines has to know, one system for each of his engines. It must be mind boggling."

"I don't want to know," answered Capp. "One system is plenty for right now. Let's get into our room; engines here we come."

They walked down the hallway.

"Remember?" said Capp. "At the end of Pre-Flight, we all went to the engine run-up stand, to start and run-up an engine so we could see and complete the procedures. The engine was secured to a big stand behind a metal fence and the controls were on our side. I followed the instructor's commands, and the engine roared to life. The sound was deafening. I had no idea how the engine worked, except that I pushed a throttle for power, mixture lever for the fuel, and a propeller lever for the propeller. I think that was just to get our juices flowing and to give us a glint of the future. It did get my juices flowing, but now I'll find out how it works."

Inside, the classroom had bright neon overhead lights, blackboards and individual wooden school desks, of which the top could be lifted to store personal supplies such as paper, pens and pencils.

The instructor, Petty Officer First Class Swenson welcomed them, took muster, and invited them over to the engine stand. Swenson was built like a football linebacker, and had large powerful hands with thick blonde hair on the back of them. He had been in the Navy for fifteen years and was an expert on reciprocating engines. His job was to explain each detail of the engine.

"Good morning gentlemen. As you can see," said Swenson, "An engine for the SNJ is set in a metal stand about belt high so you can walk around and examine every part. Some of the components, such as piston cylinders are cut open so they can be viewed in their workings and I can move a lever to make the pistons move up and down.'

'It's a complete engine with all of the electrical wiring, generators, spark plugs, fuel lines and anything else that's needed to make it work.'

'Look at it from the front. The cylinders are shaped like a large triangle and are hooked together in a circle. Air flows in the front of the engine while in flight to keep it cool and there are fins built into the cylinder sides to assist in cooling. Rods called piston rods connect the pistons inside of each cylinder to a main shaft.'

'It's amazing all of these moving parts work together without jamming up into a ball of mangled metal. Engineers dreamt up this monstrosity, but it works, we know that."

"It is a monstrosity," said Capp to Quirt. "Only Rube Goldberg could be happy with a combustion engine."

"Mr. Capp," said Swenson with a smile, "I realize you are impressed, but if you don't let me talk, we won't finish this lesson today."

"Sorry about that," answered Capp, "Just an observation."

"He talks a lot," said Quirt, "Smoothest salesman in the room, but we'll hold him down so you can finish."

"No problem," answered Swenson. "Sometimes I never know if I'm getting through to the students because no one is talking or asking questions. Ask a question, that's why I'm here. But I don't want to compete with side conversations. By the way, there's a schedule change. We're cutting this class one hour short so you can practice code topside in room 201."

A groan went through the room.

"What a way to ruin a nice day," whispered Capp to Quirt. "Code is a pain in the butt, or worse yet, in the ears. Da dit da Dit, dit da dit, dit, dit da da dit, you probably love it."

"Stop tying to impress me with your da-dits," answered Quirt. "We both hate code. Everybody hates code."

Petty Officer Swenson went through the workings of the engine; he knew it well. He finished and said, "Thank you Gentlemen, and see you tomorrow. Don't forget code practice."

"C'mon guys," said Capp. "Out of your chairs, down the passageway, up the ladder, to our most fun class, the one we dream about-code."

"I really don't want to go," said Quirt. "Listening to code in a quiet room is tough enough. Can you imagine what it's like in a noisy airplane, maybe in the stress of combat, and trying to figure out what's being transmitted into your headphones? Maybe I'll choose to fly multi-engine aircraft, which has a radio operator on board. Then I won't have to worry about code."

They entered the code practice room. There were long tables with a vertical board down the middle about twelve inches high, and smaller boards the same height perpendicular to the long center board. It divided the table into sections about three feet wide. Cadets could see over the board, but not each other's paper. Each section had a headset, a pencil and a pad of paper.

"Welcome to code. I'm Petty Officer Third Class Mankowsi and we'll practice groups of five letters. We'll start slow and then increase the speed. I understand you've had basic code in Pre-Flight so you know which dit's and da's make the letters. We'll increase speed each week until you're able to translate twenty-five letter groups per minute. The room is always open during the day, feel free to come up and practice. Eventually you'll feel the dit's and da's, and not try to think what the sounds mean. Good luck." Mankowski had glasses and was slim with intelligent looking eyes. He was more relaxed than, and not as animated as Petty Officer Swenson.

"I bet Mankowski is a math genius," said Capp. "He looks too smart to do manual labor. I think having an aptitude for code is something a person is born with; it's not natural. There has to be a system for us thick headed people."

"Like everything else," answered Quirt, "It's practice, practice and more practice."

"You know, I bet we'll never use code in all of our flying days, said Capp. "That's why we have radios. I can see practicing the visual light flashing code; a pilot may have radio failure, but this kind of code, no way."

"You're just mad that you can't do this perfectly right away," said Quirt. "You should know better than that. Some things a person just has to work harder at. Don't get negative or you'll never learn this. Just concentrate, O.K.?"

"Jeez," said Capp, "I'm the one who is usually the cheerleader. You're right. C'mon code."

It's the slow code that's easy, thought Capp. *It's getting faster. Oh, Oh, I missed a letter in that group. Great, I missed two in that group. I'll never get this. Concentrate. I got all five, keep going. Listen.*

"Take a break," said Mankowski. "Is it getting easier to feel the sounds?" There were groans from the cadets. He laughed. "You'll be surprised. One day it'll all come together, you'll see."

"How many groups can you translate?" asked Capp.

"About sixty," answered Mankowski.

"Sixty!" gasped Capp. "How do you do it? We're at ten today, and I'm behind most of the time."

"It's called practice, all the time," he answered. "It's my job and the Navy expects me to be very good at it. One more session and then we're through. Are you ready? Do I hear a No?" He laughed. "O.K., ten minutes, ready, go."

What a sadist, thought Capp. *He's speeding up, I can hear the sounds, but I'm behind. Block everything out of my mind. This is the worse thing I've ever had to do. Every Navy pilot has done this, keep telling myself that. C'mon, the ten minutes is up isn't it?*

"That's it Gentlemen," said Mankowski. "This will be scheduled every day. That's a change to your schedule. Thanks for your cooperation, see you tomorrow."

"This may sound dumb," Said Capp, "but I'm dreaming of a beer. This has been a long day."

"What's dumb about that?" answered Quirt. I'll buy the first round tonight, assuming we don't fall asleep in our chairs. Just keep thinking, tomorrow we fly, tomorrow we fly."

"Right, fly, fly," said Capp. "By the way, do you think anyone will be able to sleep tonight? One beer is all I want; we've got to sharp tomorrow. We'll celebrate this weekend. All we have for the rest of the day is hydraulics and electrical systems. It's a piece of cake."

The classes ended, and cadets streamed out of the building to the area they arrived in the morning, to line up with their platoons for the march back to the barracks.

Capp was standing by himself off to the side of his platoon, waiting for his friends who had a last minute head call. He felt someone standing behind him, turned and saw Pervis with his strange crooked smile, looking at him.

"You lost?" said Capp. "If you need some help to find where you're spot is, I can escort you. Since you weren't a class officer in Pre-Flight, you probably do need help."

"It's going to fun," said Pervis.

"What's going to be fun?" answered Capp.

"Watching you wash out of this flight program," said Pervis.

"Why would I wash out the program?" answered Capp. "I'm the sharpest cadet this Navy has ever seen."

"Naw, you've got some serious defects." said Pervis, "Serious defects that'll generate too many demerits for you to remain in the program, it's a shame, but that's your future."

Capp moved toward Pervis, his eyes blazing with an electrical blue color as if lightning was about to leap out of them.

"The only defect I have," growled Capp. "Is not kicking your butt and stuffing you in a trash can. You're sick."

Pervis stepped back, but not too far, as he knew the power of his position.

"I should give you ten demerits for threatening a class officer, but I'm going to overlook your threat," said Pervis. "I just want you to know that you're finished. Don't lose a lot of sleep over your destiny; it could affect your flying ability. Now that would be terrible, wouldn't it? Maybe your flight instructor will have to wash you out for nervousness and an inability to concentrate."

Pervis slowly smirked that sick looking smirk he had, and then gave a vicious sounding guttural laugh.

"As I said, it's going to be fun."

Pervis turned on his heel, and left to assume his position in front of the Battalion. His step was bouncy and energetic.

6

0800 Thursday, Pilots briefing room, Main hangar.

Bright neon lights on the ceiling glared on to the pilots below, also on to the desks, tables, chairs, and large blackboards, huge rectangular briefing boards covered with photos of the Florida landscape, diagrams, and flight paths.

White painted walls and concrete gray painted floors contrasted with the ever present coffee mess area with its metal coffee pots and a blue colored wooden board on which large white mugs with each cadets name on them, hung on pegs.

The air was filled with the pleasurable smell of coffee, and the pungent smell of cigarette smoke. In the 1950's, the majority of adults smoked. Pilots, who thought they were hot, smoked cigars, the international symbol of fighter pilots and persons who felt they excelled at some personal endeavor. At one time or another, every military pilot smoked a cigar. Naval Air was a fraternity of cocky, aggressive and confident pilots. That's a few of the reasons they were the best in the world.

The briefing room bustled with activity. Voices could be heard, but one was not louder than the rest. Some students and instructors sat at long wooden tables. Others stood in front of the large wall maps and pointed to the maps and flight areas, imitating airplanes with their hand gestures. To any layman who saw people make gestures with their hands-movements up, down, and sideways, it was not an indication of hearing impaired persons, but of pilots explaining their maneuvers to each other.

The flight area maps had drawn on them mandatory departure and entry patterns to the airfield, which maintained an orderly flow of airplane traffic, and reduced the possibility of mid-air collisions

Each pilot wore his full length khaki colored flight suit and boots. Some wore their leather flight jacket for warmth, but also to look hot. Sometimes the image of a hot pilot was as important to them as their skills.

The look on the student's faces gave a hint as to the success of their flights. Some were energetic and full of smiles. Others slouched and rubbed their furrowed brows with their hands.

Those on their way to the flight line for their next hop seemed quieter, with lines of concentration etched on their faces. Many complex procedures had to be memorized.

Proper sequence for each procedure was required to receive an Up grade. Failure resulted in a Down. Too many Downs and the cadet was dropped from the flight program, Washed Out.

Chuck Capp was excited for his first flight and came to the briefing room early to share in the mental and physical energy of other cadets. He sat at one end of a briefing table by himself, studying the SNJ handbook which explained what makes the plane work, also procedures for his first flight, the area maps, and observing the other cadets.

"People Watching" was as interesting as a stimulating conversation. He was trying to guess the ones that would make it, and those that wouldn't. Was there a common thread? No psychologist had found that thread and the military gave many tests trying to find that thread. It would save the Navy a lot of time and money if they could. Some tests he thought were really stupid, like the one that measured the amount of sweat on person's hands. Every cadet had to press litmus paper on his palms to see if it changed color with the amount of sweat produced during a period of stress, such as a difficult math test. They were never told the results, so obviously it predicted nothing. He knew of no cadets who were ever washed out because they had sweaty palms.

When he was in High School, this reminded him of the day the coach selected him to be the starting quarterback. Would he foul up, make mistakes, fumble the handoff, throw an interception, or call bad game plays? He was confident he knew the plays, but needed some support. His father was a large tough man, owned a successful upholstery business, never spoke much, but was a strict disciplinarian with an air of authority. Chuck still remembers the night before the game.

After supper, Chuck had asked, "Dad can we talk about tomorrow?"

"Let's go outside," answered his father, "It looks like you need some fresh air, we'll walk and talk, be good for both of us. We've got the whole evening."

They left the house and walked down the sidewalks. It was a middle class neighborhood with clean streets, neat lawns that were mowed, homes that were painted and well kept. Each home had children, which meant there were always numerous kids around to start up a game of whatever was the choice of the day. "Kick the Can" was always a favorite at night at the corner under the streetlights, and could be played all night until parents called everyone in. During the day there was always a game of football in the street, or baseball in the empty lot behind their house. Everyone knew each other, and parents watched out for all of the children. The older kids always let the smaller kids play in all the games, and were mentors and protectors of them. It was a great neighborhood to grow up in.

"What's on your mind, Chuck," Asked his father. "Girls, money, sports, school grades, but let me guess-sports?"

Chuck looked at his father who had a long, wrinkled face, heavy eyebrows over ice blue eyes, large nose, strong square jaw, and was somewhat sad looking from the fatigue and stress of running a competitive business with long work days. He also saw a twinkle in his father's eyes.

"You're right," answered Chuck. "You know I'm the starting quarterback tomorrow, and I don't want to foul up.

His father laughed, and put a large strong arm around Chuck's shoulder.

"Do you know the plays?" he asked.

"You bet," answered Chuck, "Probably as good as the coaches."

"Good," said his father, as he stepped back and faced Chuck. "Do you know anything about your opponent's weaknesses, which of your players you can rely on in a tight situation, which of your players have the desire to win regardless of the odds, and which are bums that need to be chewed out when they perform poorly? Do you have the confidence to lead your team to victory?"

"Yes, to all of that," answered Chuck. "The coaches have really helped. I believe I'm ready."

"Well then," said his father. "You're ready. Everyone has butterflies before a game. If you didn't, you wouldn't be ready. You'd be overconfident or naïve, and ready for a crash."

Chuck thought for a minute,

"You've got success all figured out, it's so simple when it's a laid out. How do you do that?"

"Well," answered his father, "Sports is kind of like business. Desire, training, hard work, and having good people around you are very important reasons for success. A friendly banker never hurts either. Now, what could be the worse thing that could happen?"

"I don't want to think about that," answered Chuck. "But I suppose having a really bad day, and being relieved of my starting job."

"Just from watching you and talking with you," said his father. "It won't happen. But if it did, guess what? Your mother and I will always love and support you as long as you live, or as long as we live. Life is hard, and if you fail at something, you just pick yourself up and go on. Eventually you'll be successful, that's a prediction. Plus you've got some damn good genes."

He laughed and slapped Chuck hard on his shoulder. "I won't be able to be at the game tomorrow due to some large contract deadlines that must be met, but you're on your way to becoming a man. I can't always be at your side physically, but you must know, I'm there in my heart."

"Thanks Dad," said Chuck, his voice choking with emotion. "I'll do my best. Thanks for the pep talk."

"Hey, you old brown nose," shouted a loud voice behind him. "What're you doing here so early, trying to get the best plane to get an edge on everyone?"

Capp snapped out of his daydream and turned around as he recognized the voice.

"You son-of-a-gun," laughed Quirt. "You weren't in your room and I thought you'd chickened out, 'First Flight Fever.' Haw, haw."

Capp punched Quirt on his shoulder, and laughed. "You jerk; I'm so ready and so good that the Navy will probably cut my syllabus in half. I came early to suck up some sun after a great nights sleep."

"Don't give me that crap," answered Quirt. "You're just like the rest of us first flighter's- couldn't sleep, tossed in your rack all night, walked the floor, and couldn't stop dreaming of procedures when you did get a little sleep. The only difference is that you came down here early, which is smart. I should've done the same thing."

"Well, Doctor Freud," said Capp, "Since you have it all figured out, let me grab you a cup of java as a reward to your deep perceptions. By the way, I slept great."

Capp walked over the coffee mess, picked Quirt's cup off of the wall rack, and filled it to the brim with hot, aromatic coffee. He walked back to the table and sat down beside Quirt.

"Thanks," said Quirt. "With all your generosity this morning, what's the catch?"

"Not much," answered Capp. "Of course this generosity in a time of stress means you buy the first round tonight at the ACRAC."

"No way," said Quirt. "Roll the dice, or you go dry, that's the rules, stress or no stress.

"You're a hard case," said Capp, "can't even beat a freebie out of you. Well, you know I'll win the roll, so you might as well offer to pay."

"Nice try," answered Quirt. "You haven't won a roll in a week, I love taking your money."

"C'mon," said Capp. "Let's go over to the assignment board on the hangar deck to verify our instructors. I don't want stay here any longer to watch guys who obviously had a bad flight. Look at Wayne Hutt, that's not a happy looking camper."

Both watched Hutt as he sat waiting for his instructor and the flight debriefing. Hutt had blond hair, about six feet tall, a good athlete in school, but was rumored to be a little lazy in studying his procedures, or overconfident, but in any event was rubbing his hands through his hair and across his forehead, no coffee, with a look on his face that looked like he had dropped the ball in the end zone; a tense, sad face.

"Out of here," said Capp. "I don't want that attitude rubbing off on us, let's go outside and fart into the wind."

"Wind or no wind," laughed Quirt. "Let's just fart."

They walked through the door of the briefing room and out on to the hangar deck, each raised their leg and attempted a large passing of gas, accompanied by loud grunts. Capp got off a small blast, and Quirt followed with a similar effort as they fell against the hangar wall laughing hysterically.

"Can you imagine," said Capp in between his gasps, "Somewhere there's an Admiral briefing a Congressman, explaining that the Navy is training diligent, dedicated, serious, Naval flight cadets who are the next line of defense to save our proud nation, and requesting funds that probably are outrageous, to help train these heroes-like us? Do you think admirals and congressmen fart? Let's keep moving to get out of this H2S hydrogen sulphide cloud; it's melting my Hershey bar."

As they walked past the sailors in their light blue work shirts and dark blue trousers, past the cadets and instructors going to and coming from their flights, they came to the assignment board. A large rectangular clear plastic board at one end of the hangar that listed the flight number, times, names of cadets alongside their instructors, the aircraft number and location of the plane they were assigned. In front of the board were the board boys, sailors who wrote the information on the board, a chief petty officer, and the officer-in-charge of the board. There always was a lot of activity in the board area, especially when there was inclement weather, when few flights got into the air, and everyone was standing by, hoping their flight would be the one to fly.

"I've been assigned Captain Fredrick," said Quirt, "Heard he was a good guy. At least neither of us are assigned a Screamer, you know, an instructor who can find no good in any student. They cause stress, and result in washouts that may not have occurred with a different instructor. Why the Navy allows instructors like that to be in the system is beyond me. Anyway, I've got to hit the Head and get rid of some of this coffee. See you later. Good luck, and have a ball."

"Thanks," answered Capp, "Same for you."

Capp was stood back from the board and watched the activity. His hop was to be assigned soon, and he was ready to go.

"Well, well," came a voice from behind Capp, which was twinged with a sneer in it. "The self-proclaimed hero is trying to find a way to get an instructor who forgives lousy flying, you'll need one. Who's your Santa Claus?" asked Pervis sarcastically.

Capp slowly turned and faced Pervis.

"You're the only guy I know that can ruin a beautiful day just by your obnoxious arrival," answered Capp. "Since you probably can't read very well, I'll help you out, as the assignment board is very complicated for a Cretin like you. I've been assigned Captain John Kranz, one of the best. I heard he drew your name, but turned it down. He felt it wouldn't be professional to barf every time he knew he had to fly with you."

"You're jealous, I knew it," said Pervis, "because you know that Rick Farr is my instructor. He served a tour with the Blue Angels-you know, the Navy's flight demonstration team filled with only the top premier pilots, and he also saw combat in Korea. The best instructor will make me the best student pilot; it just follows. I'm going to be number one. Eat your heart out."

"You don't seem to understand," said Capp. "The Navy knows you're a weak link and they hope that Farr can get you from unsafe to mediocre. The only way you'll ever be number one is if I flew all your hops. You're a loser. You know it, I know it, and all the other cadets know it. You can only blow smoke so long, and then you'll be shot down."

You're the one that's blowing smoke," said Pervis. "I'm the best, and you're afraid of me. You'll get knocked down by my jet-wash."

"Jet-wash?" laughed Capp. "You don't even know what jet-wash is. Jets are for hot dogs; you'll never see jets. In fact I'll bet you don't even finish the program. By the way, there are no barf bags in the planes for guys like you that can't cut it. Be sure to bring along your flight gloves so you can fill them up. Captain Farr will soon find out that you're not cut out for flying, only barfing. You're a loser."

"Capp," said Pervis. "As I said, some day you're going to regret making me an enemy. I'm dangerous; you won't even know what hit you."

Capp squinted and thrust his face close to Pervis's face; his eyes had turned ice blue.

"You're a psycho," said Capp. "Get away from me so you don't get hurt."

They stared at each other for a few minutes. Pervis turned and walked away with that terrible smile on his face.

7

It was time. Capp's first Naval military flight was about to commence.

Capp stood in front of the assignment board, his stomach tightened as he thought of what his first reaction to Captain Kranz would be, and he to Capp. A shiver tingled down his spine, and sweat formed on his palms, totally out of character for his usual cool demeanor. Instructors were like gods to students, and Capp placed his instructor above the rest of the gods. He would be the one to make or break Capp.

Capp walked over to one of the board boys who was standing idly near the center of the board, "Airman."

"Yes Sir," answered the sailor.

"I'm here to meet Captain Kranz for my first flight. If you know him, could you point him out to me so I won't look too surprised?"

"Yes Sir," answered the sailor. "You've got a great instructor, everyone likes him. If you look to your right, here he comes, the one that looks like a wrestler. Good luck."

"Thanks," said Capp.

Capp turned to his right, stood at attention, saluted and announced,

"Cadet Capp Sir, ready for my first flight."

"Captain John Kranz," answered the Captain, and returned Capp's salute.

Steel colored eyes bore a hole into Capp, intimidating, yet they had a glint of friendliness.

"That's good to hear," said Kranz. "I'm going to work your butt off, and make you into the best pilot in this command. I expect no less from you, and from me. Are we on the same frequency?"

"Capp thought he could handle any situation, but Kranz's words touched a deep primordial nerve. Adrenalin pumped through his body. His pulse throbbed. It felt great. He felt alive, excited, would the Captain notice?"

"Yes Sir," answered Capp with all the enthusiasm he could muster. "That's what I want to be, the best."

Capp knew Kranz's background. Two combat tours in Korea in the Grumman F9F Panther, a straight wing fighter/attack jet that had the distinction of shooting down the first Russian Mig-15 fighter in the Korean conflict. Kranz had been shot down by enemy ground fire and was forced to eject from the Panther, but was not captured. As with all Naval fighter pilots, Kranz was an expert in air-to-air combat, commonly nicknamed "Dog-Fighting." A true fighter pilot, he was Capp's kind of pilot, with a reputation of being strict, but fair.

While standing at attention, Capp saw that Kranz had the body-build of a brick outhouse, crew cut, black hair, medium height, intelligent eyes, and a scar on his chin. If there ever was a bar room brawl, this is the guy you'd want on your side.

Kranz smiled at Capp's excitement, he'd heard that Capp was one of the better cadets.

"At ease." ordered Kranz. "From this point on, we're a team. Let's brief this flight and get the bird in the air. That won't break your heart, will it?

"No Sir," answered Capp. "I've dreamt about this day, since I was a kid."

They walked into the briefing room and went over to the large maps on the wall.

"Today is an indoctrination flight," said Kranz. "We'll go over basic aircraft procedures, tour the geographical areas we're allowed to fly in, check out the emergency fields, let you get a feel of the bird, and return to Warner. Let's go over the maps, a pilot's best friend. Stop me anytime if you have any questions."

They finished the briefing and Kranz said, "Let's go check out a couple of chutes and a plane. The chutes are the crummy part because we have to carry them out to the plane. With the newer birds, we don't do that. It makes you appreciate moving onward and upward."

The walk to the flight line began; a chill of excitement ran up Capp's spine, *This is it*, he thought, *how lucky can a guy get?*

This day in November, an unusual heat hit the northwest part of Florida. It was hot and humid. Heat waves shimmered up from the white concrete tarmac, like ghosts of hundreds of past pilots. A scorpion scuttled hurriedly off of the scorching concrete and onto the cool grassy area. Cumulus clouds had appeared in the sky that looked like small white clowns. It was morning, Naval Air Station Warner field was alive, and so was Capp.

The airfield was a huge white apron of concrete, which gleamed in the sun. The control tower was off to the side, and towered over the field like a three story white giant with a glass head. Inside, Naval air controllers directed the aircraft which were taking off and landing on the runways, plus the aircraft taxiing on the taxiways. It was their job to maintain an orderly flow of traffic which at times could be very stressful, especially when there was an emergency with an aircraft in trouble. Their orders were law; no aircraft moved, landed or took off without their permission. There were separate radio frequencies for taxiing aircraft, and for those taking off and landing.

The main runway was built on an east and west magnetic heading, which paralleled the normal western prevailing wind. The second runway was orientated north and south. Taxiways were parallel to, and narrower than the runways.

Parked SNJ training aircraft all faced the same direction at one end of the airfield, close to the huge gray colored rectangular hangars.

The large windsock was in the middle of the field, a cone shaped sock that looks like a dunces cap on its side, and attached to a tall pole. Air flows in the wide round open end to show wind direction. At about 25 knots of wind, it extends straight out. Planes land and take off into the wind to reduce their distance on the runway. When the wind is at an angle to the runway, a crosswind, the sock helps pilots prepare so there are no surprises.

The panorama of the airfield took Capp's breath away. He was excited and the anticipation momentarily caused him to stop walking.

"Wow," exclaimed Capp, "Look at that, listen to that, it's unbelievable!"

Kranz looked at Capp and grinned, "Pretty impressive, huh? If you weren't affected, I'd probably wash you out right now."

In 1954, the Navy's primary trainer was the North American SNJ Texan, a two seat, 600 horsepower low wing monoplane that could, and did, take abuse. It was painted yellow, as were all of the training aircraft. The tail wheel was on the ground. Because the nose and cockpit were higher than the tail, pilots could only see out to the side while taxiing. Its engine had a unique loud growling sound that pilots recognized anywhere.

Multitudes of planes belched smoke as they started their engines and those planes that taxied out for takeoff, fish-tailed left and right, to see in front of them. Pilots with parachutes walked to their planes. Frenzied activity took place from the plane captains, sailors who were in charge of the aircraft, and who helped strap pilots in their cockpits.

And now, thought Capp, *it's my turn.*

The close-up image of the SNJ was monstrous, not like the little kite-looking planes at the civilian airport.

Their Plane Captain, Billy Joe Clements, a jovial, sun burnt, mechanical genius, grew up in Alabama, where repairing and racing cars was a religion. That hobby was a perfect fit for his Navy job, which was to prepare the SNJ for flight and Down it if there were any problems. He would start the plane in the morning, run it up and check it out completely. It seemed he could smell mechanical problems. All the pilots respected him.

Capp followed Captain Kranz as they walked around the plane, and was shown areas to inspect, and to check out.

"Pilots have been killed," said Kranz. "By being in a hurry and missing something important, like not having fuel."

He's thorough, thought Capp, *but let's get this bird in the air.*

"Crawl up on the wing," said Kranz, "and squeeze into the forward cockpit. The rear one's mine."

I know which one to crawl into, thought Capp, *somewhat irritated. Just forget it. That's probably instructor talk, to cover all the bases.*

The cockpit smelled of sweat, gasoline, and oil. The SNJ was an old weary warrior that had trained many Navy pilots which included the Top Guns and warriors of the past. It now helped to train the future protectors of the fleet, and the nation.

Billy Joe helped Capp strap on his parachute, shoulder and lap harness, patted him on the helmet, smiled and said,

"Sir, if you barf, you clean it up."

I should tell him to go screw himself, thought Capp, *but he's probably having fun with me. They work their tails off for us.*

"That's a deal," answered Capp. "By the way, got an extra glove?"

Billy Joe laughed.

"For some reason, I think you'll bring this bird back clean as a Billy goats butt."

They both laughed.

"I have no idea how clean a Billy goats butt is," answered Capp, "but I'll take that as a compliment."

"Are you ready?" radioed Kranz on the planes intercom.

Am I ready? What do you think? Capp thought. *I've been waiting sixteen weeks for this moment you idiot!* But that wouldn't have been too cool to say, so Capp answered, "Yes, Sir," and gave Kranz a big Thumbs Up.

Kranz cranked the engine. It sputtered and coughed.

Capp thought, *Oh no, don't have a problem now.*

It coughed a few more times, and then roared to life. Smoke belched out each of the black exhaust stacks that extended out the sides of the engine, surrounded the plane, and then dissipated.

"What a sound," yelled Capp. He couldn't help himself. "It's tremendous, it's powerful, and it's happening to me."

"Warner tower," radioed Kranz on the ground control frequency. "Whiskey Charlie 234 ready for taxi instructions."

"Roger," answered the tower controller. "Cleared to taxi to runway 27."

"Roger," answered Kranz. "Runway 27."

"Ready or not," said Kranz to Capp on the intercom, "We're off."

"Yes Sir," answered Capp. "This is great!"

Kranz smiled and gave the plane captain the signal to pull the chocks, both fists in front of his face with the thumbs out; he moved both fists outward sharply.

Billy Joe gave thumbs up and pulled the chocks out, pieces of triangular wood placed in the front and back of the main tires to keep the plane from moving. Finally, the plane moved. It slowly fishtailed down the taxiway. The radio crackled with instructions from the tower to the pilots. Pilots answered. It was something Capp had never heard before. It sounded confusing, but was really discipline in action.

Finally, they arrived at the warm-up area. It was an area near the runways take-off end where pilots could add full power to check out the engine and the propeller. This was the go-no-go spot. If the engine sputtered, or the prop did not cycle completely, the flight was cancelled. Kranz added power, and checked the instruments. He cycled the prop from low pitch (max RPM) to high pitch (low RPM).

My fingers are crossed, Capp thought, *I can feel my heart pound. My back's soaked from the sweat rolling down it, not from the heat, but probably from my tension. Try to relax.*

"Looks good," radioed Kranz on the intercom. "Hang on, here we go. Warner tower, Whiskey Charlie 234 ready for take off."

"Roger Whiskey Charlie 234," answered the tower. "Cleared for take off, runway 27. Wind 260 degrees ten knots, turn left after clearing the field."

They taxied into the take-off spot on to the centerline of the runway, and locked the tail wheel.

Capp felt a strange calm come over him, looked at instruments, at the airfield, the blue sky, and felt like he had always belonged here, part of the airplane.

Kranz added full power, low prop pitch, and rich mixture, "Two

Blocked" was the term, as all of the levers were pushed to the front of the throttle quadrant.

The power of the engine caused Capps's body to pulsate, and his chest to vibrate like a bass drum. The roar of the engine was a symphony of noise. Faster and faster down the runway, then, like a bird, they were in the air.

Capp gazed out from the cockpit and thought, Yeahh, *we're free! It's just like throwing off the chains of a landlocked prisoner. The lush green fields and blue waters below extend out from beneath the wings as if they were a Rembrandt painting, and we're above it all, the masters of the world. Nothing can ever take away this moment, no matter how long I live. Bring on those Gold Wings!*

8

The making of a Navy pilot was now in process. This first flight started a progression of tests to accomplish a very difficult feat, the awarding of the Navy Wings of Gold. Some would make it, some would not.

As they climbed to altitude, Capp was amazed at how small the buildings and roads looked. The roads and all of the intersections could be seen as far as the eye could see. The small cumulus clouds were at eye level, beautiful white sentinels towering above the landscape. No wonder man wanted to fly,

They climbed to angels five (five thousand feet) and leveled off. Kranz reduced the power to a cruise setting and said,

"You've got it. Make a few gentle turns left and right and keep on altitude. Follow that road below. Look at your nose position in relation to the horizon, that'll help the altitude control."

Capp wiggled the stick left and right, to show he had control of the plane.

Is this fun, or what? thought Capp. *The nose is bobbing up and down, stop that. What a feeling of power. Look at the wing; it seems to be longer than when we were on the ground. The horizon is nothing but haze, it helps, I still have to glance at the altimeter to stay level.*

"O.K.," radioed Kranz. "Now fly straight and level, and increase power to the take-off setting. In order to maintain your altitude, you'll have to roll in some forward trim tabs to take the forward pressure off of the stick."

Capp pushed the mixture control lever forward until it stopped, the rich setting; the RPM lever all the way forward to low pitch; and added power by moving the throttle lever forward. The engine noise increased and made Capp feel as if he was in control of a tiger.

Wow, he thought. *The nose wants to climb, the airspeed's increasing, and it's hard to stay level. Roll in some tabs; this is going to be more complicated than just reading about it. The nose is bobbing up and down again; this plane has a mind of its own, but I've have to be the master. Remember what Kranz told me, "No matter what happens, always fly the plane, don't let it fly you."*

"Good," radioed Kranz. "Now reduce to cruise power, the nose will want to drop, hold it up and use the trim tabs. By the way, I mentioned it in the briefing; up ahead is a wood pulp factory that makes paper. As a reminder, if you fly through the smoke coming out of the smokestacks, it's an automatic Down. Believe me, you don't want your plane full of that smoke, it'll make you barf. Also don't fly through these little cumulus clouds, there may be another plane trying the same trick from the opposite direction. It'll ruin your day."

Capp reduced power and kept the plane level. He knew of pilots who said they flew into the small clouds. They liked the kick of the plane being bumped up when the cloud was entered.

"I've got it." radioed Kranz.

"Roger," radioed Capp as he held his arms up to show he had released control. He flexed his shoulders and back, *Jeez, I didn't realize how tense I was, relax buddy, relax.*

"Below us is West Field," radioed Kranz. "That's where we'll be doing most of our landing and take-off practices. I'll bend this around so you can get a better look."

Kranz put the SNJ in a ninety-degree bank, added power, and pulled some heavy G's. The SNJ turned in a tight circle to the left.

Capp wasn't expecting the extreme bank; it startled him. The heavy force of gravity pulled his head down, it was an effort to lift his head and look out at the ground.

"How about that?" laughed Kranz. "Got to have a little fun once in a while, I had to give you a taste of what a fighter pilot goes through, that's what you want, right?"

"Yes Sir," radioed Capp. He stuck his fist in the air and gave a big Thumbs Up so Kranz could see it. "That's great, that's what I want."

"Believe me, you'll get plenty of that." radioed Kranz. "Let's head over to Sampson Field where you'll learn formation flying, then Bremer Field where you'll do bombing and gunnery, and back home. Head 340 degrees, you've got it."

Capp wiggled the stick and turned to 340 degrees.

What a blast, he thought. *I could do this twenty-four hours a day.*

"I want to show you something," radioed Kranz. "Add power and climb to Angels Niner (nine thousand feet)."

Capp added power and strained to keep the SNJ on the correct heading.

This is work, he thought. *I thought I was going along for a joy ride this morning, but who cares, he's giving me stick time, and it's great. Better than sitting here like a robot.*

They reached angels niner, Capp pulled back the power and leveled off.

"Good work," radioed Kranz. "You're a natural pilot. Don't get too cocky though, this bird can bite you when you least expect it. I'll slow down to landing speed, and then look out at the ground below. That little lake at eight o'clock is a good reference, tell me what you see."

Kranz pulled back the power, lowered the flaps and slowed to landing speed.

Capp looked behind him to the left, at the lake while the plane was in a nose high position. The lake was moving forward, from eight, to nine, and then to the ten o'clock position. The SNJ was going backward.

"We're going backwards," radioed Capp. "What's going on?"

"I checked the upper winds before we left," radioed Kranz. "Above eight thousand feet, they're about seventy knots from the West. Our landing speed is sixty, so we're being pushed backwards, crazy, huh? At thirty thousand feet they're about two hundred knots, the Jet Stream.

Just wanted you to see how much you have to prepare before you fly. This world has a lot going on and we're merely specks in this huge arena. You can't control the arena, but you can plan to have control of yourself, and not get killed. Imagine a pilot planning a cross-country flight at night, heading West, and crashing short of fuel because he didn't check the upper winds, or conversely, heading East and ending up out over the ocean, lost. It's happened. There are some stupid pilots, don't you be one of them. Let's head back to the barn, you've got it."

Capp lowered the nose, and headed east, back to the field.

As they approached Warner Field, Kranz radioed,

"I've got it; follow me through on the stick and rudder as we slow for landing."

Capp placed his hand lightly on the stick and the same for his feet on the rudder pedals. He could feel the movement but not bother Kranz.

"Warner tower," radioed Kranz, "Whiskey Charlie 234, Point Alpha for landing."

Point Alpha was the geographic location over a small lake that all aircraft passed over before entry into the traffic pattern.

"Roger Whiskey Charlie 234," answered the tower controller. "Cleared to enter the traffic pattern, left turns, runway 36, wind 010 degrees at 10 knots. Call on base."

"Roger, Whiskey Charlie 234, runway 36," answered Kranz. "We've had a wind shift since we took-off," explained Kranz. "Good experience for your first flight."

Kranz flew south to parallel runway 36, slowed down, lowered his gear and flaps as he passed the south end of the runway and commenced a left descending turn.

"Sampson tower, Whiskey Charlie 234 turning base, gear down and locked." radioed Kranz.

"Roger, Whiskey Charlie 234," answered the tower controller, "Have you in sight, cleared to land."

"How're you doing Capp?" asked Kranz, "still with me?"

"Yes Sir," answered Capp.

"There's a slight crosswind from the right," said Kranz over the intercom. "I'll lower my right wind on final, hold left rudder to keep the nose straight, tail wheel first, than the main gear, hold right rudder, and if all goes well, we'll be at the chocks soon."

The landing went as Kranz predicted, turned off of the runway on to the taxiway, and fishtailed back to the chocks. They parked, and cut the engine. The plane captains hopped on the wing and help un-strap each pilot.

"Hey Billy Joe," said Capp to the plane captain as Billy Joe helped Capp un-strap. "Clean as a Billy goats butt; you ask and you get. I'm still not sure I ever want to see a Billy's goat butt."

"You don't want to," laughed Billy Joe. "The clean cockpit will do just fine."

Capp pulled himself out of the cockpit, and stepped onto the wing, shuffled slowly and jumped to the ground. Kranz was already on the deck.

"Well," said Kranz. "Are you ready for your second hop?"

"Yes Sir," laughed Capp, who had a huge grin on his face. "This is greatest thing I've ever experienced, I'm ready right now."

They turned and walked back toward the hangar area.

"Today was fun," said Kranz. "Tomorrow will also be fun, but you're going to do all the work, so get ready for concentrated physical and mental output. You handle the plane well. Let's debrief and you can go back to your studies. Good hop."

Capp's brain was still up at angels five. He didn't hear much of the debrief and had to pull himself back to the words Kranz was speaking. He did hear his parting words,

"Any questions?"

"No Sir," answered Capp, "I'll probably have a bunch tonight, not sure how much I'm going to sleep, this is great."

"Everyone goes through the same feeling," laughed Kranz. I did, and so did every Navy pilot who wears these wings. If you didn't, you don't belong here. See you tomorrow."

"Yes Sir," answered Capp. He saluted, and Kranz left the area.

Capp looked around. Quirt had just come in and was in the process of debriefing. Quirt finished, Capp strolled over to him and shouted in a laugh,

"We made it, you son-of-a-gun, we made it. How was it?"

"Great," shouted Quirt back in return. "Up above all of the people, lakes and buildings, it's almost like a dream world, how about you?"

"Same," answered Capp. "Kranz let me get a lot of stick time, it was great. Let's get out of here and grab some chow."

As they left, Pervis was standing outside with a cigarette in his hand, blowing smoke into the air.

"Well look at the two heroes," said Pervis with a sneer. "Enjoy the few flights you're going to have before you wash out on demerits. It shouldn't be much longer now, too bad."

Capp stopped and looked at Quirt.

"You know," said Capp. "Little insignificant people, who think they're powerful, crash hard when they find out they are just that, insignificant. You're due Pervis. No one as slimy as you will ever make it, same as in Pre-flight; you have a character flaw; you're a loser."

"Just keep thinking that," answered Pervis, as he threw his cigarette on the grass, stepped on it with his shoe and slowly ground it into the green. He looked at Capp and smiled with his lip in a curl, "But remember, I've got the power, and that makes all the difference. You don't have much time left in the program. I'll see to that, tough luck."

Pervis turned and walked back toward the briefing room, stopped, looked at them and with a sinister laugh exclaimed,

"Not much time."

9

That night, Capp, Quirt, Munson and Curtin decided on a trip into Pensacola. They felt a few libations were in order, to loosen up, celebrate their first flight, and get a new perspective on life.

"C'mon you guys," shouted Capp to the others, "Get in the car; we're off to get some loving. What girl could resist true fighter pilots?"

"Yeahh," laughed Quirt. "One flight under our belt, we're the new Aces; it's all down hill now. Bring on the broads."

"Do you suppose Avalina is there?" said Munson. "I could watch her all night."

"You and about a thousand other cadets," laughed Curtin. "I think she's off limits, at least that's the rumors."

"That's no rumor," said Capp. "I tried to put a move on her, and all she did was point to the bouncer. You know the guy who looks like a throwback to a Neanderthal, the guy with no neck. She said if I didn't back off, he'd make my acquaintance. Naturally, I like my arms and legs attached in their current locations, so I decided discretion was the better part of valor."

"In other words," laughed Quirt. "You're a coward."

"You bet," answered Capp. "I may be dumb, but I'm not stupid."

The top was down, the breeze blew around their heads, life was good. After they parked, Capp put up the top.

The Gulf Breeze was the destination of choice. A military hangout, brightly lit with dark wood mahogany paneled walls, raucous and raunchy; it was a magnet for healthy boys who wanted to meet healthy girls. The large oval bar was near the front door, with a dance floor to the side of it. You could order fast food and eat at the bar, at tables, or in a separate room in the rear.

It was large, and set up so it was easy to move around and meet people. Models of military planes hung from the ceiling, along with photos on the walls of ships, airplanes and celebrities. There was a corner designated the "Blue Corner", with blue and yellow colored aircraft models placed on a shelf to honor the Navy's demonstration flight team, the Blue Angels.

Alcohol has the reputation of creating an atmosphere for fights, but since cadets would be washed out for fighting, it was probably the safest bar in Pensacola.

Besides the availability of single men and women, another main attraction was the head barmaid, Avalina, a lady with enormous breasts which were pushed up and proudly displayed in the frame of her low cut blouse. She was a beautiful bleached blonde with an hourglass figure, and nicknamed, 'Marilyn.' She would balance drinks on her head while dancing, her head never moved, but every other part of her voluptuous body did, much to the joy and appreciation of the customers. Two songs on the jukebox, one Hawaiian and one of Middle Eastern belly dancing were her trademarks which allowed her to show off her sensuous moves and physical attributes. No matter what was the atmosphere in the bar, when she took over the dance floor, it would almost immediately become loud and happy, with shouts and singing from both men and women. She created fun. To put it mildly, she was a lusty, bawdy broad.

Avalina danced among the patrons, delivered drinks, fast food, and led the patrons in all types of songs. It was the noisiest bar in town. The singing and cheering was thunderous. Some songs were raunchy, the raunchier the song, the louder the singing and cheering, with the loudest volume on the dirtiest words. The raunchier the song, the more tips Avalina would pocket, and she knew many, many, raunchy songs.

Limerick songs were the favorite as there were many creative

70

verses, but as is the case in any military genre, songs of love, death, honor and loyalty to various entities also existed. These were not sung in upper class bars, nor did persons of gentile upbringing sing them in public. But for pilots who put their lives on the line each day, it was a high adrenaline rush, and great fun. You just tilted back your head and belted out all those indecent lyrics. Two favorites began, "There was a young man from Cass whose…, Aye, yie, yie, yie, in China they never eat chili, so sing me another that's worse than the other, and waltz me around again Willie." and, "Oh dear what could the matter be, seven old ladies locked in a lavet'ry…" "Anchors Aweigh" was always sung at some time during the evening along with "Gory, Gory, what a hell of a way to die." That would go on all night, until the bar closed.

They entered the bar, it was crowded and noisy. The juke box was turned up loud, the dance floor was packed. At the far end of the room, some cadets at a table were singing the tune, "Oh the sexual life of a camel, is stranger than anyone thinks…", which went on for several verses. As usual, it was led by Avalina who was laughing and encouraging more volume. It was a funny and popular song. Normally the singing erupted when the juke box was silent, but no one seemed to mind if both were going on at the same time. Fun and frolic was the order of the night.

They found a table and sat down.

"No one who never was stationed here would believe this place," shouted Capp over the din. "It's a singles dream come true. Hey, there are a couple of women at the bar that look free. That's why we came here, to spread a little happiness among the opposite sex. Quirt, yours is the ugly one. It's time to scramble."

"Funny man," answered Quirt, "We'll see who gets stuck with the loser. Let the games begin."

"What a pair," laughed Munson. "You guys don't care about the women; it's the competition that counts- who scores first, who is number one."

Capp and Quirt got up and sauntered over to the bar.

Capp was one of the more popular cadets with the girls. Besides being handsome combined with a great personality, it was a rumored that he was well endowed.

It was a work of art, almost classic, to watch him work his seductive magic on a girl that didn't know him. After a few drinks, funny jokes, and perhaps a dance or two, he would be seen whispering in her ear. The girl would look at him with a surprised, astonished look on her face. She now knew more about him than she first had realized. Most of them were curious, and some accepted his invitation to experience the feeling of what he could perform. Several pilots had reputations as "Lady Killers" at the Gulf Breeze, but Capp was popular, and known to have a high success ratio. Quirt was going to award him a medal, "The Order of the Garter and Rear Seat-For Endurance Above and Beyond the Call of Duty." He never got around to creating it, but it was a standing joke that Capp was the leading contender for that award.

"Hi," said Capp to the better looking girl sitting at the bar. "Care to dance?"

She had blonde short hair, blue eyes and an athletic build. There was no apparent fat anywhere on her body.

"No," she answered, smiled and looked over at her friend on the other barstool. "We just stopped in for a drink on our way home, and were about to leave."

"Can I buy you one more for the road?" said Capp. "One more and a dance would be a great way to finish the evening. One more, what do you say?"

Quirt had asked her friend to dance, she also said no, and he had gone back to his table.

"My," she answered, "You are persistent, but the answer is still no." She again smiled, picked up her purse from the bar, stood up and walked to the door, with her friend following behind.

Capp stared at her as she left, in disbelief.

"Wow," said Capp out loud to the bartender. "Pete, I've never been shot down so fast in my life. What's with them two? I must be losing my touch."

"Naw," answered Pete as he filled another glass from the draft beer nozzle. He was older and been a bartender here for years. He liked the energy of the patrons.

"They come in here once in awhile, not often, but when they do, they usually leave with other girls. I was going to warn you off, but with your goofy line, who knew?"

"Give me one of those drafts," said Capp. "Maybe it'll help my eyesight. I never would have guessed. She's pretty cute."

"Well," answered Pete. "To use one of your famous sayings, 'That's why they make chocolate and vanilla ice cream.' Go have a ball. The night's still young."

"There's nothing better than a perceptive bartender," laughed Capp. "You're the best."

Pete laughed, bowed, and waved Capp off. Capp walked over to his table and joined Quirt.

"That was quick." said Capp. "Where are Curtin and Munson?"

"Dancing," answered Quirt. "While we were getting blown out of the saddle, they found some friendlies. Boy, were those two we asked to dance, cold fish. It was as if we had a pox or something."

"Not really," answered Capp, "Just the wrong sexual persuasion. Pete filled me in. And please, don't use my ice cream quote. You know, that was really embarrassing, turned down for all to see."

"Nothing ventured, nothing gained," laughed Quirt. "Let's press on. There are many targets here tonight."

"That's why we're here," exclaimed Capp. He let out a loud, 'Whoop-Forward and Onward.' There's two more over there just dying to meet us. First one there gets the best one. C'mon. Maybe we can get a quick tour in the parking lot. Then tomorrow we again fly. What a life, Yeahh!"

The parking lot was convenient, and the closest place where boys and girls could share their amorous desires. Periodically, pairs could be seen going to and from the cars from the bar, and it was laughable to see cars bouncing up and down throughout the evening hours. If a person was not one of the fortunate ones to have participated in the carousing, the anticipation of knowing there was always another time for a conquest kept a young man's primal juices flowing.

The four cadets stumbled back to the barracks, just barely ahead of bed check.

The next morning there would be a need for great quantities of aspirin and hot coffee, but for now they had a new lease on life. The stress of waiting to fly had been relieved.

Now they and their flight mates were to enter a world of adrenalin, exhilaration, and for some, a date with the Angel of Death.

10

0730, Warner Field; Navcad's ready room.

"Hey Capp," shouted Pete Pervis from the other side of the ready room, "Are you ready to be number two? The rating board has us listed as even today. Tomorrow I'll be number one, and you won't. Get used to it."

Capp was seated at a table with Quirt, Munson, and Curtin. They all looked bad, and felt bad. Too much night life along with a hangover had lowered their usual noisy chatter.

"Listen to that idiot," said Capp to his tablemates. "Is he insane?"

"Pervis," answered Capp, "There are four at this table ahead of you. Number five will be your position. Not one, not two, not three, not four, but five. Have you studied, or did you buy the answers on how to fly?"

"Nice try," said Pervis. "You tried that once. I haven't forgotten. I'll be number one. You can bet your butt on that."

"Why don't you find your instructor and embarrass him," answered Capp. "You're an embarrassment to me and to the Navy."

Pervis got up from his table and walked toward the briefing room.

"You guys are nervous, I can tell," said Pervis. "You hate to lose, but deep down inside, you know I'm right."

Quirt looked at Capp.

"Ever since Pre-Flight, you guys have been at each other. Let's hope it doesn't get any worse."

Capp pushed his coffee cup away.

"Do you know why I hate that little creep?" said Capp.

"Yeah," answered Quirt, "You caught him cheating on the Aerology weather exam."

"Pervis is a cheat," said Capp. "He's not the type of NavCad that should be in the program. Who knows what other corners he's cut, or will cut? Some may be dangerous. It's just a matter of time before he fouls up. Let's hope it doesn't hurt one of us. He really hates me, and that's O.K. He knows how I feel, and why. Who cares, time to brief. If I don't barf, I'll get to the next hop. My stomach wants to talk to my tongue, and it's not good conversation."

"We had fun last night," groaned Quirt. "But that was really stupid, especially before this kind of a hop."

"Just part of the training, another day in the life of a fighter pilot, laughed Capp. However, an extra set of gloves might not be a bad idea. I'll see you later."

Capp met Captain Kranz in the briefing room.

"Today," said Kranz, "We'll fly straight stalls, approach stalls, and spins. Have you studied the procedures?"

"Yes, Sir," answered Capp.

"Good," said Kranz. "In order to start landing practice, today's hop must be completed satisfactorily. You look a little tired. Are you O.K.?"

"Yes Sir," answered Capp. "Must be something I ate, but I'll be fine."

Kranz studied Capp's face. He recognized hangovers, and Capp had the classic look of someone who'd been celebrating something way too much, probably his first flight yesterday. He'd watch Capp close. Spins should be the fun part of the hop for him.

"As the book says," continued Kranz. "The SNJ is designed like a fighter. It loses a lot of altitude fast. Pilots have died by starting maneuvers too low, and panic into a secondary stall/spin. Respect the SNJ. Know its limitations, and you won't have any problems. Just like a woman, huh?"

"Yes Sir." Capp laughed. Capp thought, *flying with Kranz is great.*

"I'll talk you through the start, run-up, and take-off procedure." said Kranz as they walked out to the flight line. "That's why I'm here. Don't expect to be perfect. This is a complicated machine, not a Piper Cub. With practice, you'll get the hang of it. You can read all the books you want, but hands-on is a whole different ballgame."

Capp completed the Walk-Around, and then climbed into the forward cockpit. He gazed at the field, and thought, *Am I dreaming? Look at the activity, and listen to the noise. How lucky can a guy get?*

"Start the engine and let's taxi," radioed Kranz.

Capp pushed the switch. The big radial engine coughed, and then started. Smoke surrounded the plane for a moment.

Instruments O.K. Let's go, thought Capp. *Taxi straight for a few feet, and then tap the brakes which are activated at the top of the rudder pedals. Oops, too much. Don't do a ground loop, a big circle. That would be embarrassing. A little left, little right, so far so good, what a kick in the pants. Run up the engine, check the prop, all looks good.*

"Ready for take off, Sir," radioed Capp.

"Request permission from the tower," radioed Kranz.

"Warner tower, Whiskey Charlie 437, request permission to take-off." transmitted Capp.

"Roger," answered the tower. "You're cleared for take-off, runway 36. Turn left when clear of the field."

Capp slowly added power. The nose started to move to the right from the prop torque of its clockwise rotation.

"Kick left rudder," radioed Kranz, "or we'll go off the side of the runway."

More rudder, thought Capp. *That's better. Airspeed's increasing. Raise the tail. Gently pull back on the stick. Jeez, we're airborne. Gear up. Flaps up. Reduce to climb power. Turn left, and away we go. I can feel Kranz on the stick helping me out, but not enough to bother me. He's letting me fly the bird.*

"Let's climb to angels six, and do some clean stalls, no gear or flaps." radioed Kranz.

"Roger," answered Capp.

"Level at angels six," radioed Capp.

"I'll do the first one," radioed Kranz. "Reduce power, hold the nose up, it'll shudder at about 70 knots, the nose falls through, relax the stick, add power, get some speed, and gently come back to level flight, your turn."

It's hard to see the horizon due to the haze and get a reference point for level flight, thought Capp. *Here we go. Same procedure, the nose is falling through, whoa, too much forward stick, losing altitude, damn, pull back gently. Not too good.*

"You lost about 1,500 feet instead of 500," radioed Kranz. "Don't push so hard on the stick. The SNJ is very stable. Try again."

Capp did five more and all seemed to go well.

"Let's do an approach stall," radioed Kranz. "That happens in the landing pattern when you get too slow in a turn. It's very dangerous because of the low altitude. Recovery must be quick and coordinated, or you die. The best solution is never to get into that situation. You really need to practice these, understand?"

"Yes Sir," radioed Capp.

"As we briefed, gear and flaps down, thirty degree bank, then pull back the power. At the first shudder, add full power, and roll level. Don't try to be a hot dog and continue the turn. Inverted at 500 feet and out of control can ruin your day, you'll buy the farm. Better to be embarrassed and go around for another approach than to push up daisies. We had a recent fatality by a cadet ignoring procedures; you don't want to join him. Give it a try."

He had to mention that horrible crash that we saw, thanks a lot, thought Capp. *I haven't made a landing yet and if I don't get this right, I won't get to make any, Kranz will wash me out. Now do it as he said. I feel the shudder. Something's wrong. I'm inverted. What do I do?*

"I've got it," radioed Kranz urgently, wiggling the stick back and forth.

Capp raised his hands to show he no longer had control.

"Watch," said Kranz. "Add power, roll level, gear and flaps up. It's under control now, reduce power. We've lost quite a bit of altitude. Welcome to the world of Approach Stalls. That's we practice these at altitude. It can get nasty."

"What did I do wrong?" asked Capp.

"You kicked top rudder by mistake. The plane rolled around to get stable. Stable was inverted. On the next one, keep it coordinated and react faster. Try again, you've got it."

Capp wiggled the stick left and right to acknowledge he had control.

Reading about it and flying it, are two different experiences, thought Capp. *This is only the first hop. Wow, there's a lot to know. This time, keep the ball centered on the needle/ball gauge. Slower, slower, feel the shudder. Add power, roll level, gear and flaps up. Am I going to keep flying, or stall? I've lost altitude but I made it. At least the sky, not the ground is above my canopy. I'm still not comfortable, but practice will make perfect.*

"Good," radioed Kranz. "You take instructions well. Five more and we'll move on."

"Let's climb to angels eight," radioed Kranz. "Time for spins, I'll do the first one."

Everyone talks about spins, thought Capp. *The plane is basically out of control. In the ready room, scuttlebutt* (small talk, rumors) among the rookies, *this is the maneuver most talked about, the one that causes the most sweat.*

"O.K., we're at altitude," radioed Kranz. "It begins the same as a stall. When it shudders and the nose starts to fall through, kick right rudder, hard, and hold the stick back in your lap."

The SNJ lurched down and to the right, spinning.

Wow, thought Capp. *This isn't comfortable. The green earth looks like it revolves, but it's the plane, and the nose is really pointed down. I hope science works today, also my stomach.*

"To recover," radioed Kranz, "Push forward on the stick, kick left rudder until the spin stops and pick up some speed. Neutralize the rudder and gently, and I do mean gently pull the nose back to the horizon while you add power. If you pull back too hard on the stick, a secondary stall and spin could happen. Look at the altitude we've lost, double that in a secondary stall/spin. That's why you don't want to do that. Speed is your greatest friend to avoid a secondary. But you also need altitude. Low altitude spins are generally fatal. Your turn."

It's twenty degrees cooler here than on the ground, thought Capp, *but I'm sweating like a pig. Don't gag, I don't want to barf.*

Pull up, feel the shudder, kick right rudder, yuk, what a crummy feeling. Two turns, kick left rudder, forward stick; damn it works, the spin stopped. Nose down, pick up speed and gently pull up. Am I pulling too hard? We'll find out. Yeahh, I made it.

"Good work," radioed Kranz. "You lost too much altitude, but that's O.K. We've plenty of it. If you've got the speed, don't be afraid of a secondary. Just don't yank the stick back, and you'll be O.K. Spins are hard on the stomach. Many a rookie will barf from spins and rolls. Or," he laughed. "Even if you're an old pro', and have eaten some bad food. However, it's really your inner ear fluid that causes the nausea. Try a few more and we'll head back to Warner."

Capp finished the spins. He thought, *Thank God, we're done. No more heavy drinking before a flight. Kranz knows, but he's cool about it. Am I going to sleep tonight. This is work.*

In the debriefing room, Kranz and Capp sat down, both tired and sweaty. Capp's stomach was still churning.

"How's the food poisoning?" said Kranz with a slight smile. Never mind I don't expect an answer. Just be careful of what you eat before a flight, it can kill you. Next hop, we'll do landings. As you saw today, stalls and spins must be practiced until you can do them perfectly; to recognize when the plane is near the danger zone. It'll come. Sit in a chair, close your eyes, and visualize all the maneuvers, power settings, and recoveries. It's a new technique, not proven, but it seems to work. We're done, good hop."

"Thank you, Sir," answered Capp. "It's going to be hard to concentrate this afternoon in ground school. I'll be re-living this flight all day."

"Just don't fall asleep," laughed Kranz. "The instructors get testy about that. See you next hop."

Capp sat for a few minutes in the briefing room. Then got up and walked to the ready room. Quirt and Munson were there.

"Am I beat," said Capp. "I thought I was going to barf, but swallowed hard about a thousand times. I think Kranz suspected too much liquid refreshment. I told him it was some bad food. He was cool, and didn't ground me. But what a fun hop, the laws of physics were all used up today. What a blast. How'd your hops go?"

"Same as yours," answered Quirt. "I'm still in the air. What can you say? It's a blast."

"Spins scare the crap out of me," said Munson. "The only time I'm going to do any, is when it's required. But you're both right. Can you imagine when we checked into this place, just a few days ago, that we would be doing this? It is a blast. Well, back to reality, time for chow."

"Let's go," said Capp. "I'll have aspirin with my hamburger."

11

The following Saturday, Capp was out on the Grinder, a paved concrete area in the front and side of the barracks. With an M-1 Garand rifle on his shoulder, he was there to march off his demerits. It was a one-hour march, one side to the other. It was raining. Capp was miserable.

No one was allowed to verbally harass the marcher. However, Pervis was in his room gleefully celebrating his newfound power. He looked at his image in the mirror and said out loud,

"This is beautiful! That arrogant fool is finally getting what's coming to him, and there's nothing he can do about it. Capp hasn't seen anything yet, I've just begun."

Pervis had bad memories of his childhood, and his father who was a drunk. He was verbally and physically abused, knocked about, shouted at, and told he was a loser that would never amount to anything. To a little kid, the verbal abuse was horribly degrading, even worse than the physical abuse. He was never given any family responsibility, and was frightened most of the time. Little did Pervis realize that his anger against successful, popular persons like Capp was a deep-seated anger that needed professional help. In 1954, however, if you sought help for depression or anger, you might be labeled as crazy, mentally ill, and could easily be ostracized. The stigma of mental illness was socially unacceptable. It also might be a reason to be dropped from the flight program. Few considered such a drastic step as psychological therapy, or even knew it was available.

Pervis was smart enough not to cluster the demerits to Capp, which might bring it to the attention and suspicions of the Marine Officer in Charge. Pervis calculated that 80 demerits would be enough to have Capp washed out of the program. That was easy; ten demerits every week would do it. Demerits could be awarded for many infractions: sloppy clothing, bed sheets not tucked in tight so a quarter would not bounce on them, being late for muster, class, or bed checks. It should be a piece of cake. He peeked out his window again, and watched Capp march, back and forth, back and forth, in the cold drizzle.

"Yeahh," he shouted, "I love it, love it. Battalion Commander, what a great power position. My father should see me now; I'm the man in charge, the top of the heap, number one."

Capp completed his punishment, departed the grinder, and later walked into Quirts room.

"Hey friend," said Capp. "I'm through marching for that creep Pervis, ever again. Let's go over to the ACRAC and scarf down some suds along with a huge hamburger. I used up all the hot water in the showers trying to warm up after marching for an hour in that miserable cold rain."

"Great idea," answered Quirt. "I've been waiting for you."

"I'll drive," said Capp as they left the room. "Maybe Pervis will be walking and I can run him down. However, that would be too nice."

"It's a start," answered Quirt.

They entered the ACRAC, which as usual was noisy and cheery.

"This is a great place," expounded Capp. I don't know who set up the ACRACS', but he should be given the Medal of Honor. Let's sit in the corner booth where we can have some privacy."

Booths were located along the walls. A large bar and grill was in the middle. The remaining space was taken up by tables. The booths seats were brown colored and had high wooden backs so no one could see who was in the booth unless they walked directly in front of the booth. The seat backs and seats were big and soft, upholstered with Corinthian leather, very comfortable. The table was dark colored wood, which gave a macho masculine atmosphere.

Capp leaned back in his seat and started the conversation.

"Something has to be done with Pervis, he's dangerous. With his appointed new rank and warped little mind, he has a new found power, and can possibly get me washed out of the program, maybe not only me, but all of us in our group. He's not stupid. Every few weeks he'll drop a few demerits on me, not enough to bring attention to his devious plan, but enough until I'm brought before a board of inquiry. I could complain to the barracks Marine Commanding Officer, but that might single me out as someone who can't handle personal problems, or a whiner, not a good idea. Leadership mandates a solution to a bad situation. We're being trained as leaders, so let's find a solution, right?"

"Right," answered Quirt.

Jim Quirt was more upset than Capp at the bad situation. Quirt was also from Minnesota, the son of a tough construction worker. As with Capp, he had no time for phonies or self-important snobs. They met in Pre-Flight, both were irreverent, iconoclastic, and became friends immediately.

"There are a lot of swamps around here," said Capp. "Do you suppose we could shanghai Pervis and feed him to one of the alligators?"

"Naw," answered Quirt. "That would be animal cruelty. The alligator would have indigestion the rest of its life. Not a bad thought however. Any ideas that are non-fatal?"

Capp grabbed a napkin, looked around to make sure no other person was close, scribbled some words on it and pushed it over to Quirt.

Quirt read the note, leaned back in his seat, and roared with laughter.

"This is great, you a son-of-a-gun," said Quirt. "P-Day- Pervis the Pervert day will soon arrive. Capp, let me buy the master of intrigue another beer. We've got some exploring to do."

They left the ACRAC and drove to one of the inlets that were swampy, not the place that normal persons would go for a walk to experience the wonders of nature. The drizzle was falling in sheets of miserable wetness.

"Hey Quirt, said Capp nervously as they walked on the soggy turf. "Maybe this wasn't such a good idea. Maybe we should call this off, I don't like this place. It gives me the creeps."

"Just watch where you walk," answered Quirt. "There's got to be a prize here that we're after. Stay close."

They shuffled along; both tense, aware of the dangerous area they were in.

"Stop," said Quirt quietly. "I think we've found what we want. Hand me the stick and the bag."

"Are you sure?" answered Capp. "We don't want to screw up, that could be dangerous."

"Quiet," answered Quirt, "Don't move. I'm sure."

He jabbed with the stick, pinned his prey against the ground, lifted it for Capp to see, held out the bag, and then deposited his wriggling adversary to the bottom of the bag.

"A beauty," said Quirt, "One that will go down in history."

"Keep that damned thing away from me," said Capp. "Are you sure that bag is safe, it won't escape? This is gross; maybe we should let it loose?"

"Are you kidding?" answered Quirt. "This is perfect, and what a background. A depressing, dreary, drizzly day, it's better than a Frankenstein plot. Let's get out of here. This is not the place I want to be when it gets dark."

"You don't have to ask me twice," answered Capp with relief in his voice. "This isn't the place I want to be when it's daylight."

About 2130, 9:30 PM, Capp met Quirt at Capp's car. It was dark, the drizzle had stopped.

"Open the trunk," said Quirt. "You create a diversion in the passageway, and I'll do the rest."

Capp walked in the front door walked down the passageway and into the duty office. The BSOOD (battalion student officer of the day), Brett Mayfield, was reading a book.

"Hey Mayfield," said Capp. "Do you smell smoke?"

"No," answered Mayfield. "What are you talking about?"

"I don't know," said Capp. "Maybe it's just my imagination, but I swear I smelled it down the hall. With these old wooden barracks, maybe you should clear out the first floor. Talk to Pervis who's the senior cadet and we can take a look around. If we find something, the fire alarm can be sounded. What do you think?"

"You'd better be right," answered Mayfield. "This is going to be a pain in the butt clearing everyone out. But I'd better check it out, just in case."

Mayfield walked down to Pervis's room. He was lying on his bunk, reading a book.

"Hey Pete," said Mayfield. "Sorry to bother you just before lights out, but Chuck Capp thinks he smelled smoke in this area. We should clear the rooms and do a search. Other cadets can help."

"What a crock," answered Pervis. "Is this one of Capp's practical jokes? I wouldn't put it past him."

"Who knows, but it's best we check it out," said Mayfield. You can stand by the duty office while I look around. Capp agreed to help, since he's the one that smelled it."

"O.K., O.K." answered Pervis. "But be quick about it."

Mayfield and Pervis walked back to the duty office where Capp was standing.

"C'mon Capp," Said Mayfield. "Let's do a quick inspection, it shouldn't take too long. Let's get some help from other cadets."

"Right," answered Capp. "Hope I'm wrong, but you never know."

"Get going," said Pervis. "It's almost lights out."

"Well, we don't want to deprive you of your beauty sleep, would we?" said Capp. "A real concerned leader of the troops."

"C'mon," said Mayfield. "You two can fight each other at a different time. Let's go."

Mayfield cleared out the rooms, and Capp followed.

Quirt stood outside, behind the door at the end of the barracks watching the scene unfold through the glass partitions; Capp turned and gave him a thumbs-up. Quirt entered quickly, entered Pervis's room, and left again without being noticed.

"Nothing here," said Mayfield. "Let's call it a night. I'll check the passageway throughout the night, just in case. Thanks Chuck, better safe than sorry, right?"

"Right," answered Capp. "I swear I smelled something, but you're a good man, a true leader. Some people in charge I know wouldn't be as diligent." He looked over at Pervis.

"Get lost," said Pervis. "What with all the beer you drink, I'm surprised you even have a sense of smell. Let's hit the sack."

Lights out was at 2200, 10:00 PM. The barracks were dark except for the dim glow of hallway night lights.

Now, no one had ever tested the sturdiness of the walls of the barracks from sound wave vibration pressure, but at about 2205, there came the most blood-curdling scream at a volume that only Joshua at the walls of Jericho must have heard.

Pervis was screaming,

"Get that thing out of here, get that thing out of here, I'm going to die, I think it wants to bite me, O God I'm going to die!"

Pervis had crawled into bed, felt something moving under his body, threw back his covers, leaped out of bed like an Olympic athlete, turned on the lights, and there on his bed sheet was the ugliest, thick, black and brown striped snake he had ever seen. Its yellow slit eyes seemed to focus on Pervis, and it slithered off of the bed toward his feet.

Pervis went nuts, screaming, terrified, and afraid to move for fear it would bite him.

Cadets from the other rooms in the barracks flooded into his room to see what was wrong. When Pervis stopped screaming long enough to tell them there was a poisonous snake on the floor, the room emptied faster than it had filled up, including his room mate. Everyone was in a panic. Many so-called heroes decided that fighting snakes was not what they had signed up for, and Pervis had no guardians.

As the snake continued toward his feet, Pervis knew he had to move before the snake bit him. His rigid panic ridden body would not move. With an extreme effort of mind of over matter, he mentally took back control of his muscles and jumped to the side, and then out the door. He slammed the door and leaned against it, limp, whimpering softly from fear, the terrifying suffocating fear prehistoric man must have felt just before being caught and devoured by animals in the dark of the night.

Security was called. Nervous military police were ordered to find the snake, which they did, under Pervis's bed. It was dispatched with a blow from a nightstick, and then carried to the sick bay where it was determined not to be poisonous.

Pervis was in a state of terror and fright. He wouldn't go back into his room. Instead, he went into the Head in the event he had to throw up.

Capp heard where Pervis was, made his way to the Head by his room, and pretended to relieve himself.

"Damn," said Capp. "That was terrible. Maybe you should have given it a demerit. But then again, if you did...it might have a poisonous friend pay you a visit."

"You did this, you did this, you miserable freak!" screamed Pervis. "That smoke scare was just a screen so you could put that in my rack."

"Are you crazy," shouted Capp. "Snakes scare the crap out of me. I wouldn't come within a thousand miles of one. Besides, I was with Mayfield the whole time. That must have been one lonely snake, to get into your bed."

There was an investigation, everyone was interviewed, but since no one was found to have placed the snake in Pervis's bed, the assumption was it got there by itself, as Florida has plenty of snakes.

Sunday afternoon, Capp and Quirt were enjoying a beer at the ACRAC, discussing the events of the previous nocturnal encounter.

"You know," said Capp, "I would never lie to such a fine upstanding cadet like Pervis; snakes do scare the crap out of me. You however..."

Laughing, they clicked their glasses and toasted the many varieties of snakes, which included those that wear cadet officer's bars.

Capp and his friends never received another demerit from Pervis, no matter how unmilitary they acted.

Pervis, however, was not one to drop a grudge. He was sure that Capp was the culprit, and this was not going to be the end of his revenge.

12

Chuck Capp was sweating and grunting, trying to turn the SNJ onto the landing field, but it was as if the plane had a mind of its own. This was his second full working flight. His indoctrination flight and first working hop were over and behind him. This now was serious.

The sky was a brilliant blue, with bright sunlight, a beautiful day to fly, but enjoying the scenery was the last thing on Capp's mind.

Landing practice was at West Field, a large square field. Because so many planes used the field, it was a good idea to keep your head on a swivel.

"C'mon Capp," Captain Kranz encouraged him, "Keep turning, don't level out or you won't get to the line-up. Reduce power, that's the way, don't reduce too much. Keep turning, watch your altitude, you're getting low, add some power, keep it coming, O.K. roll out. You're close to the ground, start rotating the nose up... faster or you'll bounce."

Capp rotated the nose up, but not high enough. The main wheels hit the ground and the plane bounced high. The nose started to rotate back toward the ground, the beginning of a dangerous porpoise, a series of out-of-control bounces which could end up in a crash, sometimes fatal.

"How do I get out of this?" shouted Capp into the intercom.

"Add power!" Pull back on the stick gently, and get back into the air!" responded Kranz sternly.

"Roger," answered Capp, fighting off the feeling of panic.

Capp did as ordered; the plane hung in the air for a moment, and then began a slow climb back into the landing pattern, an imagined rectangular area to the runway.

"Sorry Sir, it won't happen again." radioed Capp.

"Don't bet on it," answered Kranz. "Just know how to get out of it. I haven't lost a student yet, and you can bet your boots, you're not going to be the first. Now turn downwind and let's keep practicing."

Capp called the tower, "Baker One One Four, turning downwind."

"Roger, Baker One One Four, answered the tower, call the base."

Capp leveled off at one thousand feet and paralleled the landing area, lowered his gear and flaps. *Get it together, a lot going on, but each step is separate, think dammit, don't get behind by even one step. Here we go, concentrate!*

Capp radioed, "West tower, Whiskey Charlie One One Four turning base."

"Roger, One One Four," answered the tower, "Cleared for touch-and- go's, call downwind."

Capp reduced power, and started a thirty degree left bank toward the runway area.

Capp kept talking to himself,

"Looking good, check the instruments, keep it turning, watch the altitude, want to land one third of the way down the runway, I'm on the straight-away, ground coming up, pull nose up, reduce power, don't drift, hold it, hold it, c'mon, it should stall, need that tail wheel to hit first, hold it…Yeahh, just like in the book."

The tail wheel contacted the ground with a thump, and the main gear made impact a second later, a perfect carrier-type landing.

"Great," radioed Kranz. "That's the way the first team does it. Now do ten more of those before we head back home."

Capp was elated. He completed the practice landings, most of which were above average and headed back to the base. To finish off a good day, he made a good final landing at Warner Field.

Capp and Kranz walked back to the hangar for their de-briefing.

"Thanks for letting me to work out my problems without chewing me out." said Capp. "At this stage, I need to feel the plane, and make the right corrections. It's a feeling, hard to explain."

"You're doing fine," answered Kranz. "And might I add, you did good by keeping cool and not losing control of the plane. That can be dangerous. I never like to take the plane away from a student, but sometimes it's necessary when it gets too hairy. It's my job to help you get those gold wings, not shake you up. As I said before, we're a team. By the look on your face, I can read your mind. The answer-one bounce, that's all. On the second one, I take control."

Capp smiled. "You read me right."

The debriefing was thorough. Kranz reviewed everything; nothing was left to guesswork or chance.

"Thank you Sir for your help," said Capp. "It's a pleasure having you as my instructor, I really mean that."

"I'll take that as a sincere statement," answered Kranz. "And that you're not trying to blow smoke up my backside. However, remember, I expect every hop to be better than the previous one. Maybe you'll change your mind next week."

They parted, and Capp looked for some of his flight mates. In the corner, he spotted Curtin, who had also finished de-briefing.

"Hey Cy," said Capp. "How'd it go?"

"Well," answered Curtin with a sigh. "If this was World War One, Baron Von Richthofen would not be losing any sleep over me."

"You never know," laughed Capp. "All you have to do is get on his six and it's all over."

"The way I handled take offs and landings, I never want to see combat." said Curtin. "Man, was I all over that runway, bouncing, drifting, and generally loosening every bolt in that bird. The mechanics will have their work cut out tonight, putting everything back together. I hope it gets better, soon."

Capp laughed again. "Hey, I bounced my first landing so high I thought I'd get a nose bleed. You're not alone. Stop worrying. The way the Navy trains us, step by step, it'll all come together quickly. Relax, let's go quaff a few cool ones and exchange war stories with the rest of the guys."

Pervis was at the next table and overheard their conversation.

"So you fouled up and bounced a big one," said Pervis as he leaned over Capp. "What a loser you both are. My hop was perfect."

"Back off you jerk," said Capp. "Your breath stinks. One of these days you're going to blow a procedure big time. When I hear about it, guess what? You won't get any sympathy. What is your problem?"

"You're my problem, Capp," answered Pervis. "You think you're the best, but little do you know that I'm the best. What a crushing blow that's going to be when you finally have to admit that."

"Pervis," said Capp. "The only thing you'll ever be the best at is being a jerk. Go find yourself a mirror. That reflection is the only person that thinks you're great. Go away."

"Getting to you, huh?" said Pervis with his vicious sneer. "Just wait, this is just the beginning."

"Get lost," said Capp. "Come on Curtin; let's go socialize with normal human beings."

Capp walked to the door, twisted the knob, opened the door slightly, turned, looked at Pervis, and said. "Do you know that perfectionists make mistakes? Can you handle that?"

Pervis's face brightened up with that strange twisted smile,

"I don't make mistakes."

"Oh yeah," said Capp. "Remember the Pre-Flight marching drills? You couldn't figure out your left foot from your right, always out of step, always making a mistake. Remember? You provided me with more laughs than watching the Three Stooges. The difference is, they try to be funny. Remember the chewing gum I gave you? I wanted to observe someone who couldn't walk and chew gum at the same time, and you didn't even appreciate my help."

"You're obnoxious," answered Pervis. "Besides, that was marching, not flying. This is now, not then."

Capp jabbed the air, his finger pointed at Pervis,

"As I said before, when you do finally make a mistake, it's going to be spectacular. Bet on it. And I want to be there."

Capp closed the door behind him.

13

The ready room was noisy as usual, with cadets trying to relax prior to their morning flights, drinking coffee, laughing at jokes, and putting each other down with friendly verbal jabs. The weather was cool and sunny with a slight wind from the northwest, ideal for regular and crosswind landing practice.

"Curtin, are you ready to impress your instructor with perfect three point landings?" asked Capp.

"After yesterday," answered Curtin. "I'll be happy just to walk away from any landing. My problem is that I look directly out to the side instead of looking along the front edge of the fuselage, and that fouls up my depth perception. I don't know how far above the runway I am; my rotation for landing is either too high or too low, too soon or too late. It's a habit I've got to break. It's a problem."

"It's not a habit yet," said Capp. "Habits take twenty-two days to form. If you keep looking out the side, it'll become permanent. Stop doing that! Force yourself to look out the front side along the fuselage. That's the habit you want. C'mon, it's early in the game, and nothing's permanent. This is all new to us, so listen to your instructor. He wants you to be good because it's a feather in his cap to see you succeed, O.K.?"

"You're right," answered Curtin. "Being a Pro after one landing practice flight is expecting too much. By the way, where'd you get all this in-depth knowledge?"

"Were you asleep in ground school?" laughed Capp. "I only know what I'm taught. That's one of the classes we had. The instructors tried to pound that into our heads, "Don't look directly out the side while landing."

Capp knocked on Curtin's head with his knuckles. "Pay attention, some day it may save your life."

"Sorry I asked," answered Curtin. "Next time I doze off in class, give me a kick."

"Have you studied cross-wind landing techniques?" asked Capp. It's going to be a long embarrassing hop if you haven't."

"I think so," answered Curtin. "I've read through the manual a few times, plus my instructor does a good brief."

"Don't be too casual," answered Capp. "You should have it totally memorized so it's an instinct in the air."

They checked their wristwatches.

"Time to brief," said Capp. "Time to live, or time to die from a severe butt-chewing, let's live."

They both laughed and walked over to the briefing room. Capp was seated when he saw Captain Kranz approaching.

He stood up and said. "Good morning, Sir." as he stood up and saluted, "Ready for briefing."

"Good morning Mr. Capp," answered Kranz returning the salute. "You look roaring to go. That's good. Sit down and let's go over a few items. First, there's wind drift. If you're flying along a road with a wind blowing from the left, your plane will drift to the right. How do you correct that?"

"You crab, or turn your plane into the wind," answered Capp, "Just enough to stop the drift."

"That's right," said Kranz. "When a large airplane lands, that's the technique that's used. Just before touchdown, the pilot uses rudders and ailerons to straighten the nose, but keeps the upwind wing lowered into the wind to keep it straight on the centerline of the runway. Large planes have a longer straightaway on final. That technique is easier than keeping a wing down for a long distance."

"Sounds complicated," said Capp.

"It is," answered Kranz. "It takes a lot of coordination. I've seen some hairy landings, where the pilot wasn't too good at that method. Like everything else, it takes practice."

"We only use the wing-down method, because our final lineup is much shorter. Is that right?" asked Capp.

"You've read the book," answered Kranz. "Although in a strong wind, you may have to use the crab method.'

'In the wing-down method, on final approach, the upwind wing is lowered into the wind, just enough to stop the drift. Opposite rudder is used to keep the planes nose from turning. The stronger the wind, the lower is the wing, and more rudder is needed.'

'At touchdown, the upwind landing gear will make contact with the runway first, followed quickly by the downwind wheel. Remember, keep the stick into the wind and hold opposite rudder, or a ground loop can happen. That's not a pleasant experience. You could flip the plane and possibly be injured, or killed."

"I've seen planes ground loop when taxiing out for take-off," said Capp.

"Right," answered Kranz. "And that's at about five knots. Imagine that happening at sixty knots. As I said, it's not a pleasant experience. Ground loops also happen on the roll out after landing, when the tail wheel is unlocked to turn off the runway. A pilot can lose control fast if he's not alert.

"The book doesn't give any certain way to get out of a ground loop. What would you do?" asked Capp.

"It happens so fast," answered Kranz, "that about all you can do is hang on and hope it doesn't flip. Rudder, brakes, and opposite aileron can be tried, but most of the time the pilot just rides it out.'

'When you get into advanced training, the planes have tricycle landing gear, which eliminates the ground loop because the nose wheel is on the ground."

"I can hardly wait," said Capp.

"It's great," answered Kranz, "But for now, you're stuck with a tail wheel plane, a tail dragger. We'll fly over to West Field and do some into the wind landings, then over to Halsey Field, which is the crosswind runway. Let's go fly."

Capp took off and took up a heading for West Field. After five landings, Kranz radioed. "You've the hang of that; let's fly over to Halsey Field. Most winds are from the west or northwest and Halsey has a runway that heads north and south, which provides crosswind-landing practice.'

'I'll do the first ones, and then it's your turn. Remember, if the wind is from the left on final, you must have a greater bank when starting your approach on base leg. If the wind is from the right, you must have a shallower bank. On final, do the wing into the wind or wing down method. Follow me on the rudders and stick."

Kranz completed two landings, which were perfect, just as briefed.

"Your turn," said Kranz. "On final, recognize your drift and stop it with the stick. Use rudder to keep the nose straight down the runway line."

The wind is from the west and I'm landing to the north. I'll have to use left wing down on final, thought Capp.

O.K., I'm on final all lined up with the runway, put the left wing down. Oh no, that's too much; I'm drifting left of the runway, I can't land.

"Add power and let's try that again," radioed Kranz. "Give yourself more straight away on final so you can see the drift. Then stop the drift. The centerline of the runway is painted. Use that as your reference to judge the drift."

Here we go again, thought Capp. *O.K., I'm on final all lined up again. I'm drifting right, put in some left stick to lower the wing. Good, that stopped the drift. Hold right rudder to keep the nose straight. Hey, I'm flying straight down the runway, only too far to the right side. Can I land? Let's try it. Touchdown, the left wheel landed first just as the book said, then the right one. Keep left stick into the wind, add power and go around. It's complicated, not much room for error.*

"That was O.K.," radioed Kranz. "With a left crosswind, it's better to be slightly to the left side of the runway, but the middle is best, keep making touch-and-go's."

Got to keep it in the middle of the runway, thought Capp, *O.K., I'm on final, left wing down, hold some right rudder. I'm lined up on the painted centerline, reduce power, good landing, I'll take it.*

"That's better," radioed Kranz. "Do a few more."

Capp completed two more landings that were acceptable, not great, but safe.

"I've got it," radioed Kranz. "I'm going to do a full stop landing, then taxi over for a take off. Follow through on the controls."

Kranz did a full stop landing. As he slowed, he unlocked the tail wheel and turned off the runway onto the taxiway, which is beside, and parallel to the main runway. He S-turned the plane for forward vision and taxied all the way to the takeoff end.

"Your turn," radioed Kranz. "Keep the stick into the wind and use rudders to keep the nose straight down the center line. Concentrate."

What does he think I'm doing up here, sleeping? thought Capp. *Of course I'm concentrating. Let's go.*

Capp taxied onto the runway, stick left, added power and was airborne, then turned left, downwind, parallel to the runway. He approached the landing end of the runway, dropped his flaps, landing gear, and banked left to begin the landing procedure.

I'm on final approach, the straightaway, and I'm lined up with the centerline, thought Capp. *It looks good. Hold the nose up and yeahh, a terrific landing but keep the nose straight with the rudders. The planes almost at a stop, time to unlock the tail wheel. Whoa! The nose is coming around, stomp on the brakes, keep the stick left. Is it going to stop? Oh man, it stopped, thought I had a ground loop. Jeez, I'm sweating like two pigs.*

"Welcome to the world of almost a ground loop," radioed Kranz. "Good reflexes, but slow down more before you turn off the runway. Let's go home. Good hop."

"Yes, Sir," radioed Capp.

Capp was ecstatic. *When an instructor says, "Good Hop," it makes your day.*

They landed, checked in the plane, their parachutes, and walked to the debriefing room.

"I need black hot coffee," said Capp. "That was work trying to keep the nose straight down the runway."

"Bring me one too," said Kranz. "We both need it."

Capp brought the coffees. They both leaned on the long, wooden, and highly varnished briefing table.

"You flew a good hop." said Kranz. "A few more of those and you'll feel more comfortable. An airplane's not like a car because wind moves it around. That's what makes flying fun and a challenge. I don't have a lot to debrief, any questions?"

"No, Sir," answered Capp. "But now I have an idea what a ground loop could be, it's a helpless feeling."

"You held on," said Kranz. "Let's hope that's the closest you ever get to one. See you tomorrow."

"Good-by, Sir," answered Capp, "Looking forward to it."

Capp walked over to the ready room to relax before going to lunch and ground school. He knew Curtin took off right after him, and thought he'd wait for him. There were always plenty of flying magazines to read and take up time.

About a half an hour later, Curtin walked in, sat down beside Capp and said,

"What a bunch of crap!"

By the look on Curtin's face, Capp couldn't help but laugh.

"You look like someone just stole your last beer and your girl," said Capp. "What's up?"

"Worse than that," answered Curtin. "I ground looped!"

"Well, it couldn't have been too bad, you're sitting here," said Capp. "At least you survived."

"It was so embarrassing," said Curtin. "You told me to keep the stick into the wind, my instructor said to keep the stick into the wind, the book says to keep the stick into the wind, guess what I didn't do?"

"Keep your stick into the wind," answered Capp.

"How'd you guess," said Curtin. "I did the touch-and-go's and then the instructor cleared me for a full stop landing. As I rolled out, I looked to the right to see where the taxiway was. The stick moved over to the right, and with right rudder, the left wing lifted up. The plane rotated and did a nasty circle. The wing tip almost scraped the ground. It happened so fast the instructor couldn't stop it. Man, was he pissed. He chewed me out on debrief so bad, my butt will be in shreds the rest of my life. Now I know why you keep the stick into the wind. Jeez, do I need a coffee, and tonight a taste of the keg."

"I wish I had a movie camera," said Capp laughing out loud. "Your face, voice, and hand waving would win an academy award."

"It was scary," said Curtin. "A person forgets how fast you can get into trouble with these birds."

"Forget it," said Capp. "Chock it up to experience. I bet you'll never leave your stick on the downwind side again."

"Hey Curtin," came the sound of an unfriendly sounding gravelly voice, it was Pervis. "I had to wave off because some dork ground looped in front of me. Wonder who that was?" He laughed sarcastically. "Can't cut a little cross wind?" He again laughed.

"Pervis, if you weren't such a jerk, I could really learn to hate you. Capp, do you mind if I kick his butt?

"Be my guest," replied Capp, "but be sure to get a few of his teeth from old butt face."

"You guys are hilarious," said Pervis. "With the way you all fly, I'll never run out of things to laugh about. I can't wait until tomorrow to get the laugh of the day. I'm leaving before I hurt myself from laughing too much."

Curtin looked at Capp.

"He really is an asshole, isn't he?"

"The biggest," answered Capp. "He's a case study in assholinest. I don't what that means, but that's Pervis."

14

Sue Ann Crawford pensively blew cigarette smoke into the air. She watched it rise slowly and dissipate, swirling into blades of the ceiling fans in Jacques restaurant and lounge. She was dressed in a dark blue skirt, white sleeveless blouse, pearl necklace, black high heel dress shoes, and silk stockings. Her long legs were crossed at the ankles. She sat straight on the velvet covered bar chair, both hands holding a strawberry daiquiri, and stared into the dim light of the room.

Jacques was an upper class lounge, dimly lit with a maroon and black décor; it boasted of having one of the better restaurants in town. The movers and shakers of Pensacola society along with military officers were frequent patrons. It had a quiet, warm feeling, and a pervasive friendly family atmosphere.

She set her drink down on the bar, and with slender delicate hands, brushed her long dark hair back from her shoulders. Her brown eyes surveyed the other patrons on the opposite side of the bar and wondered what were they thinking, and why they were here so early in the afternoon?

The doctor's words resonated in her consciousness, but like a dream that was hard to recall, she mentally struggled to recall every syllable after his first words were spoken, the ones that put her into a state of shock. His remaining words were a blur, advice mainly, but of little consequence at this present moment. She missed her menstrual period and made the appointment to find out if what she had feared was true. The doctor was kindly, and with a gentle voice exclaimed,

"Congratulations Sue Ann, you're going to have a baby, you're going to be a mother."

She sipped a drink of a her daiquiri, placed her hand on her flat stomach, and tried to feel any movement that could manifest a life form in her body. A tear appeared at the corners of her eye, and rolled down her exquisite high cheekbones.

Why me? She wondered. *Now what do I do? Single pregnant women are not welcome in society, they're ostracized, a permanent black mark on their character. I have to leave Pensacola before it shows. Where do I go to have the baby? I have no close friends, and my parents will never forgive me if they find out. I know who the father is, but will he understand? Will he marry me? I doubt it. It was an evening of dancing and romance, not a serious relationship. He was so handsome, so persuasive, and I wasn't able to say no. A one-time fling, I've never done that before, never went all the way. One time, why me?*

Pete Pervis sat in his room, and stared out the window. It was Saturday afternoon, a day off from the stresses of flying. He had been studying the navigation syllabus manual, a boring mental exercise especially on a beautiful day of sunshine and gentle breezes. He felt it was time to get away from the military atmosphere for a while, and give his brain a rest.

"Hey Dirk, I'm going into Pensacola," he said to his room mate. "Want to go along for a beer and catch a movie? I've had it with studying today."

"Thanks for the offer," answered Dirk Maybon, a fellow class officer from Los Angeles who had majored in English at college, "but my instructor invited me for some tennis. Guess he found out I was on the tennis team, and wants some competition. Evidently he's pretty good, as no one here has beaten him. He's kind of arrogant; not sure if I should destroy him, or be a politician and let him win in a close game."

"You've got guts," said Pervis. "I wouldn't play him, he grades you. If you destroy him, it could leave a sour taste in his mouth. If you tank the match and he thinks your patronizing him, that also could bad. Why don't you call him, tell him you're not feeling well and come on with me. It's safer."

"You're probably right," answered Maybon. "I'm not even sure an instructor should be associating with Navcad's, but I feel obligated. I'll do the socially gracious thing, play him once, and then make excuses for future matches. A good tough match is fun. I know where he's coming from, playing half speed with people who aren't very good is actually harder than going all out, and much less fun. It'll be OK."

"Boy, talk about arrogant," said Pervis. "He'll probably kick your butt from here to the moon. Anyway, have fun, I'll see you later."

As Pervis drove out of the main gate, he thought, *where can I go to get away from the military? It's a beautiful day; maybe the beach would be the thing. No, half of the Navy's Navcad's will be there, that's not the place. Let's start out at a nice bar, one that doesn't have all the rowdy military creeps in it. I've heard Jacques is nice. Then who knows where, maybe the animal shelter? I miss my dog. Fair enough, Jacques it is.*

He pressed on the accelerator, and roared off toward Pensacola.

Sue Ann thought she may have one more drink, and then go back to her apartment and sleep. She could feel the effects of the alcohol, and knew this was not going to solve her depression.

"Bartender," she said. "One more daiquiri and then don't give me any more after this one."

"Yes Ma'am," he answered as he mixed the proper ingredients and placed it on the bar in front of her. As a bartender, he was skilled at observing the characteristics of the many people who came into the bar area, and could see that this attractive young lady was perplexed. Tears were not common when a person was having a good day, and she obviously was not having a good day.

Pervis found a parking spot in front of Jacque's. He got out of his car and walked up to the large oak door, pulled it open and stepped inside.

Say, he thought, *this is really nice, much nicer than the ACRAC, and besides the ACRAC doesn't have lovely young ladies at the bar.*

He walked over to the bar, and sat two seats away from the attractive girl. She was slim, intelligent looking, sitting up straight, not slouched over like some sloppy women he'd seen in other bars, very pert, and appeared to be about his age.

"Cutty and soda," he said to the bartender who promptly poured scotch into a low glass full of ice, squirted in a blast of carbonated water, and placed it in front of him. He took a drink and smiled contentedly, knowing he had made the right decision to come here, gazed at the other patrons on the other side of the bar with no particular interest, and turned to the girl next to him.

"Beautiful afternoon," he said with a laugh. "Makes you wonder what all of us are doing in here?"

Sue Ann had noticed a man in a military uniform took a seat near to her, but she didn't expect to engage in any conversation. She hesitated for a moment, and then turned to him, and answered in a quivering voice,

"You're right, it is kind of silly."

"Are you all right?" asked Pervis. "I don't mean to be nosy, but is there anything wrong?"

Her voice and the crumpled handkerchief on her lap indicated she'd been crying. He normally didn't care much about other people's troubles even though he had a background in psychology, his own problems were more important to himself, but she was beautiful and here.

If he was polite and curious, he thought, *maybe this could be an interesting afternoon, a target of opportunity, who knows?*

"Nothing I want to talk about," she answered. "But thank you."

"You really look as though you should talk to someone," said Pervis softly. "And I'm a great listener. Is it money, a relationship, health, or a job? Any of them can cause stress. Care to share it with me? I was a Psych major in college; maybe I can help. Don't let this Naval cadet uniform mislead you, I really do have an education."

She looked at Pervis calmly.

He's not very handsome, she thought, *a somewhat rough looking face with acne scars, thin nose and intense brown eyes, strange mouth, however he seems very nice and has a comfortable way of speaking. I've no one else to share my anxieties with; maybe he could be a good*

sounding board. After all he is an officer candidate and should be of good moral character. A few girls at the office dated Naval flight cadets, and said they were the sharpest guys they ever went out with. Who knows, with his background he may have some ideas I haven't thought of. What's the harm? It couldn't get worse; people are going to find out anyway.

"Normally, I wouldn't share my thoughts with anyone," answered Sue Ann. "Can you keep a secret?"

"Of course," said Pervis. He moved to the stool next to her, sat sideways and leaned slightly toward her, just close enough so he could speak in a low confidential voice, but not close enough to be threatening.

"If you don't know, I'm a cadet officer. One of reasons the Navy gave me these bars, is that cadets can come to me and share their secrets without having to go to the higher brass. We can sometimes work out problems in confidence without getting formal, just thought that might help if you're concerned about privacy."

"I don't know," she said, "It's embarrassing. I've had a few too many drinks, and I don't know you at all. Some secrets should be left just that, secrets."

Pervis looked at her and thought,

This is getting interesting, now I want to know. Do you think she bought that crap about me being a father confessor to the other cadets? What could be embarrassing to her? Certainly not losing a job, that's no big deal; she's obviously single because she has no ring on her finger, so it's not a divorce. Hmm, either she picked up a venereal disease, or she's knocked up.

"You're pregnant," said Pervis.

Sue Ann's head jerked back and tears came to her eyes.

"How did you know," she gasped. "Is it that obvious? Oh, my God, this is terrible." Her voice choked from emotion and she dabbed her eyes with the handkerchief. "Even a stranger can figure it out."

"I'm sorry, said Pervis. "It's not obvious. Let's just say I've got a sixth sense about misfortunes. It's a dark gift, not sure I like it, but nevertheless, it's there. Sometimes, I also feel I can predict the future.

There's a situation I'm involved in at present and I know there's going to be a tragedy, not to me, but to another cadet."

"I don't know who to talk to," said Sue Ann. "And I'm not sure what my next step is. Perhaps you're a blessing in disguise, or should I say, in uniform." And with that, she chuckled, "My goodness, that's the first time I've laughed since the doctors office, you must be good luck."

"That's great," said Pervis. "You need to keep your spirits up. You know, your condition really isn't the end of the world; it's the wonder of nature and can be dealt with. Can I be personal, a little bit?"

"Sure, answered Sue Ann. She was beginning to like this stranger, who seemed to be an elixir in the nick of time.

"Have you told the father yet?"

No" she answered.

"Are you going to tell him?

"I'm not sure," answered Sue Ann.

"Why not?" said Pervis? "Shouldn't the two of you share your secret?"

"He's the son of a very influential businessman," answered Sue Ann, "and is being groomed to take over the business. He's a friend, but I doubt if this is what his parents have planned for him."

"Why don't you let him decide that?" said Pervis. "He sounds intelligent, and a businessman accustomed to make decisions. Wouldn't it be easier on you if you were married, and had a husband?"

"That would be ideal," answered Sue Ann. "But I'm not sure that could ever happen. He's not going to marry me. I basically have a few options, as does anyone who's expecting: Get married, have the baby out of wedlock and try to raise it myself, adoption, and the worst would be an abortion at some location where it's legal." She started to cry again, "What have I done, one weak moment, Oh, to go back in time; I knew better, but here I am, and have to handle it."

"Just knowing you for this short time," he must be a special type person, I can't picture you slumming."

"Thanks," she smiled. "Yes, he's tall, dark haired and handsome, an athlete, with a great personality, one of the most eligible bachelors in Pensacola. I hate to admit it, this is embarrassing, but it was hard to resist his advances. It was flattering just to be with him. I'm sure he's had many conquests, but a moment of weakness, a lack of common sense, and here I am. Experience is not always the best teacher."

Well, thought Pervis, *my original thought about having a spectacular afternoon affair won't happen. Is this a one time happening, or an opportunity that fate has dropped on me if I can figure it out.*

He sat quietly beside her, and then, a smile that turned into a sneer enveloped his face, he turned again to Sue Ann with breathless anticipation,

"Are you strong?" said Pervis. "Can I suggest a solution that is just about perfect, but you'd have to be strong and persistent."

"Tell me, please," answered Sue Ann. "I'll do anything within reason."

"How would you like to be married? Not to the father, but to the most handsome, desirable cadet in the Navy, a true hero who has deep compassion for the trials and tribulations of persons in need. Your child would have a father; and knowing him, the two of you would be a perfect match."

"Here's the plan," said Pervis. "But it must be a secret between you and me; he mustn't know I'm involved even though we're good friends. Care to listen?"

15

Chuck Capp slammed the green colored pool ball into the side pocket. The loud 'thunk' sound as it hit the mark was adrenaline to Capp.

"Yeah," shouted Capp at Jim Quirt. "Watch this, I'm going to run the table, it's a perfect setup. Get your money out Quirt, there's a new eight ball champ in the room. Your reign is over; you're going down in flames.

It was Sunday afternoon, right after lunch. Capp and Quirt were the finalists in their cadet barracks eight ball tournament. This game decided the winner; best two out of three, each had won one game.

Cadets crowded the rectangular table, but not close enough to bother the players. Jeers and hoots were heard above the din of the television on the far wall, gambling side bets went down, and no one really cared who won, as both Capp and Quirt were popular.

"My butt," laughed Quirt. "You've said that before, but I always win. Pool is my game and mark my words; this just isn't your day."

Capp bent over with his eyes looking down the length of the pool stick, lined it up for the proper angle on the cue ball and the yellow ball. He moved the stick back and forth under his spread fingers, so the flesh under his forefinger, which braced the stick, also moved back and forth, holding it firm but in the correct position.

"Perfect," said Capp as his focus went from the stick, to the cue ball, to the yellow ball, and then to the corner pocket.

"A perfect angle, just like making love, this is going to hit the spot, and then a new champion is born."

"C'mon," challenged Quirt. "We don't have all year. If that's the way you make love, I pity your girlfriend; she'd need something to keep her awake."

"Relax," answered Capp. "I make love slow, tender, and long. As opposed to your caveman technique of wham, bam, thank you ma'am, mine is professional, just like this shot. Watch this, and eat your heart out."

Capp drew the stick back and stroked it forward into the white cue ball, which traveled across the green colored felt table and hit the yellow ball, which bounced against the corner of the pocket. It ricocheted back, into the black eight ball, which slowly rolled, and rolled, and rolled, and dropped with a plop into the side pocket.

"What the hell was that?" growled Capp as he threw down his stick on the table.

"That, my friend," shouted Quirt as he fell against the side of the pool table laughing uncontrollably. "Was the lousiest shot ever made by man. And guess what, the games over, you lost, a lousy lover and a lousy pool player."

Quirt turned to the crowd of cadets, "Let's hear it for the worst shot of the tournament," as he waved his arms up and down for them to make some noise, which they did by a loud cheer for Quirt.

"Hey Capp," shouted one of the cadets. "Next time I've got an extra girl, I'm taking Quirt. He knows what to do."

"Get lost you ingrates," laughed Capp as he waved them off. "Make one mistake and you change sides. What loyalty. What a bunch of bums. See if I go with you guys on a double date, I'm just going to take all the girls for myself."

Quirt slapped Capp on the back, "C'mon, let's go to the ACRAC, you owe me a beer for that crummy shot."

They were about to leave when the BSOOD (Battalion student officer of the day, each cadet had to stand desk duty at various times), came into the lounge,

"Hey Capp," you've got a phone call; it's a girl. How'd you line up a date so fast after blowing the game? It's the main phone in the passageway."

"Takes talent my man," answered Capp. Capp turned to Quirt, "Who could this be, I haven't called any girl for a date today?"

"Why are you asking me?" said Quirt. "Go answer the phone."

Capp walked down the passageway, the public phone was attached to the wall, and the receiver was lying on the shelf below the main part of the phone.

"Hi, said Capp. "Naval cadet Capp Sir, can I help you?"

"Is this Cadet Chuck Capp?" said the voice, which was low and sensuous.

"Yes," answered Capp. "Who's this?"

"Sue Ann Crawford, we met at the Gulf Breeze a little over a month ago, remember?"

"No," answered Capp. "It doesn't ring a bell, but from the sound of your voice, how could I forget?"

"Are you free?" asked Sue Ann. "Could we get together this afternoon for awhile?"

"Sure," answered Capp. "What's this about? Anything I should know?"

"Just want to see you again," said Sue Ann. "How about four o'clock at the Chuck wagon, it's a little restaurant down by the wharf."

"I know it well," answered Capp. "It serves up some of the best hamburgers in town. Anything I should bring?"

"Just yourself," breathed Sue Ann. "That's all I need"

"Four o'clock it is," said Capp. "See you in awhile."

"Bye now," answered Sue Ann.

Capp walked back to the cadet lounge, which was full of cadets playing pool, ping pong, and watching television. He ambled over to Quirt who was watching a pool game.

"What's up?" said Quirt.

"Ever heard of a girl named Sue Ann Crawford? asked Capp, "Or remember anyone by that name? Strange, she says I met her at the Gulf Breeze about a month ago."

"Doesn't sound familiar," answered Quirt. "But that doesn't mean anything. Most of the time there, I'm so crocked that Rita Hayworth could dance, and I wouldn't remember. In fact you're generally worse off than me, so why should we remember?"

"Well, said Capp. "If the rest of her is as sexy as her voice, I want to see her. We're meeting at the Chuck wagon at four o'clock, for what reason I don't know, but it could be a wild weekend finish to a crummy pool game tournament. Why else would she want to meet on a lazy Sunday afternoon? Keep your fingers crossed, I may get seduced."

"See if she's got a friend," said Quirt. "I'm free."

"Today," answered Capp. "With all my adrenaline, this could be a long night. But back to reality, she wouldn't tell me why she wanted to see me, could be she wants to borrow money. I like the first thought better."

"Jeez," laughed Quirt. "You've got the wildest imagination I ever saw, go take a cold shower. If you're not back in two weeks, I'll send out the posse. Better get going or you'll be late. I hope she's ugly, it'd serve you right."

"Thanks friend," said Capp. "You're a real jerk."

As Capp drove into Pensacola, he kept thinking,

Who in the world could she be? What does she want? Well, I'm here, and about to find out.

The Chuck wagon was a typical small Mom and Pop type restaurant. A counter with stools, a few small square tables with red and white checkerboard table cloths, several booths on the side wall, light pink colored walls, and a white colored ceiling with the ever present ceiling fans slowly revolving to keep the air moving. The menu was ample and offered full meals, a daily blue plate special, which could be served quickly-usually meat loaf or a hot roast beef sandwich with grits, some seafood, and great hamburgers. It was owned by a married couple, Ralph and Mary Gadston, large full-bodied people who laughed a lot and carried on a friendly banter with their customers, many of who were regulars.

Capp opened the door and stepped inside. Not knowing what Sue Ann looked like, he assumed she'd be sitting by herself. He gazed around, saw two young ladies, one in the booth, very pretty, and the other at a table, not as pretty. He stood for a minute, and hoped Sue Ann would see him.

Mary Gadston was behind the counter, waved at Capp, smiled and said, "Welcome Mr. Flyboy, sit where ever you want and I'll take your order in a minute. Make yourself at home."

The pretty girl in the booth waved at Capp, "Over here Chuck."

"Well," said Capp as he walked over and sat across from her in booth. "You must be Sue Ann, and if I might say, a welcome relief to look at after spending time with a bunch of ugly cadets."

"I bet you tell all the girls that," answered Sue Ann, smiling. "Thanks for coming. And if I might say, you look quite handsome in the daylight. Sometimes that's not always the case when the only time we've seen each other is in the evening, under dim lights. Care for some coffee?"

"Sure," said Capp, "Black."

"Two black coffees Mary," said Sue Ann to the owner as she held up two fingers.

"Coming right up," answered Gadston. She poured two coffees and brought them to the booth, "Anything else?"

"Thanks," said Sue Ann. "Not right now."

"Nice place," said Capp. "Come here often? That's an old pickup line," laughed Capp. "But I'm not sure what else to say, especially since it seems I'm the one that's being picked up."

Sue Ann place a quarter in the jukebox selector on the wall next to them, pushed the buttons, and selected five songs. She wanted background noise to cover their conversation.

"I know you're curious as to why I called you," said Sue Ann.

Capp nodded.

"Do you mind if I ask you a few questions?" said Sue Ann

"Shoot," answered Capp, "As long as we can go dancing later on. You're quite pretty, you know, and that's not just a line, you are."

Sue Ann blushed, the red moved from her cheeks to her whole face. First impressions were important, and she liked this brash cadet, Pervis was right.

"How do you feel about family?" said Sue Ann.

"The most important thing in the world," answered Capp, "The greatest support group that exists. Friends come and go, but family is the rock. They'll forgive bad decisions, and there are always hugs, family is immortality."

"How do you feel about parents?" said Sue Ann.

"Parents," answered Capp. "Set the ethical, moral, and self confidence standards for the family. Parents with low standards can ruin a family; the opposite is true for families with parents of high standards. Why are you asking these questions?"

"In a minute," said Sue Ann. "How do you feel about children in a family?"

"Great," answered Capp. "But parents have to want them. I don't know about you, but I've got friends whose parents, I think, never wanted children, but had them only because of the social pressure that married folks should have kids. Those friends, some of them, well, were abused, physically and mentally. It's not a happy situation."

"How do you feel about marriage?" asked Sue Ann.

Capp eyed her warily and answered, "I don't know where this is going, but eventually most people get married."

"What's the responsibility of a man to a woman, when he is the father of her child?" asked Sue Ann.

A crawly feeling started to raise the hair on Capps back;

"The man has total responsibility to raise the child with the mother. It takes two to tango, he can't abandon her."

"So, single mothers are not expected to raise their child alone, with no assistance from the father." said Sue Ann.

"No," answered Capp. "The father should provide assistance, both monetary and physical. Marriage is best for the kid, but sometimes that's not feasible if there's no love between the parents. However, fathers who abandon the mother are the dregs of society, they should be shot. There's a responsibility and parents should get married for the sake of the kid. What kid wants to grow up being called a Bastard?"

"A little over a month ago, and that's the reason I asked you to come today," said Sue Ann. "I went to the Gulf Breeze. I heard it was a fun bar with fun people. I met you there, or should I say you met me. It was just about closing time and you were about one beer away from passing out, maybe two, but to put it mildly, you were feeling no pain. I also had a few too many drinks.'

'You were funny and very sexy. I had heard rumors of your physical attributes from girls around the bar, and have to admit I was curious. To make a long story short, you convinced me to go out to your convertible. I had never done the act before, and have never done it since, but you were gentle and skillful. However, you were too uncoordinated to put on protection, we both were passionate, so we did it anyway. After it was over, I went back to my car, and drove home. I've never been back to the Gulf Breeze again. I was embarrassed for what had happened. This month I found out I'm expecting. I'm the mother. And," she paused, smiled, and gently placed her hand on Capp's as she gazed into his eyes, "You're the father."

16

Capp's jaw dropped, he stared at her incredulously, not believing what he had just heard.

"You're insane!" blurted out Capp he pulled his hands away from hers. His eyes turned an icy blue. "I've never met you before in my life. What kind of con job is this? You can't find the real father, so you're going to pick on a helpless cadet? Well I'm not helpless, and I'm not the father, and you know it."

Pervis said he would react angrily, but to keep on him, as he really was a softy inside. But she didn't expect this much reaction; maybe she should forget the whole thing. She'd try once more.

"I'm sorry," she said in a humble tone of voice. She looked down at her hands, then back up at Capp. "I know it's a shock, but it's true. I've only done it once. You've got to believe me. I wouldn't lie to you. We both had too much to drink."

She was so beautiful, and so sincere; Capp had a moment of doubt. He knew some nights he'd drunk so much, that the next morning he didn't remember what had happened. Could this be one of them?

"I don't believe you," said Capp. "But why'd you ask me here, other than to ruin my day? What do you want, money?"

She seemed relieved that he backed off a bit.

"I don't want to give birth to a child out of wedlock. You know what people would call our child, and it's not a nice word. I want to get married."

"What?" gasped Capp? "Are you crazy? Cadets have to be single. If I get married, I'm kicked out of the program, out of flying."

"No one would know," answered Sue Ann. "I'd stay in my apartment, and you in the barracks, just like now. I'd not tell anyone. After you get your wings, then we'd live together as husband and wife. Look at us. Your son would be strong, and if a girl, she'd be beautiful. We'd work it out; we both seem to be compatible."

"Got it all figured out, don't you," said Capp disgustedly. "What if I told you to get lost, go have your child by yourself, then what?"

This was the moment of reckoning, she thought. *Pervis said to keep pushing.*

"I'm not a cruel person, but I'd have to call the Navy," answered Sue Ann." I don't want our baby to be called that awful name."

Capp felt sick to his stomach. He stared at ceiling, not sure what to do next.

"You seem to have me in a box," said Capp. "Let me think about it. I'm not sure the Navy would believe you. But here's an option, just a thought, not an agreement. If we got married to protect your child's name, I'd want a divorce right after the birth, and a blood test to prove my relationship to the baby. If I am the father, I'd provide money to raise him or her, but that would be all, nothing more. It's too risky to be married the rest of my flight training. All my life I've wanted to be a military pilot. You've got to compromise, and after I get my wings, who knows, but that's a long ways off."

Sue Ann felt empathetic toward him, but the plan seemed to be working. She'd have a marriage to protect her child's name. If she confronted the real father, she knew she'd get no satisfaction, and would end up being a single mother, giving birth alone. If this works out, she'd owe a lot to Pervis. She would keep the marriage a secret. Capp would get what he wants and I'd get what I need.

"That might work," answered Sue Ann. "I need to know soon. This all would be kept a secret, I promise you."

"What's the hurry," said Capp. "We could get married in your eighth or ninth month of pregnancy? That would satisfy your desire to have a child born to married parents, right?"

"I don't know," answered Sue Ann. "That almost sounds cruel. We need to be married for our child and my peace of mind. Don't you agree?"

"No I don't," said Capp. "The longer we're married, the greater chance there is that the Navy could find out, and I don't want to take that risk."

"There are only two people who know," answered Sue Ann. "And I know you won't tell. So what's the worry, right? Here's my address and telephone number. Give me a call when you're ready. As with most stressful situations, a firm decision dissolves the stress, and then you'll be fine."

"This is unreal," said Capp. "You're too in control, too cool, I still don't believe you, but I'll let you know."

Capp picked up the paper with her address, turned, and left the restaurant with quick, long strides. He had to talk to someone he trusted, a confidant, and that person is Quirt.

17

Capp strode into Quirt's room,

"C'mon, said Capp in a firm voice, "We've got to talk, now."

"Jeez," answered Quirt. "I just finished chow, give me an hour of rack time, then I'll be free to listen to all your fantasies."

"Now," said Capp throwing Quirts shirt at him, "I need to talk."

"All right, all right," answered Quirt. He'd never seen Capp so uptight. He buttoned his shirt, grabbed his cap and motioned to the doorway. "Just because I whipped your butt in pool, don't let it get to you."

"Let's go," said Capp, "Outside."

Capp walked quickly down the passageways, down the ladder, and out the front door, followed by Quirt. They went out on to the sidewalk in front of the barracks, and walked toward the hangar area.

"Slow down," said Quirt. "I can tell you're mad about something, but I don't like to be ordered around, even by my best friend. You want to talk, let's talk."

"I just want to get away from the barracks," answered Capp. "So no one can hear us. This is really confidential."

"Normally," said Quirt. "I'd give you a smart-ass remark, but you're way too serious. What's up?"

"I'm being charged with paternity," said Capp. "This broad, Sue Ann Crawford is pregnant, and claims I'm the father of her baby. She wants me to marry her so the kid isn't born a bastard or she's going to tell the Navy. Either way I'm screwed. If I'm married and the Navy finds out, I'm kicked out. If I don't get married, she makes the charge and I'm kicked out because of un-officer like conduct. Talk to me buddy, what the hell do I do?"

"Are you the father?" questioned Quirt.

"Oh man, jeez," groaned Capp. "I don't think so, but who knows? She has too many details, knows too much about me. I'd probably lose in a Captains Mast hearing. The Navy isn't going to wait seven or eight months for birth to get a blood test, they'd kick me out on a morals charge, regardless if I'm the father or not."

"Makes a person want to stop drinking," answered Quirt.

"That's not the answer I need," said Capp angrily. "Stop trying to be funny, and tell me what you'd do?"

"Will she keep it a secret?" answered Quirt. "That's the key to the whole situation, sounds like she's got you over a barrel. I wonder how many innocent guys are forced into marriage, just because the woman makes a charge. Is she a prostitute?"

"Naw, she's too sharp," said Capp. "Actually great looking with a great body, but yes, she promised to keep our marriage a secret. She says she only got laid once, with me, who knows, I swear I've never seen her before. She may agree to a divorce after the birth, that's where I'm coming from."

They walked along the white sun bleached sidewalk for a while, not speaking, their minds mulling over the options and consequences of each.

"Well," said Quirt. "She has all the marbles in her court. If it were me, I'd try to get married as close to the birth date as possible, and then a divorce immediately after the birth. That's the safest, it's crummy, but the safest-if she can keep a secret. If you think she's going to tell the Navy anyway, I'd stay single and take my chances at a Captains Mast hearing. Can you trust her?"

"Who knows," said Capp. If she were a man, I'd punch her out. I don't think I've got any choice but to marry her, and hope she keeps her end of the deal, secrecy. What a crock. I'll try to put her off as long as possible, but I don't want her to get nervous and make a call to the Navy."

"What about an abortion?" said Quirt. "I'm catholic so I can't recommend it other than a last resort."

"Not me," said Capp. "I'm not asking her. That could push her over the edge if she's nervous. Besides, I doubt if it's legal in Florida. Not an option unless she brings it up, and the way it sounds, she wants the baby."

"Well then," said Quirt. "You're back to negotiating for a marriage and divorce option. I'm glad it's not me, good luck."

"I'll call her tonight, said Capp. "Thanks for letting me bounce this off you; you're the only one I trust."

"Do me a favor," said Quirt. "Don't let this affect your flying. Make a decision and then move on. It's the only way."

"I won't sleep much tonight, but thanks for the advice," said Capp. "Hope I can follow it. I've never been in a situation where I didn't have control. This is scary."

"You'll do fine," said Quirt. "I'm here anytime you want to talk, scream, pound the wall, or whatever. Just don't screw up flying, O.K.?"

"Right," answered Capp, "Time to make a phone call."

Capp drove into the closest town, and called Sue Ann on a telephone that seemed to be private.

"Sue Ann?" asked Capp as she picked up her phone.

"Yes," she answered. "Are you O.K.?"

"Not really," said Capp. "It's a shock, but if you want to get married, and later a divorce after the birth, I'm agreeable to that. How does that sound?"

"I'm really sorry to have dropped this on you," as she choked up with tears. "We both have a life to live, and that would probably be the best. I know your concerns; maybe we'll get to know each other better. Did you have a date in mind?"

"How about next month?" he said. "I'm really in the middle of a tough part of the syllabus, is that O.K.?"

"Yes," she answered quietly. "Call me, and thanks for understanding."

She hung up the telephone. Tears had streaked her face; she went into the bathroom and placed a cool wet towel on her face. She looked into the mirror, slapped it sharply, and said out loud,

"Capp's really a nice guy. What have I been talked into?"

She went to the telephone and dialed the Navy barracks.

"Battalion Student Officer of the Day Richards Sir, can I help you?

"Cadet Pete Pervis," she asked. "Can I speak to him?"

"Just a minute," answered Richards. "I'll see if he's in."

There were a few minutes of silence and then a gravelly voice answered,

"Cadet Pervis Sir," Can I help you?"

"Hi," said Sue Ann. "Can you talk privately?"

"I can listen," answered Pervis gently. "Go ahead."

"Chuck Capp agreed to get married," she said. "I can give you details later. But I just wanted to call and thank you for all your help. You were right; he does have a soft spot."

"When will this take place?" asked Pervis.

"Sometime next month," answered Sue Ann. "I'll let you know the date."

"Great," said Pervis. "It makes me feel good that you're happy. Glad to be of help."

"I'll talk to you soon, said Sue Ann. "And again, thanks, you're a lifesaver. Goodbye."

Purvis's blood pressure and heartbeat bounced to a new high. He did a dance down the passageway, jumped and clicked his heels together, and started to sing to the tune of "It's raining, it's pouring",

"I've got him, I've got him, the smart fart, I've got him. Yahoo."

I'll wait until the marriage is official, he thought, *and then call the Navy, and Capp will be gone, kicked out. Yeahh, My quest is over. How could I be so lucky? Sue Ann, I love you. What a saleslady, Yeahh. That S.O.B. Capp has finally got what's coming to him. I've won. Yeahh.*

Neither Pervis nor Capp slept much that night.

18

This was the day all pilots dreamed of, and Capp saw on the assignment board in large letters next to his name-Solo Check!

Captain Kranz had challenged Capp.

"Get an Up on this hop and you'll be in control of a high powered aircraft, all by yourself. That's what you want, that's why you're here."

Capp stared at the board as if hypnotized, and fantasized flying by himself, alone in the SNJ.

Quirt, walked up beside him.

"Get the moon glow out of your eyes, Chuck. The moment of truth is here. It's best you brush up on your procedures. This isn't going to be a joy ride. If you don't cut it, you're out of here."

Capp snapped back to reality,

"Thanks for ruining a great dream," said Capp. "I visualized myself taking off alone. Guess it would be a good idea to first get an Up on the check ride."

As they stood there, the board boy walked to board, erased Captain Kranz's name and replaced it with Lieutenant McCoy.

"Oh no", said Capp. "What's this? That's not fair. McCoy is a screamer, a hard nose. He gives more Downs than all the instructors combined. The scuttlebutt is that he's afraid to let the students take total control. What a revolting, crummy development!"

"Look," said Quirt sternly. "Fly your damned hop the way you know how, the best, right?"

"I really wanted to fly this hop with Captain Kranz", answered Capp. "He's the one who got me here. Well guess what, I'll just have to be perfect so McCoy can tell Kranz what a great job he's done. That's the least I owe him. Bring on McCoy."

"Jeez, that's what I like about you," laughed Quirt. "You're not cocky."

The board boy again walked to the board. Captain Kranz was assigned to Pete Pervis, who also had his solo check ride today.

"What's this crap?" asked Capp. "Pervis doesn't deserve a nice guy like Kranz, he deserves McCoy."

"Evidently you didn't read the bulletin board this morning." said Quirt."

"What about it?"

"No student can be assigned a check ride with his regular instructor," said Quirt. That keeps a level playing field. It also takes the pressure off of the regular instructor in the event of personality differences. A neutral check pilot supposedly can be objective. There must've been some problems in the past."

"Well, let me get at the procedures book," said Capp. "McCoy should be here soon."

"Good luck," said Quirt.

"You too," answered Capp.

Quirt left to study at the other end of the ready room.

Capp was reading the procedures book, when he felt a presence beside him. It was Pervis.

"What do you want," snapped Capp. "I'm trying to study, so don't bother me."

"Do you know that McCoy has given a Down on his last three check rides?" said Pervis with a chuckle and that strange crooked smile on his face, "Just thought you'd like to know that. By the way, Kranz will probably drop you after he flies with me. As the old saying goes, 'The cream always rises to the top.'"

"Really," answered Capp. "Well don't forget the cream gets removed first. Besides, McCoy doesn't bother me. I'll fly a 4.0 hop."

Capp clasped his hands behind his head, stretched, and then put his hands on the table.

"Pete, you know we both want to get an Up on this check ride, why don't we try to bury the hatchet? I'll tell you what. Captain Kranz has some procedures he likes. It may help you. You don't have to do them, but listen."

Capp leaned over toward Pervis, and lowered his voice. Pervis also leaned forward, two men sharing a secret.

"Just before you turn base on your landing approach leg, rock your wings and move the nose of the plane up and down." said Capp. "That way he knows you have control. He likes confidence."

Pervis, deep down inside wanted to be one of the guys, he thought for a moment.

"As his student," he answered warily. "You must know what he wants. Let me think about it. If that gives me an edge, I'll take it. Thanks for your help. You have a good check ride, not as good as mine, but a good one."

"Good luck." said Capp.

After they separated, Capp went back to his studies. His flight was scheduled earlier than Pervis's or Quirt's.

Quirt walked over to Capp.

"I saw you talking to your buddy Pervis. What's on his weird little mind?"

"I hope I didn't screw him up," said Capp. "I gave him some really bad procedural advice. I meant it as a joke; I can't believe he'd be dumb enough to do it? Kranz is a stickler for exact procedures. I'll really feel bad if Pervis gets a Down. Maybe I should tell him to forget it."

"What did you tell him?" asked Quirt.

Capp told him, and held both of his hands palms out, up by his shoulders, with a quizzical look on his face.

"What do you think? Would you do that if I told you the same thing?"

Quirt looked at Capp in astonishment, and then burst out laughing.

"That's beautiful, just beautiful, I love it. Pervis may be a total jerk, but no, he knows you; and no, I don't think he's dumb enough to deviate from the procedures. Forget it. As much as we dislike Pervis, I hear he's a pretty good pilot. He won't do it."

"I don't know," said Capp. "Pervis had this puppy dog look on his face. Just like girls get when they want to believe you, but know they shouldn't. Well, as you say, we have to assume he's sharp enough not to believe me. Let's go fly."

Lt. McCoy walked up to Capp who was seated, studying. Capp saw him, and quickly stood at attention,

"Cadet Capp, ready for the check ride, Sir."

McCoy looked at Capp, and coldly eyed him up and down as if measuring a corpse for a coffin. He had sharp features, with a nose that bent downward at the end like a hawk's beak. His eyes were piercing, and he never seemed to blink.

"At ease," said McCoy. "Let's get on with the briefing."

The briefing was very complete, professional, with no humor or small talk.

"Once we leave the hangar," said McCoy. "I won't speak unless a problem is apparent. This is your solo check ride. My job is to ensure you can handle the plane and procedures by yourself, any questions?"

"No Sir." answered Capp.

Capp went through the normal pre-flight procedures, climbed into the front cockpit, and strapped in. McCoy strapped into the rear cockpit.

Taxi and run-up was completed. Capp transmitted,

"Ready for take-off, Sir."

"Roger," answered McCoy.

Capp requested clearance for take off, received it, taxied into position, added power, controlled the left and right nose position with rudders, raised the nose at the correct airspeed, raised the gear and flaps, and took up a heading for West Field.

Capp approached West Field and transmitted to the tower, "Permission to enter the landing pattern for touch-and-go's."

Permission was granted and Capp felt great. Everything was going as briefed.

McCoy is too quiet, thought Capp, and that's scary. He's a screamer. Instructors always are talking. Has he given up on me?

On the next touch-and-go, McCoy radioed to Capp,

"Make the next landing a full stop and taxi over to the parking area. Leave the engine running."

Now what have I done wrong? thought Capp.

Capp landed, taxied where told, and stopped.

"It's all yours," radioed McCoy. "Make two touch and go's, and a final landing. It really is in your best interest to come back and get me."

"Yes Sir," radioed Capp.

McCoy climbed out of the rear cockpit and on to the wing. He gave Capp's helmet a solid pat, smiled, gave a thumbs up and jumped down to the ground."

Capp's grin almost split his ears.

Capp was alone.

He looked back at the rear cockpit.

It's empty. This is for real, the day I've been waiting for, but I feel like I'm outside of the womb. My security blanket is gone. Man, is it lonely. What if I get in trouble, the engine quits, or the gear doesn't come down. I'll have no one to help me. McCoy's watching me. Let's get back to the take-off area and get this plane in the air. You can't live forever.

Capp took off, made the two required touch and go's, and a final landing. He taxied over and picked up McCoy.

"Well, how was it?" radioed McCoy on the intercom after he'd strapped in.

Capp laughed and answered, "At first it was a little scary, but what a blast!"

"I still remember it like it was yesterday," said McCoy. "And I felt the same way."

Back in the air, McCoy radioed,

"For a pilot with your time in the air, I'm impressed. Let's go back to Warner Field, you have an Up."

Capp was so happy he sung to himself the Star Spangled Banner.

The adrenaline made his body quiver and his heart pound like a trip hammer.

He thought crazily,

Where's a Russian MIG when you need one, I need something to kill, something over which I can celebrate. Yeahh!

There are two traditions when pilots solo. The first is that your flying mates cut off your tie, just below the knot. The second, which may be unique to the Navy, is that you give your check pilot a quart of the best booze money can buy, his choice of course. McCoy wanted Jack Daniels Black Label. Capp also bought a quart of Chivas Regal scotch for Captain Kranz.

The tie cutting took place at the ACRAC after evening meal.

Quirt also got an Up on his check ride.

Capp walked into bedlam. Quirt, Munson, and Curtin, plus other cadets filled the room. Many had soloed today. The merriment, shouting, and laughter were contagious, raucous, and a joy to the ear. The beer was flowing freely. It was going to be a long night.

"Stand still before I get too drunk, and cut off your Adams apple." shouted Capp at Quirt.

The tie was cut off, held high for all to see, and a rousing cheer was given.

"Capp," laughed Quirt. "Here's to a miserable excuse for a pilot, but a hell of a friend. Observe how quickly your phallic symbol is removed."

With that, Quirt cut off Capp's tie, held it high for all to see, which prompted more cheers, and a cry for more beer.

Capp was standing near the bar, when someone roughly pushed him from behind. He was almost knocked down.

It was Pervis, with a cut-off tie, his teeth bared in a snarl, and his eyes red from too much beer.

"Capp, you son-of-a-bitch, you almost got me a Down, almost made me flunk my check ride. And to think I trusted you!"

Pervis pulled his fist back to hit Capp.

"Hold it, hold it," said Capp. "You should be happy, you got an Up. What's the problem?"

"I thought you were my friend," Pervis shouted. "You told me to rock my wings and move my nose up and down on the approach leg because Captain Kranz liked that. He not only didn't like that, he went crazy. After the second time, Kranz shouted over the mike, that if I ever did that again, the flight was over. He said it was the stupidest thing he had ever seen, doing dangerous maneuvers at low airspeeds. He scared me. I thought he was going to give me a Down. How could you do that to me?"

"I'm sorry, it was a joke," answered Capp. "But I didn't think you'd do that, you're too good of a pilot."

Quirt was laughing so hard he almost fell down and had to lean against the bar.

"You mean you believed Capp, the world's greatest practical joker. Man, are you gullible. I can picture Captain Kranz, beet red face, veins popping, wondering what kind of an idiot was up front." Quirt was in hysterics.

Pervis was furious.

"It's not funny. Forget friendship, this is war! You crossed the wrong guy, Capp. I'll, get even! You wait and see."

Pervis knew better than to start a fight, shook a fist at Capp and staggered back to the bar.

Capp looked at Quirt, shrugged his shoulders and with an innocent look on his face, said,

"I don't suppose this is a good time to tell him that Kranz doesn't drink, and to only buy him a six pack of coke?"

"Yeah, yeah!" laughed Quirt in hysterics, and pounded on the table. "Can't you see the look on Kranz's face when he got some pop instead of booze? It'd be worth a months pay. You probably would tell that to Pervis, and he might be that dumb again. Great idea, but not tonight, that could be dangerous. Even Pervis has a breaking point. Jeez, waggle your wings and raise your nose up and down, man, that's unbelievable. Wish I could have been there."

They both raised their glasses and clinked them together,

"To Pervis," laughed Capp. "May he continue to provide entertainment."

19

"This almost feels eerie," said Capp to Jim Quirt as they stood in front of the scheduling board.

"Why?" answered Quirt?

"Here we are, about to sign out our first SNJ, all by ourselves. Imagine, the Navy allowing us to do such a thing. A few months ago, we had no more responsibility than eating and breathing. What a difference. What a change. What a Macho builder."

"Yeah," said Quirt. "It is amazing. But remember, we're just like a baby learning how to walk. It's easy to stumble and fall, remember that. The morning flights were cancelled due to low clouds, be careful out there."

"You know," answered Capp. "In the Battle of Britain, a lot of the Spitfire pilots had less hours than we have. And they went up against experienced Luftwaffe pilots. Is that impressive, or what?"

"I think it's crazy," said Quirt. "That's why so many of the British pilots got creamed."

"You're right," said Capp. "Well, with our hours, at least we can get the bird up in the air and back down again. Be glad there are no Messerschmitt's out there. However, it would've been fun to tangle with them."

"Just remember to put your gear down, and your zipper zipped," said Quirt. "Bad things can happen quickly. We don't have an instructor to bail us out. We're on our own."

"Are we getting apprehensive?" answered Capp. "Where's that devil-may-care spirit?"

"Still there," said Quirt. "But it's just my luck to get some tired old SNJ that wants to go the junkyard, instead of hauling a bunch of cocky cadets around."

"Be careful what you wish or think about, it may come true," said Capp. "Well, my hop is getting close to launch time. See you later."

Capp walked across the hangar deck. It was a warm afternoon, and he was feeling great.

The hangar in the rear area was full of SNJs' in various states of repair. The smell of gasoline and oil hung in the air. The mechanics in their blue dungarees working uniform were crawling over, under, and beside the planes.

Those sailors are amazing, thought Capp as he waved at some he knew. *Without them, the whole aviation structure would collapse. When I get assigned to a squadron, I'm going to make damned sure they're well taken care of.*

Cadets in their khaki one-piece flight suits, walked to and from the ready room. The area was always busy and invigorating.

Capp went to the locker area and opened the metal door. He removed his uniform and put on his flight suit. It had numerous pockets to carry items such as pencils, leather gloves, maps, and whatever else a pilot wanted. Every pilot had them full. He retrieved his flight helmet, an ugly gold colored hard hat with raised grooves on the exterior. Snaps held the inside of the soft helmet to the hard exterior. Ugly as it was, it saved many concussions and head injuries. The kneeboard, a small rectangular plastic board, was strapped to a pilots left thigh if they were right handed. The right thigh was used as an arm brace, if needed. The kneeboard was like a Bible. Checklists and procedures were clipped to it. There was a clip on the top and bottom to hold papers and maps from blowing away. Lose the papers in the air, and a pilot was in some trouble, hoping his memory was intact to remember all of those items. An open cockpit would suck out most loose items. Sometimes they flew with the canopy back, an open cockpit, so securing loose items was a must.

Capp went to the line shack and signed out his SNJ. He then proceeded to the parachute loft and signed out his parachute.

I don't care what Quirt said, this is eerie, there's no one with me.

Capp inspected his plane within an inch of its life. In fact, he went around twice, just to make sure he hadn't missed anything.

The plane captain knew this was Capp's first flight by himself, and recognized his nervousness.

"Don't worry, Mr. Capp," said Airman Third Class Anderson. "I've gone over this bird three times and I guarantee it's solid as the day it was built. In fact, I'm scheduled to fly in it later with an instructor to get my monthly flight time. So I want it to come back just like it is now, perfect."

"Thanks Anderson," Capp laughed, "I needed that. You've probably seen your share of rookies trying to look cool, but inside their guts are boiling with the apprehension of looking bad or flying stupid."

"You'll do fine Sir," answered Anderson. "Climb in, and I'll help strap you in."

Capp hooked up his seat belt and shoulder harness with Anderson's help. He put on his helmet, hooked up the radio cords, then gave a thumbs up to Anderson, who positioned himself to the front and left of the nose of the plane with a fire extinguisher by his side.

Anderson returned the thumbs up.

Capp moved the switches and levers. The engine coughed into life.

No matter how many times you start an engine, Capp thought, *there's always a surge of emotion and a thrill when smoke roars out of the stacks on the sides of the engine cowling. What a blast.*

Capp received permission to taxi from the tower and gave the signal to pull the chocks.

Anderson removed them, stepped back and gave a thumbs-up. He then used his hands in a waving motion for Capp to taxi forward, and pointed with both hands to the taxi way.

Capp added power, followed Anderson's directions, and headed out and down the taxiway, toward the take off area.

Why's my stomach churning? thought Capp, *I've done this many times, but this is different. This plane is mine. What a sense of power.*

I wonder what my fraternity brothers are doing at this time, probably washing their cars. I wish they could see me now. I'm a Navy pilot.

Capp went through all the pre-take off procedures.

The engine sounds good, he thought. *Let's go.*

Capp got permission to take-off, taxied into position, added full power, checked instruments as he rolled down the runway, and was airborne.

So far, so good, thought Capp.

Capp glanced out the side of his cockpit and saw all the yellow SNJ's that covered the field.

What a sight, he thought

Capp headed to West Field to practice landings. This was not scheduled to be a long flight, just enough to get experience by himself. There was a standing rule; 'At this stage of the game, don't go anywhere near another aircraft. If you got close enough to make another pilot nervous and it was reported, you may never have another flight.' Safety was paramount.

Capp entered the landing pattern and made three touch and go landings. It was time to head back to Warner Field for a final landing and some beer.

"Warner tower," Capp transmitted, "Whiskey Charlie 254 approaching Point Alpha for landing, over." Nothing was heard except silence, no sound of a friendly voice. Capp again transmitted, "Warner tower, Whiskey Charlie 254 approaching Point Alpha for landing, do you read me? Over." Again, silence was all that Capp heard.

Great! thought Capp, My *crummy radio just crapped out. What a ridiculous predicament, first solo, why me? I can't barge into the traffic pattern, that would make some people very nervous, including me. Let's get out of here and dig out the procedures manual.*

Capp flew away from the field, and flipped through the pages of his kneeboard to the emergency procedures.

I'm sure what to do, but since there is no hurry and I've got plenty of fuel, no sense to rush it. Read what to do a couple of times. The worse that can happen is that I have a mid-air collision and die along with another pilot. Let's skip that option.

OK, fly over the field in the direction of the traffic at 2500 feet and rock my wings. The traffic pattern is 1000 feet, so let's hope everyone is watching their altimeters. Watch for the green light from the tower and enter the traffic pattern at the far end of the field, so I won't descend into anyone. Why me? Why the first solo flight?

Capp followed the book, saw the green light, and proceeded to land. All the other aircraft were cleared away until he touched down.

Oh man, is this embarrassing; but at least I made it back OK.

Capp picked up Anderson's hand signals and was directed into the shutdown spot, and cut his engine.

Anderson jumped onto the wing, and helped Capp un-strap.

"Well," said Anderson, "I guess I missed something, sorry about that."

"Anderson, you're worth your weight in gold, trying to be humble and make me feel good," answered Capp. "Everything worked as advertised until the end of the hop. You can't second-guess a radio that is older than Methuselah, and on its last legs. You can be my Plane Captain any day."

"I appreciate that," said Anderson with a smile and a look of relief on his face. "See you tomorrow."

"We'll find out about that as soon as I hit the debriefing room," answered Capp. "I know the operations officer is talking with Captain Kranz. You know Kranz, 'There's no such thing as a bad procedure, only good procedures screwed up by bad pilots.' Wish I could go directly to the ACRAC."

"Good luck Sir." Anderson laughed, "I'm sure I'll see you tomorrow."

"Thanks," answered Capp.

He turned in his parachute, filled out the yellow sheet in the line shack, listed the radio problem, and proceeded to the ready room.

Captain Kranz was waiting for Capp.

Here we go, thought Capp. A small shiver ran up and down his spine.

"Welcome aboard," said Kranz. "Have you changed your shorts yet?"

Capp saluted, laughed a nervous laugh, hoped that was not out of order, and answered, "No, Sir, but if that engine had coughed; my butt would have sucked up the whole parachute, big time."

"Fair enough," said Kranz. "Pull out your emergency procedures and let's review them."

They reviewed the Radio Out procedure. When they had finished, Kranz said, "What do you think?"

"Well Sir," answered Capp. "I think I followed the emergency procedures correctly. The kneeboard was worth its weight in gold, everything was there for me to read."

"You're right," said Kranz. "You did fine. The main thing you did was to stay cool and follow the first rule in emergencies, 'Fly the airplane.' This won't be your last emergency. Always be prepared. They happen when you least expect them. Hopefully, the ending will always be this good. See you tomorrow."

Capp breathed a sigh of relief. His shoulders and neck hurt. He didn't realize how tense he was. It was time for chow. He went back to the barracks, showered, ate, and headed over to the ACRAC.

Quirt saw Capp enter and shouted for him to join them at a booth, which included Munson and Kirk.

"What are you trying to do?" asked Quirt. "Get some publicity for a DFC (Distinguished Flying Cross)? We heard your radio was out. Hell, I bet you turned it off just to get some recognition."

"You'll never know," laughed Capp, "But the funny thing is, you were the one that worried about an emergency, and instead, it happened to me. I'm staying away from you."

"Have a beer," said Quirt. "I'm buying."

"Let's hope Pervis isn't here," said Capp. "I'm really not in the mood to talk to that idiot and let him revel in my flight problem."

"Guess who's spotted you," laughed Quirt. "And he's headed this way."

"What a phony emergency," sneered Pervis as he stood beside the booth. "Trying to get some brownie points with the instructors? An engine failure would have taken guts, why not that?"

Capp just sat there, staring at the tabletop, not sure if he was going to punch Pervis, or just ignore him.

"You know something, you little freak," said Capp deciding not to punch him. "Even though we don't like each other, that's a terrible thing to say. Little emergencies can turn into big ones if they're allowed to get out of control.'

'Well, it proved one thing," Capp continued. "I'm a better pilot than you are. You would've panicked, wet your pants, and cried for your instructor. Probably, would've flown into the traffic pattern and killed someone. You know how I know-because you think your crap doesn't stink. You're overconfident and don't think anything will ever happen to you. Some day you're going to pay for your indifference. Go away."

"I am a better pilot than you." said Pervis, his anger rising causing his face to get red. "Someday you're going to have to admit it. Think hard about that, you'll see. Don't get up for a superior person, I'm leaving."

As Pervis left, Capp shook his head slowly side to side, "You wonder why God would create such a weird character as him. I bet He wishes He could take back that union of sperm and egg. Who knows? Forget it. Let's get back to jokes and drinking- Skoll."

And they did.

20

"Turn down the volume on that damnable country hick music, you miserable redneck," shouted Capp. "It's attracting cockroaches!"

Capp hated country music. Cool jazz, Dixieland, and big band music were his passion.

It was 1000 Sunday morning in the barracks. The humidity seemed to increase each minute of the day, which did not allow perspiration to evaporate, only run down a person's skin; it was muggy. To add to Capp's discomfort, he was nursing a hangover.

"Hey, since I know you like it so much, you need more volume, it gets into your soul and your bones," shouted back Moose Redmond, Capp's roommate. "Listen to this sad son of a gun. It's his best record, 'Here stands the glass, fill it up to the brim.' It breaks your heart; he's just lost his girl."

"Don't you rebels ever listen to anything else?" groaned Capp. "The record stores are full of music that has nothing to do with losing your girl, dog, horse, or pickup truck to another drunken slob. Ever heard of Dixieland, Jazz, Dave Brubeck, Glenn Miller, or Louis Armstrong? I'd even suggest Mozart, but you'd probably think he's a Martian."

"C'mon Capp," answered Redmond. "You just don't understand music of the earth. I'll take you to a good ol' country bar; check out the women in their tight jeans, lots of dancing, mucho beer, and an occasional fight. You'll never go back to those prissy jazz places where everyone sits around, looking like their bungholes are wound too tight. You'll love it."

"Hey, I'm all for a party bar," said Capp. "Next time you go, I'll take you up on your offer. But in the meantime, turn down the volume; you're not converting me to country music. Plus, my head is telling me it may blow apart. If you don't, I'll report you to Cadet Battalion Commander Pervis. He'll put the fear of the Lord in you."

"Damn Sam," answered Redmond. "That makes me shake in my boots. You know, we could really have a blast. I know you don't like him, but we could take him with us, have him dance with the girl of the meanest, toughest redneck in the bar, and watch as he gets the crap beat out of him. We could just sit at the bar and enjoy the show."

"You sly old raccoon hound." laughed Capp loudly as he pounded his hand several times on the top of his desk. "I can see it now, that little fart thinking he's in love, doing the slow dance, and then this big brawny, hairy Neanderthal picks him up, and throws his butt halfway across the room. I like it, I like it."

"See," said Moose. "You really have some good ol' boy blood in you, but don't know it. We'll just have to work on you."

"Just turn down the volume," said Capp. "That singer is going to have to cry in his beer without causing pain in my head."

Moose turned down the volume on the radio to a lower roar.

"Next weekend," said Moose. "I'll invite Pervis to go with me. You don't have to be in the car with us. You just meet us there with a few of the guys. We'll be at the wildest country bar in Pensacola. It's up on the north side." Moose rubbed his hands together gleefully, "Are we going to have fun, or what?"

"Or what," said Capp, still laughing. "We don't want anyone thrown in jail; just want to see Pervis have to change his shorts."

Their two roommates, Sam Sibley and Bob Marino strolled into the room, having finished brunch at the mess hall. They hadn't heard what Capp and Moose had planned.

Marino had been to church earlier, put his hands over his ears and said to Moose and Sibley, "If you guys keep listening to that country crap, with its out of tune fiddles, the Lord is going to send one of His avenging angels to whisk you off to damnation, and you're going to spend eternity forced to listen to Lawrence Welk."

"Haw, haw," said Sibley. "You Yankees sure are a sensitive bunch; don't know how y'all won the war."

Jim Kennedy and Sam Johnson sauntered into the room. They lived down the hall with two French cadets who were part of a NATO exchange program.

The French cadets were notorious as wild pilots who did some crazy things in the air. They did loops all the way from Warner to West or other airfields where they practiced landings. Then, when they were through, they again did loops all the way back to the Warner. They must have had cast iron stomachs. They also had a great sense of humor, which was about to be tested.

"Do you mind if we sit here for awhile?" asked Kennedy. "So we can breathe some unpolluted air?"

"What's with the unpolluted air?" said Capp. "Check out our southern boys' feet, they stink. Now that's pollution, but you're more than welcome to sit a spell if you can stand it."

"Do you know what's it's like to live with those two frogs?" said Kennedy. "They think we Americans are too sanitary, and that washing all the time is unhealthy."

"For instance?" asked Capp.

"At night, when we throw our dirty clothes in the laundry bag, they fold up their undershirts and shorts and put them back in their dresser drawers. In the winter, they put their stockings on the radiators to dry. Guess what that smells like? Old rotten fish smell better. After the stockings are dry, they roll them up and put them in the drawers with their other underclothes. It's horrible. Sam and I have almost come to blows with them. We don't know what to do."

"Well, let's think for a minute," said Capp, rubbed his hand on his chin, looked at Moose and said with a smirk on his face. "Moose, if one of your old cows ambles into a manure pit and gets stuck, what do you do?"

A smile crossed Moose's face.

"Capp," he said. "You are a country boy, and one who really is the devil in disguise. Well, we do what all good cowboys do, throw a rope around the cow, pull it out, and hose it down."

Everyone looked at each other, and then roared with laughter.

"Are we all thinking what I think you all are thinking?" laughed Kennedy, "A shower party!"

"Let's do it," shouted Capp.

Down the hall they went, opened the door to Kennedy's room, and there were Jacque and Francois lying in bed, each reading a book.

The six of them circled the beds, while Capp whistled 'Anchors Aweigh.'

"Hi fella's," said Capp. "Welcome to sanitation 101."

The French cadets looked puzzled, but that only lasted for a second.

Capp pulled Jacque out of his bed by his feet; Marino grabbed him under the armpits, lifted him waist high, and proceeded down the passageway to the showers. Moose and Sibley did the same to Francois. Kennedy and Johnson emptied the French cadets underclothes into laundry bags, and followed the parade behind the roars of laughter from the Americans.

The French cadets were having none of this, screaming, swearing and shouting in French, which no one understood. The noise could be heard all over the barracks.

"Here we are," shouted Capp, "On with the water!"

"Hold them under the water," shouted Moose.

Kennedy and Johnson emptied the laundry bags of dirty clothes on the shower floor and proceeded to soak them down.

All of them had their uniforms on. So with everyone grappling with each other, the French trying to get out, and the Americans pulling them back in, it was hard to see who was winning. They all, however, got very wet.

The word spread throughout the barracks, and other cadets arrived to help, or just to join in the fun. Someone brought a box of laundry soap flakes and poured it over everyone. The suds were monumental.

Pete Pervis heard the commotion and ran to the second deck shower room to see what was going on.

He was in his uniform, bars glistening on his collar lapels, and he couldn't believe what he was witnessing. About that time, he saw Capp.

"Capp, you hoodlum, stop this immediately or I'll have you and your buddies thrown in the brig. Attention! Attention! Stop it! Stop it right now."

Someone, no one knows but Moose or Capp were suspected, pulled Pervis into the pile of soapsuds and wet humanity. He fell down, someone rubbed soap in his face, and Pervis was soaked.

Pervis got free. Dripping wet he ran down to the duty office and called the military police. Pervis said a riot was in process, which was not the case. He told them that Cadet Capp was the ringleader.

The MP's arrived and broke up everything very quickly. No one in his right mind went against the MP's.

The Officer in charge, a Marine Captain, demanded to talk to Cadet Capp.

Capp stepped forward.

"What in the hell is going on here?" demanded the OinC?

"Well, Sir," Capp answered, (He was very apprehensive as to what was going to happen. He didn't want to be in the brig, lots of demerits). "There was a reported odor problem with some of the French cadets, and we were just helping them get rid of it. No one was hurt, and no property was destroyed."

The MP OinC looked at the wet soapy irreverent looking cadets, and shook his head.

"You are the sorriest looking group of officer candidates I've ever seen. Where are the French cadets?"

Jacque and Francois stood at attention in front of the OinC, both dripping wet.

"Are you hurt?" asked the OinC. "Do you want to press charges?"

"No Sir." answered Jacques. "These are my friends. They just felt we needed a shower, and everything was done in fun. You Americans always have a good time."

"I want them all thrown in the brig." chimed in Pervis. "They were involved in a riot. Do your duty, Captain."

"I don't see a riot here, but I do think a few demerits should be in order." answered the OinC. You soggy dredges of humanity, give your names to Sergeant Callahan. I'll have to report this as an incident."

Names were given and the MP's left. Capp was sure he saw a smile on the face of the Marine Captain as he left.

Pervis was still standing in the passageway as everyone filed back to his rooms.

Capp walked up to him and put his face in Pervis's,

"You little anus," growled Capp. "You'd better hope none of us gets kicked out. If anyone does, you'd better reserve a room in an extended care hospital. We're just having fun, but you don't know what that is. You are the most miserable excuse for a leader ever known to the Navy."

"Don't push it, Capp," answered Pervis. "I call it as I see it. Next time you won't be so lucky. I'll get you kicked out."

Capp stopped by Kennedy's room, to apologize to the French cadets.

"Jacque and Francois, sorry about that," said Capp. "We were just trying to have some stupid fun."

The French cadets both laughed,

"Maybe someday if you ever visit Paris, and we detect an odor, perhaps we can return the favor. We had a great time. Forget it."

"Thanks guys," said Capp. "You really could have gotten us in deep trouble, but you didn't. We owe you one."

Capp walked back to his room where the other five perpetrators were still talking and laughing.

"Great show," said Moose, "Never had so much fun in a long time. You know, I'm really going to enjoy introducing Pervis to the bad rednecks lady. Maybe we can even have him dance with two of them. Damn, it's really going to be something to see. I can hardly wait."

"Yeah," said Capp, "If the little fart lives that long."

21

"Sixteen flights ol' buddy, sixteen terrific flights," shouted Capp as he hopped on one foot into Dwight Munson's room and landed with two feet next to Munson's bunk, and pounded his hand several times on the mattress. "Sixteen flights in the precision phase, and then we move into acrobatics.'

'C'mon, let's get moving, get out of the bunk. It's 0700, the sun is shining, the engines are warmed up, you ate too many eggs and bacon, and you cannot lie down. You'll turn into a whale, not that you aren't already.'

'Look at you, your gut hanging out over your shorts and undershirt, pillow wrapped around your head, and wearing socks. What the hell is that all about? A poster boy for Naval Aviation, you're not!"

"You scared me half to death with enough noise to wake up half the barracks," groaned Munson irritably. "Who gave you a pep pill? It's too early to have that much energy. Go away and let me think about lunch, now that turns me on. You're screwing up the contemplation of my fantasies. Besides, my gut is a sign of gracious living, and I just never took off my socks last night, big deal."

"C'mon, let's get down to the hangar," said Capp. "I've got a 0900 hop. We can talk about what we're going to do today."

"My hop isn't until 1000," answered Munson. "Why do I want to go so early?"

"Because," said Capp. "We can talk about wingovers, chandelles, precision landings, engine out landing emergencies, steep turns, and women. Not necessarily in that order."

"I'll take women any day," said Munson. "The rest is boring."

"Boring? Boring?" exclaimed Capp. "Think about it, completing a perfectly executed wingover, on speed, on altitude, and magnetic heading, doing a perfect reversal to get on the tail of an imaginary bogey. That's exciting, not boring.'

'Munson, you're the only person I know that can wake up, get into uniform, eat, get out of uniform, and get back into the sack within an hour. If I had that kind of dedication, the world would be mine."

"It takes practice," answered Munson. "You have to get a life Capp. Eating, sleeping, and women are priorities. All else is secondary. Some day you'll thank me for the advice."

"Well," said Capp. "Women I'll agree with, but there's small item called flight training. It's sort of important, don't you think?"

"But it's too early." answered Munson. "I bet Pervis doesn't harass his friends like this. Maybe I'll change friends."

"Pervis would like that," said Capp, "since he doesn't have any friends to wake up. However, I'll bet he's been up since 0500, doing pushups or something stupid like that. He'd probably wake you up and make you join him. Come to think of it, that would be funny. Think I'll suggest to him, that you want to be his friend."

"Now don't get any dumb ideas," said Munson. "You'd do that and think it was hilarious. You're perverted."

"Well, get off your blubbery butt and out of that rack that's starting to form on to your body," answered Capp, "and we'll keep Pervis out of this. We don't want to ruin a good day."

Capp went to Munson's closet and threw a shirt and trousers at him.

"C'mon," said Capp, "Get dressed and we'll go the briefing room. There are charts and diagrams on all of the maneuvers. It'll be good for both of us to explain them to each other."

"No wonder you're listed number one," said Munson. "You really eat and breathe this stuff, don't you? You're either a real pro', or, as is the case this morning, a spectacular pain in the butt."

"Do you realize how much the U.S. Government is spending on us," said Capp. "At least we can give them their money's worth. Who knows, some day we may have those Gold Wings, and it's free!"

"Yeah," said Munson. "And all we have to do is put our bodies on the line."

"That's part of the deal," said Capp. "There are hundreds of white crosses at Normandy, of servicemen and women that had the same contract. We'd be speaking German or Japanese if it weren't for them protecting our country. Now the Communists are trying to end our freedom. Our bodies are on the line. That's the price of freedom. That's why this country was founded. It's just amazing how many people in this country have forgotten that. But we can't."

"First you wake me up," said Munson. "And then you give me a patriotic speech. My stomach hurts."

"Just wanted to clear the air," said Capp. "Your stomach hurts because of all the bacon you ate. I'm amazed how someone could eat that much."

"Let's go." said Munson. "Maybe tomorrow I can sleep."

As they left Munson's room and walked down the passageway, Munson noted,

"These are the squeakiest wooden floors I ever heard. It's a wonder that anyone could sleep."

"I think they leave them that way," said Capp. "So we can't sneak in after Lights Out. It's really underhanded, and a crime against party people. Remember, the more you weigh, the more the deck is going to squeak. Does that ring a bell? Oink, Oink."

"At least I'm happy," said Munson. "Go screw yourself if you think I'm going to deprive myself of man's basic rights, 'Eat until you burst.'"

"I always feel a sense of pride when I walk down the streets of a military base. Look at this place," said Capp, as they walked down the street toward the hanger area. "The sidewalks are bustling with sailors, cadets, and officers going in various directions. Everyone is well groomed; their uniforms are neat and pressed.'

'The white frame two story buildings shine in the sunlight. The buildings are old, but they look good and are kept in immaculate condition. The grass is cut and the streets have no holes.'

'A military base is always neat. It emanates pride and radiates the very high values of the servicemen and women who are stationed here. An old Navy saying, I like old Navy sayings, 'Don't stand still for too long of a time or someone will paint you.' It's great, just great."

"Wow," said Munson. "Are you on a tear this morning. What brings all this out?"

"I don't know," said Capp. "Some days it just hits me. What a great country. It's not perfect, but I've never heard of anyone trying to get out of it, however, there are a lot of non-citizens trying to get in. That says something. And the government has placed their trust in us to keep it free from those that want to bring us down. Why would anyone want to do bring the U.S.A. down?"

"I can think of lots of reasons," said Munson. "I minored in history, and the world's always been full of greed and conflict. Let's just become the best pilot's we can. Some day we'll have to go into combat, you can make book on that."

"Here's the hanger," said Capp. "We can kick around procedures on the blackboard in the briefing room. When the instructors show up, we can fine-tune it with them. It should give us an edge to fly a perfect flight."

Capp knew Munson was not the most dedicated student. This was one way to keep his head in the program.

"O.K.," said Capp. "Let's start with a wingover and finish up with a chandelle. Explain both of them to me. What are they?"

"A chandelle is a climbing turn," answered Munson, "with a 180 degree reversal in direction. A wingover is also a 180-degree reversal in direction, but with the nose of the plane pulling up and around. The wings are perpendicular to the ground at the 90-degree or halfway point. Then the plane rolls out, ending up at the same starting airspeed and altitude, but flying in the opposite direction. It's a beautiful maneuver."

"Great," said Capp. "Now memorize the power settings of the throttle, and use your hands to fly through the maneuvers. You have to visualize the maneuver, and practice until the maneuver becomes a reflex."

"Why is that?" asked Munson.

"If you constantly think mechanically by the numbers of what is coming next," said Capp, "you'll mentally get behind the procedure, instead of flying mentally ahead of the procedure. That can get you killed. For example, your plane stalls in a turn at low altitude. You want an instant recovery reflex, not a mental discussion of what to do mechanically. Let's take a break and head over to the ready room."

"Wow," said Capp as they entered. "Is it crowded, everyone must be is flying today. Let's try to find a corner table, away from the bridge players, that card game goes on all day."

"Guess who's at the next table?" said Munson. "Our favorite Battalion Commander, Pervis."

"Hey Pervis," said Capp. Haven't they washed you out yet?"

"Fat chance," answered Pervis. "When a person is number one, all Cretins follow my lead."

"Everyone knows about you," said Capp, "Too bad."

"What are you talking about?" asked Pervis."

"The word is," said Capp. "That you sleep with your socks on."

Munson groaned.

"That's ridiculous," said Pervis. "Only children do that."

Munson groaned again. He wasn't sure where this was going.

"By the way," said Capp. "Munson wants to be your friend in the morning. What were you doing early this morning?"

"None of your business," said Pervis. "But if you want to know, as a real man, I was doing pushups."

"Wow, that's what Munson wants to do, right Munson?"

"Are you kidding?" said Munson, who finally had enough of the practical joking. "Only a sick person would do pushups in the morning. And no, I don't want to be your friend, especially in the morning."

"Pervis," said Capp, "When the word gets around that you sleep in your socks and do pushups in your socks, your macho image may be in jeopardy. What a shame. What do you think Munson?"

"Yup, you're right," said Munson. "That is a little weird."

"You guys are crazy," barked Pervis. "Who the hell let you in the ready room? I don't do that, and don't spread any rumors or I'll start spreading some of my own."

"Your secret is our secret," said Capp, "Too bad, such a nice boy."

Pervis got red in the face, "Capp, you think you're funny, but you're just a pain in the butt. I'm out of here."

After Pervis left, Capp said, "Sorry about the socks Munson. It's O.K. to wear them to bed. I just like to find new and better ways to get under that little farts skin. He probably wears his gold bars to bed along with a teddy bear."

"That's O.K.," said Munson. "But no more practical jokes, Pervis may have believed you."

"Wait until tomorrow morning," laughed Capp. "You'll find out."

22

Wednesday, April 1955, 0800, weather cloudy, humid, 75 degrees, 10 knots of wind from the southeast, time to fly.

It was the eighth hop in the syllabus of sixteen, required for the precision phase at Warner Field, Florida.

Chuck Capp and Jim Quirt strolled into the ready room. It was noisy as usual, full of cadets waiting for their briefing times.

Capp noticed Pete Pervis sitting by himself at the end of the room.

"Get you some coffee, Pete?" asked Capp.

"No thanks," said Pervis. "Why are you suddenly interested in my well being?"

"Everybody in the Navy needs a cup of Joe in the morning," said Capp, "Gets the blood flowing, makes you a hot pilot."

"OK," answered Pervis suspiciously, "Cream and sugar."

Capp walked to the coffee mess, filled a cup with hot coffee, poured in some cream and salt, lots of salt.

"Here you go Pete," said Capp. "That'll get the cobwebs out."

"Pervis took a large swallow, got a pained look on his face, ran over to the sink, and spit out the coffee, accompanied by a loud *'Aagghh.'*

"Damn you, Capp. You put salt, not sugar in my coffee. That's a crummy trick. I should've known you'd pull something like that. Thanks a lot."

"I'm sorry," said Capp, looking as innocent as a choirboy. "Jeez, I got the wrong bottle. That must have tasted terrible. Here, let me get you another cup."

Quirt and the cadets who were nearby, tried to hide their muffled laughter.

"Are you kidding?" answered Pervis, "What the hell would you put in that one, saltpeter?"

"Man, you are taking this too hard," said Capp. "Anyone can make a mistake. Hmm, I never thought of saltpeter. You're just full of information Pete."

"Don't go getting any stupid ideas," answered Pervis, "And especially with me. Revenge is sweet you know. It's my turn."

"Boy, you sure are sour," said Capp. "By the way, it's time to brief. Better wash out your mouth, Pete. You look all puckered up."

"Capp, you really are a dork," said Pervis.

"Hey, that's better than someone who drinks salt in his coffee," answered Capp. "Thanks for the compliment. Let's go fly."

Even though the eighth hop was a solo, the instructors briefed the cadets as to the procedures to complete the hop. Practice, practice, practice, makes perfect. That was the Navy way.

At the end of the briefing, Captain Kranz said, "Capp, keep your stick movements small, smooth, and rudder coordinated. You don't want to horse the plane around. If you horse it around, you'll get ahead or behind the maneuver. It'll be sloppy, and you'll have to start the maneuver over again. Your hop is only one hour long, use the time to your best advantage.'

'As you know, the restricted area is full of planes doing acrobatics. Clear the area above and below before you start maneuvers, any questions?"

"No, Sir," answered Capp.

"Our next hop is dual," said Kranz. "We'll see what you practiced."

"Yes sir," answered Capp. "I won't let you down. It'll be perfect."

"Only one person in this world was perfect," said Kranz. "And He didn't fly airplanes. Outstanding would be O.K. Have fun."

Capp did his normal pre-flight, taxied out to the runway, and roared off toward the restricted area used for acrobatic maneuvers.

What a beautiful day, thought Capp, as he banked over the lush green foliage below, which contrasted with the deep blue sky and fluffy white clouds. *To think the government is paying me to do this. How lucky can I get?*

Well, this is the area. Let's clear it for other planes. A 90-degree bank left and right, no planes below and none above, seems to be safe.

A wingover is always a nice way to start the day. Set the power, small movements, pull the nose up, kick a little rudder for a coordinated turn. Keep it coming, halfway there, and 90 degrees of bank, slowly let the nose fall through and slowly roll out. There, perfect. Opposite direction, ending up at the same altitude and speed that I started at, am I hot, or what?

Now for some Chandelles, which I never liked, but it's part of the syllabus, a climbing turn to the opposite direction, boring, but probably a combat maneuver of sorts.

Simulated engine failures are more fun. Chop the throttle at anytime, then try to simulate landing on a field. It takes a lot of practice and patience. You try to land safely in an open field, or die. Trees don't forgive planes that crash into them. Back to Warner Field, it's been a good hop.

Pervis, on the other side of the restricted area, was not having such a good day.

Time to do a wingover, thought Pervis. *Add some power and, Damn! What was that? The engine's running rough. A backfire. Smoke's coming out of the stacks, the engine has quit, and I'm alone.*

C'mon, remember the emergency procedures. Reduce power to stop the backfiring, trade airspeed for altitude, turn toward a field, I think West Field is off my starboard wing, there it is! What luck!

"Mayday, Mayday!" radioed Pervis. "Whiskey Charlie 354, engine failure two miles west of West Field at five thousand feet. I'll attempt to land at West Field. Clear the field."

I knew I should've gone back to the chocks after the run-up check at Warner. That's what happens when you get in a hurry and not read the checklist. Farr warned me about that. I added full power without the propeller lever being at high RPM. Probably over boosted, and ruined the engine. I didn't want to taxi back to the flight line and admit I fouled up. And here I am, without power. Damn.

Keep circling. Now do S-turns and keep the approach end of the field in sight. Hope I don't let down on any other planes.

O.K., flair out. I'm too high and slow. Oh, Oh, going to hit hard. Oomph. Hold on. Kick rudder so I don't cartwheel. It's going to cartwheel. No it's not. It stopped. This is a tough bird.

Turn off the switches and sit on the wing. An instructor will be here soon to fly me back to Warner.

Last night, I dreamed about death. I couldn't tell who died. Dreams never tell you that. It frightened me enough to wake up. I wonder how Freud would interpret my dreams. I bet my father would have found out I fouled up. I can see him yelling at me in the casket. I'll never tell anyone about the over-boost.

Well, here comes the Ready plane with the flight surgeon and a second SNJ with an empty rear cockpit, my seat. Jeez, miss one lousy procedure, and face the gauntlet of an investigation board. They may guess what happened after inspecting the engine, but I'll never admit to anything.

The flight surgeon leaped from the ready plane, and ran over to Pervis.

"Are you all right?" he asked, "Any broken bones, pains?"

"No, Sir," answered Pervis. "But my hands and knees are still shaking."

"Let me do a quick examination," said the Flight Surgeon. He pushed and pulled on Pervis's body. "It doesn't appear you're injured. When you get back to Warner, check in at sickbay. I'll meet you there."

"Yes Sir," said Pervis. *What a crock, thought Pervis. I hate physical exams, it's embarrassing having someone put his hands all over me.*

The second plane taxied up. The instructor let the engine run. He motioned for Pervis to get into the rear cockpit.

On the flight back to the field, the instructor radioed,

"You did a good job Mr. Pervis. You got your plane down in one piece. I've seen some bad crashes and injuries from Dead-Stick landings; it's not always the best way to go. The option to bail out is always there. Sometimes it's safer than taking a chance on a bad crash. But you made it, that's what counts."

"Thank you, Sir," Pervis radioed back. "I guess practice does pay off." Pervis thought, *What idiot would bail out of a plane that wasn't on fire or totally out of control? I didn't even consider that option.*

After they landed, Pervis was given a clean bill of health at sickbay. As he walked back to the barracks, Pervis thought,

I don't want to see Capp. That vulture. I know he's just waiting to pounce on me. He'll have something insulting to say. Guess I'll have to insult him more than he can insult me. I'll try to avoid him as long as possible.

The accident investigation board cleared Pervis of any fault. He was given an outstanding commendation on how he handled the plane, and followed correct emergency procedures during an engine failure. They did not discover that Pervis over-boosted the engine. And Pervis didn't tell them.

23

Capp shouted across the room to Dick Price, "Price, c'mon over and join us at our table. Don't sit at the bar by yourself."

"Hey, thanks," answered Price. "I just got here and looked for some friendly faces. Since you guys don't look like the enemy, you'll do in a pinch. Let me buy you a round."

"You know the rules," said Capp. "Only the loser on a roll of the dice can buy. Here, you start the roll. We'll play, 'Ship, Captain, and Crew.' Low man buys. No fair rolling sixes or we'll send you back to the bar stool."

"Hey," said Price, "I never win at this game. But go over the rules again, maybe there's something I missed."

"O.K., said Capp. "Five dice in a cup. You get three rolls to qualify and get points. In order to qualify, you need to roll a six, a five, and a four in order; that's the ship, captain, and crew, and you keep those dice out as they come up. The two remaining dice are your points; two sixes are the highest and two aces or ones are the lowest. If you never qualify, you'll lose."

"Why delay the results?" answered Price. "But since you're so honorable, let's give it a roll. Look at that." moaned Price as he banged the brown leather dice cup on the bar. "Three rolls and all I got was one lousy six and a five. I didn't even qualify. Better put my money on the table."

152

"Not so fast," said Capp. "Where's your competitive spirit? I thought you guys from Chicago were tough. Quirt, Munson, Curtin, and myself have to roll. Quirt cheats. Other than that, you've still got a shot."

"C'mon dice," shouted Munson, as he slammed the dice cup with the five dice on the table. "Six, five, four, and two fours-eight's my point. I'm out, yeahh! Can't get much better than that."

"Do it baby," said Curtin, as he slammed the cup even harder than Munson. "Third roll- six, five, four and deuces, hey, I qualified with a four, looks good."

"Here goes," said Capp. "Six, five, four, and treys, my points six, I'll take that."

"You lucky turd," said Quirt. "Watch this. I'm going to slide them out instead of trying to put a hole in the bar."

"Get lost," said Capp. "No sliders at this table. Nice try, grease ball."

"Bam, Bam, Bam." yelled Quirt at each of his three tries. "What's this? I didn't even get a six. I didn't qualify. I'm smoking and burning."

"See," said Capp. "I told you, sliders pay. It breaks my heart. What a shame."

"Wait a minute," said Quirt, "Pricey-Wicey didn't qualify either. I get one more shot at him."

"I'm thirsty," said Capp. "Let's cut it down to one roll each. High dice points win, O.K?"

"No way," said Quirt. "I want my three rolls. That's the rules."

"Order the beer," Price said to Munson. "Quirt, you're going down."

"That's the spirit," said Capp. "I hate a happy loser."

"O.K. dice, do it," said Price. "Six, five, four, a five and a deuce; beat that Quirt, sevens my point."

"No problem," said Quirt. "What! Six, five, four, a trey and an ace, what a bunch of crap. Next time we change the rules so I can win."

"Start them over," said Quirt. "I can't lose twice in a row."

"Give the waitress a big tip," said Capp, "If you're not going to lose again, at least share some of your profits with her."

"Capp, stop trying to spend my money," said Quirt. "If I'm going to share something with her, it won't be profit."

"Quirt," said Capp. "She goes for class, somebody like Pervis."

"Hey, that hurt," said Quirt. "Speaking of Pervis, there he is, sitting at the end of the bar. What do you suppose he's thinking about, his engine failure?"

"He did a good job landing the bird on the ground in one piece," answered Capp. "But it's just not fair, not to razz him about it. There must be someway to irritate him. He's so arrogant."

"Jeez," said Quirt. "Look at the pot calling the kettle black. Go ahead. We'll drag your body over to sick bay if he decides to open a beer bottle on your head. You two just love to grind on each other, don't you?"

"All we cadets have to do is fly, chase women, and drink beer," said Capp. "There has to be more to life than that. Not much more, but something. Pervis is that something that rounds out my personality. It just feels good to see him lose his cool. He thinks he's such an ace. It's fun to knock him off his pedestal once in awhile. I'll be right back."

"Be gentle," laughed Quirt.

Capp walked over to the bar and sat down beside Pervis.

"Pete," said Capp. "Good job on how you handled your engine emergency.

"Shove off," said Pervis.

"I really mean it."

"Yeah, right," snarled Pervis."

"Can't you handle a compliment?" asked Capp. "What's the problem?"

"Not from you," answered Pervis. "I don't trust you, or anything you say."

"I can't blame you," said Capp. "But you're a good pilot. If an engine failure ever happens to me, I'd like to do as good of a job as you did. Maybe I can learn something from you. You don't have to tell me, however I'd sure like to know how you handled it."

"Let me think about it for a minute," said Pervis.

He stared at the wall for a moment, looked down at the floor, exhaled in an expression of boredom and exasperation, and then looked back over to Capp.

"O.K., let's make this quick. I started a wingover. The engine backfired. Fire and smoke belched out of the engine stacks. The engine started running rough."

"What did you do?" asked Capp.

"Didn't you read the accident report?" answered Pervis.

"Sure," said Capp. "But I'd like to hear it firsthand. Let me buy you a beer."

Pervis relaxed and appeared to loosen up. He continued,

"I pulled back the power, and looked for a field to land on. Luckily, I was close to West Field. What a break. I've only practiced simulated dead-engine landings a few times. If nothing but a small field was available, I don't know if I'd have made it."

"Luck always seems to be with the lucky," said Capp.

"Who said that?" asked Pervis.

"Me," answered Capp, "Very original."

"Sounds good," said Pervis. "Does that also mean that bad luck follows the unlucky?"

"It's an attitude," said Capp. "I've noticed that negative, pessimistic people always seem to be losers. Positive optimistic people seem to handle the pile of crap that life so brutally dumps out."

"You should have been in my psychology classes," said Pervis. "That's a dark science, you know. The instructors would've hated you. They only dealt with, 'why people are screwed up.' Not with, 'why people are happy and well adjusted.'"

"Glad I missed those classes," said Capp. "Economics was dark enough. So finish the story."

"Due to my superior skill and airmanship," said Pervis. "I S-turned and slipped the SNJ, to a perfect landing."

"I think it's getting a little deep in here," said Capp. "What really happened?"

"Jeez," said Pervis. "What a skeptic. O.K.—I almost ground looped, scared me to death. I got to the field in good shape, but was high and fast. Lots of rudder was the only thing that saved my butt. I thought

I might flip over, maybe burn to death. It's strange how many things can go through your mind in such a short time."

"Have another beer," said Capp. "You deserve it."

"Thanks," said Pervis. "I haven't had this many beers in a long time, feels good to relax. It's been hard to sleep at night. All I can see are those ground loops in my dreams. Maybe by talking about it, they'll be gone. Capp, you ever thought about going into psychiatry? You'd be good."

"Naw," said Capp. "Flying is all I want to do."

"I'm getting a little crocked," said Pervis. "My precision stage check ride is tomorrow. I should get back to the barracks. Don't want to accidentally over-boost the engine again."

"What!" said Capp?

"You didn't hear me say that!" stammered Pervis, in a state of panic. "It was a mistake."

"You over-boosted the engine," growled Capp, "And didn't go back to the flight line and Down the plane. Tell me, if you didn't have an engine failure, would you've reported it? Would you? Because if you didn't, the next pilot would've had the engine failure. Well, would you have reported it?"

"Hell, yes," moaned Pervis. "I just didn't want to cancel my hop."

"This is our secret, right?" said Pervis as he narrowed his eyes in a threatening manner.

"For now, it is," said Capp. "But, if I ever find out, you've put a pilot's life in danger by fouling up and not reporting a problem, I'll tell the accident board what you did. I'll take my lumps for not reporting this now. You'll be washed out."

"Don't be stupid, Capp," sneered Pervis. "I want those Gold Wings. If you tell, you'll never know what might happen to you."

"You little psycho," said Capp, his teeth clenched. "Don't threaten me! I should knock your butt right off that barstool. You're disgusting."

Capp turned and went back to his table, his fists clenched in anger. He then went back to the barracks, alone.

Pervis left the ACRAC immediately, he didn't want Capp to come back and embarrass him. It was time to make a fast exit, and he did.

24

Sue Ann Crawford knew there was a problem. She bent over in pain from cramps in her stomach as waves of nausea swept through her body. She stumbled into the bathroom, and screamed. Blood flowed from her private part. She was terrified.

The phone, the phone, she thought as she stumbled back into her kitchen. Her hand and fingers trembled as she frantically tried to get her fingers into the holes; her trembling made it hard to dial. Finally the connection was made, the phone rang and a pleasant voice answered,

"Doctor Mastic's office, Can I help you?"

"This is Sue Ann Crawford. I'm pregnant and have severe cramps. I'm bleeding. Help me, what should I do?"

"Don't hang up," exclaimed the nurse with a calm but urgent tone in her voice. "I'll get Doctor Mastic."

A brief pause, "This is Doctor Mastic. Sue Ann, I understand you've got cramps and bleeding. Is that correct?"

"Yes, yes," answered Sue Ann. "I'm scared, what do I do?"

"You need to come to the hospital's emergency room, immediately, said Dr Mastic. "I'll meet you there. Do you need an ambulance?"

"No," answered Sue Ann. "It's only a few blocks; I can drive, is that all right?"

"Don't be a hero. If you can't drive we'll send an ambulance." said Mastic, "Are you sure you can drive?"

"Yes, I'll leave right now," answered Sue Ann, "What's happening to me?"

"Just meet me at the emergency room." said Mastic. "Try to stay calm. Don't speed. We don't want you to have an accident. I'll be right there. You'll be all right, O.K.?"

"All right," answered Sue Ann. "I'm leaving now; it'll take me about five minutes."

She hung up the phone, grabbed her purse, car keys and then wobbled to the doorway. Her car was in the driveway.

"Ohh, it hurts," she groaned.

She turned the ignition key; the car started, she backed out, and drove toward the hospital.

"Just a few blocks," she said out loud. "Don't speed, Ohh it hurts. There's the emergency entrance. Pull up to the door; I don't think I can walk from the parking lot."

The emergency room personnel were waiting for her at the doorway.

"Just stop there," shouted a nurse. "We'll take care of your car. Just get out and get on the gurney."

"O.K.," groaned Sue Ann.

"I'm dizzy." she said as she stepped out of her car.

A blackness spread over her eyes, she slumped to the ground.

Chuck Capp had just returned to his room. The loudspeaker blared from the passageway,

"Chuck Capp, you have a phone call in the Duty Office."

"You hear that Capp," said Moose Redmond. "You get more phone calls than all of us in this room together."

"How can I not hear that," answered Capp. "It's loud enough to rattle the ceiling. If you feel bad about not getting any calls, you go down and answer it, be my guest."

"Naw," said Redmond. "It's probably some enraged husband that wants to take you apart. I'll let you take the heat."

"I don't chase married women," answered Capp. "However, it could be some girl's large boyfriend; sure you don't want to answer it?"

"Will you get out of here," said Redmond. "I'll give you a military burial if you lose the fight. Even a Yankee deserves a proper ceremony."

"Yankees, Rebels," answered Capp, "I still don't understand, the war's over, never mind, I'm out of here."

Capp hurried down the passageway and into the Duty office.

"Capp here," Where's the phone?"

"You can take it over on that vacant desk, answered the cadet on duty, "Try to keep it under five minutes. If it's going to be a long call, hang up and call them on the public phone in the passageway."

"Yeah, right." said Capp sarcastically.

He hated cadets that were by the book in minor matters. He picked up the phone, "Cadet Capp Sir, can I help you?"

There was silence for a moment, then a woman's voice, sobbing, and choked with emotion was heard.

"Chuck, It's Sue Ann. I'm in the Pensacola public hospital; can you come over to see me tonight? I really need to talk to you. It's important."

"The hospital?" gasped Capp. "What's the matter? Are you all right?"

"Yes," she said. "I'll tell you about it when you get here. Please come."

"Sure, sure," answered Capp. "I can be there in about half an hour. What room?

"253," said Sue Ann.

"I'm leaving now," said Capp. "See you soon."

"Thanks," said Sue Ann. "I'll be watching for you."

Capp ran out the door and to his car.

I've got a check ride tomorrow, thought Capp. *This had better be important. It's probably about the baby. I hope she isn't going to push marriage this soon; I'm not ready yet. Well, let's find out.*

Capp found the hospital, walked down to room 253, not sure what to expect, and slowly entered the room. Sue Ann was in the bed next to the window. The other bed was empty.

"Hi Sue Ann," said Capp softly. "How are you?"

"Oh Chuck," whispered Sue Ann looking up at him with tears in her eyes, she sobbed, "You're a sight to behold. I know you're busy and under stress, but I really needed to see you tonight. I have a confession to make."

"What happened?" said Capp. "Are you sick?"

"Not now," answered Sue Ann. She smiled and wiped tears from her eyes. "I had a miscarriage. There no longer is a baby."

The impact of her words hit him in the face as if he had received a punch to the jaw. His body jerked back. He stared at her for a moment.

"A miscarriage?" said Capp. "That's serious, you could have died." He put his hand gently on hers, "A mother losing a baby is horrible, I'm sorry. I really am."

You're such a gentleman, and I'm such a witch," answered Sue Ann. "You don't deserve what I've put you through."

"I have to admit, said Capp. "It's caused me a lot of stress, but a deal is a deal. I would have honored our agreement together."

"I know. I was going to call you later this week and let you out of our agreement," answered Sue Ann. "My conscience got the better of me; I couldn't sleep. This was unexpected. It makes it easier, but you've got to believe me, I really was going to call you. You're free Chuck. You would have been, with or without this happening."

"That's fair enough," said Capp. "I believe you. But why would you have let me off? You know I was sincere. I also believed you'd hold up your end, and keep it a secret."

"Because," answered Sue Ann. "You're not the father."

Capp was stunned. His back muscles tightened, his eyes turned ice blue.

"Also," said Sue Ann. "Someone else knew of our agreement. Someone we could trust to keep our secret, but it complicated things."

"You, you mean," said Capp stuttering, he pulled his hands from hers, rubbed his forehead hard and ran his fingers through his hair. "You put me through all of this when you knew it was a lie? What the hell kind of a person are you? My life has been nothing but misery since we met. My flying has suffered, and my friends think I've turned into a wimp. It's been a living hell. Deep inside, I knew you were wrong. What else? Who's this other person? Why did you do this?"

"Oh God," cried Sue Ann. "Please forgive me. I was embarrassed and scared when I found out I was pregnant. I didn't know what to do. I told you the truth that I only had done it once. It wasn't fair. I felt so dirty. I knew the real father would never agree to marry me and give my child a proper birth.

"Go on," said Capp.

"One afternoon, at a hotel bar I was trying to decide what to do. A Naval cadet came in and we struck up a conversation. He knew you quite well, said you were a softy, and would probably agree to marry me. That's when it started."

"Who's this cadet? demanded Capp. "Did he also tell you I could get kicked out of the flight program if the Navy found out I was married? What went through your mind?"

"No," he didn't," answered Sue Ann sharply. "And I'm not going to tell you anything about him, I'm afraid you might hurt him."

"You got that right," said Capp. "That cadet held all the power. It would be an easy way to get rid of me. And I know of only one person who could be that vicious, Pete Pervis. Is that who it was?"

"I'm not going to tell you." answered Sue Ann. "I don't know who this Pervis person is. If I had known the marriage restriction at the beginning, I probably wouldn't have called you. But after meeting you, well, you and the birth father have a lot of similarities. You were so nice. I thought you'd be a great husband and father to my child. Besides, the other cadet promised me he'd keep our marriage a secret, he just wanted to see me happy."

"Get you head out of the clouds lady," barked Capp. "This was a setup from the beginning, but you were too gullible and naïve to see that. That cadet wants me kicked out of the program. He's selfish. He could give a crap-less about you."

"No, he's really nice," said Sue Ann. "He thinks a lot of you. I can't believe he would've betrayed my trust."

"Believe it." growled Capp. "He was a psych major in college, and knows how to manipulate a person, especially a vulnerable person like you. He's a scumbag. That's who it was, Pervis, wasn't it?"

"No," she answered. "Chuck, it's over. Go on with your life. I know you hate me and maybe that other cadet too? But don't let your hate

JOHN SCHLETER

destroy you; you've got too much going for you. But please, can you forgive me? It's important to me."

Capp relaxed and sat back in his chair.

"You know," said Capp. "You're beautiful, intelligent and have a great personality. Maybe at a different time, or place, or circumstances, it might have been different. Believe me, you were tricked. You were offered a solution to an embarrassing problem, and didn't know what was really on his warped little mind. For that I can forgive you, sort of, but not that cadet. Whoever he is, I still think it was Pervis; he took advantage of your innocence. Do me and yourself a favor; if you ever do it again, use protection. Thanks for telling me right away. You could have strung me along and I wouldn't have known you weren't pregnant. You're a classy lady, but I don't ever want to see you again. I hope you understand."

"Yes, I do." answered Sue Ann. "It's a shame. In this great big world, a person crosses paths with only a few people, and of that few, there are the rare instances that two people are compatible. I wish we had met earlier, before this happened. But I understand. I won't ever bother you again.

She offered her hands; Capp reached out and held them, gently.

"Take care," he said.

He turned and left the room, relieved, but sad for Sue Ann.

She was really excited at the thought of being a mother. He shuddered, Jeez, how easy it was to suck him in. Scary, but thank heavens for natures little miracles, it wasn't meant to be.

At the barracks, Capp walked into Quirt's room. Quirt was in his rack, as usual smoking, and listening to classical music on the radio.

"Hey, hot shot," said Capp. "Let me buy you a cool one. It's for a minor celebration."

"You always know when to interrupt me when I'm enjoying life." answered Quirt. "Listen to that, it's Beethoven, it's beautiful. And now you want me to go to ACRAC, with all its noise, loud music and noxious smells?"

"You got it," said Capp.

"Sorry Beethoven," sang Quirt. "I need some French fries. You said you're buying, right?"

162

"Right," answered Capp. "I'll tell you about my celebration on the way."

They got into Capps convertible and headed toward the ACRAC.

"I'm free," said Capp. Then he shouted at the top of his lungs. "Do you hear me, I'm free!" He pounded the top of his dashboard. "Crawford had a miscarriage, I'm free!"

"All right!" shouted Quirt back at Capp. "You son-of-a-gun, are we getting our old Capp back? Or are you still going to mope around like you've been doing lately?"

"I'm free, damn," said Capp. "And you know what, I wasn't even the father. How about that crap, I was set-up."

"Jeez," laughed Quirt as he pounded Capp on his back. "What happened?"

"Some cadet talked her into accusing me." said Capp. "I think it was Pervis, but she wouldn't tell. I think he was going to inform the Navy when I got married, and get me kicked out. All I want to do tonight is find him and beat the living crap out of him. He's probably at the ACRAC, that little pervert."

"Hold it, hold it," shouted Quirt. "Stop the car. Pull over here, now! Are you crazy? You'll be out of the frying pan into the fire. You punch him out, and you'll get kicked out. If it was Pervis, he'd still win. Turn this car around. We're not going to the ACRAC."

Capp stopped the car, rested his hands on top of the steering wheel, and then his head. He sighed.

"You're right," said Capp. "This is really stupid. All I could think about on the way back from the hospital was how good it was going feel, to smash my fist into his face. You're right again, as usual. I'm not even sure it was him."

"Even if you could prove it, said Quirt. "Leave him alone. He's not worth it. You're free. Put this behind you and move on. It's been a nightmare, but it's over. It'll be just a memory in a few months. Don't screw up now. Move on."

"That's what Sue Ann said," answered Capp. "O.K., I promise not to punch-out Pervis. Some day, mark my words; he'll get what's owed to him. I don't know how, but he will. He's too evil.

25

Warner Field, Florida. Friday, 0800 Sunny, Hot, Wind from the Southwest at eleven knots, Good Navy weather.

Capp was in the briefing room studying procedures for his final check ride in "B" stage, precision flight.

"Hey Capp," hollered Quirt. "Where have you been? I've looked all over for you. Since last night, you've been a phantom. What's the problem? You should be a happy camper now that you're free."

"No problems," answered Capp. "I just want to get through this check ride."

"That's baloney," said Quirt. "You've never sweated anything. C'mon. I'm you're old buddy who knows you like a book. What's up? You left the ACRAC last night without stopping for a final brew. Is that Sue Ann thing still on your mind? You ate breakfast before all of us. And here you are. You're not turning into a loner, are you?"

"Look," said Capp, "I'm not a loner. I'm not fouled up. Just back off. Do that as a friend. I've got some other things on my mind which I have to sort out."

"I'll bet it's got something to do with that jerk Pervis, hasn't it?" asked Quirt. "You were talking to him at the bar, and you looked angry. What was that all about?"

"If you want to talk about broads, booze, or flying," answered Capp. "That's O.K. But knock it off, or I'll move to another table."

"Boy, are you testy, but as a friend, consider my cross examination closed." said Quirt. "By the way, you have Lieutenant Rick Farr as your check-ride pilot. He's really good. Show him your stuff."

"An ex-Blue Angel," said Capp. "I'll bet he can show me a few tricks, maybe after the check ride. Who knows? That lucky Pervis has him for his regular instructor. Captain Kranz is great, but Farr would be outstanding."

"First you've got to get an Up on the check ride," answered Quirt. "By the way, Pervis got Captain Kranz for his check pilot."

"That's terrific," said Capp, "He had him for his solo check too. Remember how I screwed with Pervis's mind, almost got him a down. Damn, that was funny. I'll bet Pervis is scared to death. That's great."

"I'll let you go without a confession," said Quirt. "But whatever's bothering you, don't let it get in the way of your check ride. Good luck, See you later."

Capp tried to study, but it was hard.

Quirt hit it on the head, he thought. *Didn't know it was so obvious. Between Sue Ann and Pervis, I couldn't sleep last night. Pervis did something that was dangerous to him and other pilots, plus I'm sure he was behind the baby plot. Should I turn him in for over-boosting his engine? Forget it. It's all over, got to get my mind in the cockpit. Here comes Farr, show time.*

"Good morning Lieutenant," said Capp.

"Good morning," answered Farr. "We've got a beautiful day to go flying. Let's brief, and get on with it."

"Yes, Sir," said Capp.

The brief completed, they signed out the SNJ, picked up their parachutes, and walked out to the flight line.

"Isn't this great," said Farr as they walked, the planes taxiing, the roar of the engines, the smell of the gasoline. Capp, I hope you appreciate the elite club you're in. It's an honor to be here."

"Yes, Sir," said Capp. "I agree. Sometimes I have to pinch myself to believe this can happen to me. All I want is those Gold Wings."

"Well," said Farr, "This is the next step. Just as we briefed, you'll have control of the plane for the hop. I'll only observe, unless there's a problem."

They took off and flew toward the restricted area assigned for acrobatics and unusual attitudes.

"Let's start off easy to get a feel of the plane," radioed Farr. "Do two, Power Off stalls."

"Roger," answered Capp. *This is a piece of cake. But concentrate. Pull the nose up, reduce power, a buffet, and let the nose fall through the horizon, add power and recover. Good.*

"O.K," radioed Farr. "Now let's do an approach stall."

Capp was mentally going through the procedures.

Start a turn, and pull off power. Pull back on the stick, let it stall, add power, roll out, and recover with a minimum loss of altitude, so far so good.

"Now, let's do a chandelle," radioed Farr.

A reverse climbing turn, this isn't my best maneuver, thought Capp. *Just don't be dangerous. Don't stall. O.K., I got through this one. Let's keep up the effort. Man, am I sweating, relax.*

"Next on the list is a wingover," radioed Farr, "Whenever you're ready."

My favorite one, thought Capp. *I'll knock his socks off with this one. Oh, that's beautiful. Opposite direction, right on heading, altitude, and speed, that should impress him. Maybe he'll sign me up with the Blue Angels.*

"Let's try another Chandelle," radioed Hall. "That needs some fine tuning."

Great, thought Capp. *He found my weakness. Do it good. I don't want to get hung up on this.*

"That's better," radioed Farr. "Let me try it. I'll talk through it."

Is this guy good, or what, thought Capp as Farr completed what could be the best Chandelle he ever saw. *What a natural pilot. Jeez, he's like silk. Someday, I'll be like that. It takes practice, practice, and practice.*

"Let's do a few simulated dead engine landings," radioed Hall. "I'm chopping your power."

The engine went silent, punctuated with popping sounds of an engine at idle power.

Farr didn't give me a chance to set up, thought Capp. *Quick, trade airspeed for altitude, then get the nose down to gliding speed. Bank left and right to find a field. All I can see is that short one to the left side. Not good, but that's all I've got. Don't pull a Pervis, and land high and fast. Where's the wind from? Not good, I'll have a crosswind. Wish I could see another field.*

Nothing, O.K., concentrate. Keep doing circles to get to a good ninety-degree approach spot. I'm too high, now I know how Pervis felt. Do an S-Turn; now straighten out, too high. Damn, I blew it.

"Add power, add power!" radioed Farr with urgency. "We're too high and long."

"Let's try another one," radioed Farr. "You would've touched down at the far end, into the tree line. Get more distance on your approach spot at the ninety."

C'mon, thought Capp. *If I think long, I'll be long. Get Pervis out of my mind. Let's do a Capp landing.*

"We're at two thousand feet," radioed Farr. "I've chopped your power."

Find a field, thought Capp. *There, that's a good one. If worse comes to worse, I'll land on the road. No, that would be a Down. Farr wants a field; it's tougher.*

Fly to the ninety-degree position. Keep S-turning. Plan to be lined up at the approach end. I'm going to be short. What a crock. I'll be in the trees on the approach end. This isn't good. I could get a Down if I don't make it. Leave the flaps up until the last minute. The trees are too close. I think I'll make it. Pop the flaps! I'm ballooning over the trees. Hey, it looks good.

"Add power, add power!" radioed Farr, "It wasn't pretty, but I think you'd have made it. Let's go home."

My hands are shaking, thought Capp. *I've never worked so hard in my life. My brain's numb. Relax, but not too much, this is still a check ride.*

"When you get into advanced training," radioed Farr. "You'll be flying jets. They're not the type of planes you want to ditch. There isn't a big engine in front of you with a propeller to take the initial hit. In jets, the pilot takes the hit. So practice your dead engine landings while you're in props. But once you get into jets, you'll eject instead of a dead-stick landing. Some jet pilots have dead-sticked to a runway without dying, but the odds are low. By the way, Congratulations, good hop. Now that you're officially in C stage acrobatics, let me show you my favorite maneuver, the Barrel Roll."

"Yes, sir," answered Capp. "Anything you want to do is great; I could stay out here all day."

Did you hear that, I'm in acrobatics, I made it. Yeahh. O.k. get my brain back in the cockpit. My hands are shaking, an Up from the best flight instructor in the Navy, Yeahh!

"You start just like a wingover," radioed Farr. "But go inverted at the ninety degree position, keep rolling through and slowly roll out, pull up your nose and end up at the same initial heading and altitude. In combat, when you have someone at your six, close in, you do a high-G barrel roll and try to get on his six. But that's for a later date, in advanced training."

"I can hardly wait," radioed back Capp.

"I got ahead of myself," radioed Farr. "But it's good to show you what's coming. In the meantime, learn your procedures perfectly. Take this training one day at a time. You'll do fine."

They landed and debriefed.

Capp sauntered into the ready room and announced,

"O.K. you A and B stage pukes, stand at attention for a real C stage pilot!"

Several cadets shouted, "Booo," and threw donuts at Capp; they ended up on the deck which wasn't too clean.

"That's the thanks I get for being a hot pilot," said Capp, laughing, while ducking the donuts. "You're all jealous."

Capp bent over and picked up the donuts. He noticed Pervis at a table in the corner.

"Hey ace cadet," said Capp as he walked over to Pervis. "What're you doing here? You're supposed to be on a check ride. Want a donut, they're fresh?"

"You're such a Dork," said Pervis. "Why do think I'm sitting here?

My plane went down. They're trying to reschedule the hop, or I've got to fly it Monday. What a crock."

"Why'd it go down?" asked Capp.

"I know what you're thinking," answered Pervis. "It was the radio."

"Just remember," said Capp, "I'm watching you."

"Don't watch too closely," answered Pervis. "It could be your undoing."

They both glared at each other.

"Someday," said Capp. "We're going to tangle."

"I'm waiting," said Pervis.

Capp left the ready room. He couldn't stand Pervis.

26

Capp had just finished his bacon and eggs at the chow hall, yawned, stretched his arms toward the ceiling, crossed his legs and said out loud to Quirt, Curtin and Munson who were finishing seconds on their eggs,

"It's Saturday; we've all got a hangover, what should we do today? I vote for the beach. Anyone have any ideas?"

"That sounds great." mumbled Munson through a mouthful of scrambled eggs. "However you forgot one small item, we're scheduled to run today."

"You're right," answered Capp. "I forgot. Let's run this morning and hit the beach about noon. We can do both. Run when it's cool, and swim when it's hot. Plus we can call some girls and see if they're free. Can't lie in the sun all day, or we'll look like a lobster."

"O.K., that's affirmative on both items," said Quirt. "But we have to decide on which group of girls to call. One group is average looking but lots of fun. The other group is terrific to look at, but kind of dull."

"I vote for the fun group," answered Curtin. "They aren't that bad. Nothing I hate worse than some great looking chick expecting me to provide her entertainment; let her go home and gaze in her mirror. Wish we could find some great looking broads that also were fun to be with. They're out there, but we haven't found them yet."

"We'll find them," said Capp. "We've only been in Florida for a few months without much time off. Let's make do with the groups we know. I agree with Curtin, I'd rather laugh and have a good time than spend money on girls who think they're cool. Laughter, that's what makes for a good time."

"Sounds like I'm outnumbered," said Quirt. "Myself, I want someone who's great to look at, but the majority rules. I'll call Mary Jane and see if her friends are free. If not, we'll try to pick up some women at the beach."

"Good luck on that one," said Capp. "There are four men to every girl in this town. But you never know, luck has a way of smiling on us. Finish your breakfasts and let's go. We'll lie around for an hour to let your guts digest that disgusting second course of bacon, eggs and cinnamon rolls, and then we'll head over to the track."

"I may barf," said Munson. "I hate to sweat, but the big Navy wants us in shape. I'd rather leave that to the infantry."

"Just wait until you get to acrobatics and formation flying, said Capp, "You'll wish you'd run every day instead of once a week."

As they walked back to the barracks, Capp said,

"Do you remember the obstacle course in Pre-Flight? That was tough."

They all laughed as the memories flowed.

"I remember," said Munson, "that I thought I'd be washed out because I was always in last place or close to it. My time got better but never enough to give the record time a challenge. The horizontal ladder above the ground that you had to travel hand over hand was almost my undoing. I kept losing my grip."

"Climbing up the log wall was the worst," said Curtin. "I couldn't get over, just up to the log before the top. Finally the cadet behind me pushed me over, or I'd be hanging there yet."

"Running through the soft sand at the end of the course was always the killer," said Quirt. "Your legs were tired and the sand was almost a final blow."

"My worst was after the soft sand when you were exhausted," said Capp, "You had to jump over a water trench, which few made to the other side. Your shoes were wet which made them feel like they weighed a thousand pounds, more soft sand, and then the rope swing over another water trench followed by a sprint through more soft sand to the end. I almost barfed. Come to find out later that I almost set a course record, but I've never been so tired in my life."

They walked back to the barracks to digest their food. Later Capp went to each room and woke each of them up.

"It's time to run; get out of your rack, the hour's up."

"Maybe I don't want to run," said Quirt. "I was having a great dream, and you weren't in it."

"Thank God," said Capp. "All I want to be is a great pilot, not a porn star."

"Why do you think it was erotic?" said Quirt. "It could have been about a Porsche, or a Jaguar."

"I don't want to know," answered Capp. "But I bet it wasn't about cars. C'mon, get up."

They each changed into shorts and t-shirts, which were colored Navy blue and gold. The tennis shoes were black.

"Let's drive over to the course," said Munson. "We don't want to get too serious about this physical stuff."

"It's only a mile," answered Capp. "We don't need to drive, we walk it every day."

"Today is different," said Munson. "My eggs are still percolating. Besides, it's a weekend."

Quirt and Curtin agreed with Munson. It was a weekend, if that was any excuse.

"Get in the car," said Capp as they walked to the parking lot. "Do you believe this? We drive to a track to get exercise, is anyone else in this world that stupid? Do you suppose this'll start a national trend?"

"It's already here," answered Quirt. "People drive to the Pensacola athletic club to sweat for an hour. If they jogged to the club, they wouldn't need to spend all that money to belong to a club. It's stupid, but people jog at the club instead of using public outdoor facilities located all over town, and then drive home."

They drove out of the parking lot to the running track, located by the runways. It was a dirt track, two miles around, and the cadets had to complete it in 30 minutes. Not an Olympic requirement, but enough to burn off a second helping of eggs. After the run was finished, ten pull-ups, 30 pushups and 30 sit-ups were required. Some of the more athletically motivated cadets ran it every day, but they were in the minority.

They parked near the check-in shack, a small white frame building located at the beginning of the track. Beside the shack was a grassy area to complete the sit-ups.

They signed in with a petty officer who was on duty for the weekend, and was assigned to special services. Special Services was the division where many athletes were assigned. They manned the athletic facilities on the base, and most belonged to Navy athletic teams. During World War II, some of the military's athletic teams could beat many college teams due to the quantity and quality of the personnel. Boxing champion Joe Louis was in the Army's special services division, and boxed in exhibitions for the troop's morale.

"Hi," said Capp to Third Class Petty Officer Erickson, a tall redhead with freckles and a very muscular build. "Want to change places for about thirty minutes? You look in good shape."

"You're the tenth cadet to ask me that this morning," laughed the Petty Officer. "Evidently once you start flying, running isn't one of your favorite pastimes."

"You got that right," answered Capp. "Never was."

"Sign on the line," said Erickson. "See you in thirty minutes. If you want to set a goal, the track record is fifteen minutes."

"Jeez, who set that?" said Capp. "A gazelle? I couldn't make it in fifteen minutes if I drove my car."

"Some cross country jock from Blake University in Iowa who went through the program about a year ago," said Erickson. "He was quite a runner."

"I guess," answered Capp. "Well, we're off. Send out the St. Bernard rescue team if we're not back in an hour, and make sure a cool keg is attached to its collar."

"If we had one of those, no one would make it back," laughed Erickson. "Not a bad idea though."

"C'mon young jocks," Capp said to the other three who were

signing in, "We're off to get sunshine, sore muscles and heavy breathing without any broads."

They ran for about a half a mile, and Munson gasped,

"Hey, stop. Let's walk for a bit and not try to break the record."

"We've just started," said Quirt. "You can't be in that bad of shape. I'm going to have to hide a bicycle out here for you."

"Don't be a smart ass," gasped Munson. "I was built for loving, not running. Let's walk twenty paces and run twenty paces, how about that?"

"Well, we can't leave you behind," said Capp. "So that's O.K. The goal is to finish, not to die. Besides, it's the weekly event we all love to hate, other than code. Who's got a new joke?"

They finished the course and walked over to the grassy area to finish off the exercises.

"Do you want to count the exercises as we complete them?" said Capp to Erickson.

"Naw," said Erickson. "You're officers and gentlemen. Let me know when you're done. Is Mr. Munson all right? He's awfully red in the face. Maybe he should sit down for awhile."

"You know," said Munson, "You're the first intelligent being I've met on this planet today. Normally I'd play the macho bit, but my heart is pounding so hard that it feels like its coming out of my chest. Think I'll sit for a minute. Did we set a record? I feel like it."

"You finished in twenty five minutes," said Erickson. "Not bad. There's always next time."

"The way you drink beer at night," said Capp. "We'll need to start putting you in a wheelbarrow to get through in thirty minutes."

Capp, Quirt and Curtin finished the exercises, and waited until Munson completed his.

"Let's get into the car and motor back to the barracks, shower, and off to the beach." said Capp.

They all cheered, "To the beach."

27

Capp pulled into the barracks parking lot, turned off the Pontiac's engine and ordered,

"Everybody out. Quirt you call the girls, and we'll meet in my room in an hour. Sand, sunshine and sex, what a day this is going to be."

"I can guarantee the sand and the sunshine," answered Quirt as he exited from the back seat. "But the sex has been all yak and no shack. We've got to find some horny girls. The ones we know are too pure. I'll call them this time, but next time someone else does it."

"Where's your spirit of competition and the chase?" said Capp. "Most of the fun is in the pursuit of the forbidden fruit. Girls like to be pursued, hear sweet nothings whispered in their ears, close dancing to sentimental music, moonlit nights, and then the final culmination when she submits her tender soft body to your advances. Jeez, I get all excited just thinking about it."

"You're not as horny as I am," said Quirt. "Right now all I want is a quick One-Nighter, wham, bam, thank you ma'am. Nothing tender, just lots of physical activity and heavy breathing. At this point, I'll even take on a two bagger."

"What's a two bagger?" asked Munson.

Both Capp and Quirt laughed out loud.

"You've been too sheltered," said Capp. "You don't know what that is?"

"No," answered Munson.

"A two bagger," said Capp. "Is the amount of bags you put over a really ugly girls head while you're making love to her. The second bag is there, in case the first one breaks."

Munson bent over in laughter, tears rolling down his cheeks,

"I like that, reminds me of my high school prom date. I'll never live that down, but I was desperate. It was a last minute thing; I really wanted to go to the prom so as not to lose face with my friends. As the old saying goes-'If they don't meet your standards, you lower your standards'; and did I lower them. However it was innocent and we had a good time. Didn't get any, and didn't want to. If I had known about the bag trick, maybe things would've been different."

"An hour," said Capp. "Let's go. On the way to the beach, we'll pick up some bags for Quirt."

They all arrived in Capp's room about the same time. Quirt came in first and sat on the wooden chair at the desk. The hot summer wind blew through the windows, rustling the papers on the desk. Quirt put a book on top of the papers.

"I called Mary Jane, and Rhonda was over at her house. She said Mary Sue and Sally had to work, but was sure they could make it. They'll try to be there by about three o'clock. She was excited. I really wish she was horny."

Being excited is the first step," said Capp. "You never know, just keep pushing and keep the target in sight."

"I heard that," said Curtin as he and Munson entered the room. "She's Catholic. You'll never get to first base because her priest at confession will tell her to back off. You've got to find a nice Baptist girl and let her shout, Hallelujah."

"Curtin," said Capp. "You don't say much, but when you do, you're right on target. Now we know what to look for, Baptist girls, there're millions of them down here. C'mon, we're out of here."

They left the room, walked through the passageway with its squeaky wooden floors, down the stairs, out the front door, and into the bright Florida sunshine.

"Let's put the top down," said Capp. "So we can suck up this great weather."

The four of them piled into the convertible and headed out to the main gate. The Marine gate guards stopped them for a moment, glared at them, and then waved them through. The guards seemed to enjoy trying to intimidate the cadets, and the cadets knew it, but when you can burn to death in an airplane crash, glares meant nothing. They were ignored by the cadets and chalked up to the immaturity of the young guards.

The Pontiac roared down the highway, through a few small towns, and over a long bridge that led to the beach.

"Most of the southern states are reclaimed swamps," said Capp. "On the panhandle where we now live, if you can disregard the stifling summer heat, insects, alligators, snakes, oppressive humidity, hurricanes, and the cool clammy winters, it's a nice place."

"Be sure not to apply for a job at the chamber of commerce," said Quirt. "You wouldn't last a week."

"One thing it does have," said Capp. "And it overrides all the other problems, and that's the beach."

"When I get older," said Curtin. "I'm going to build a home on the beach and just stare at the blue ocean for the remainder of my life."

"Roger to that," answered Capp. "I wonder how much beachfront land is worth and what's available for sale. Some realtor is going to make a killing on beachfront sales."

"They probably are now," said Curtin. "If flying doesn't go good for me, that's not a bad idea. Everybody likes sun, especially us Yankees that hate to shovel snow. I've been thinking that now is the time to buy some of this land, it would be a great investment."

"You're right," answered Capp, "But for now, the beach is right ahead. I'll park in the parking lot, on the end behind the bar so the girls will see the car."

Capp got out of his car, opened the trunk and pulled out blankets, towels, suntan lotion and shower shoes.

"Look at this, said Capp as he walked onto the beach, "Isn't it great.

Wow, the sand is hot," He hopped up and down to prevent burnt feet. "Let's get a blanket down and some shower shoes on."

After donning their shower shoes, Capp continued his chatter.

"What a picture, fluffy white clouds on a pure blue sky that seems to glow, an ocean as far as the eye can see with blue water the same color as the sky, whitecaps breaking onto the beach, not enough to surf but just strong enough to push a person slightly backwards. Bright blinding white sand, a gentle breeze that evaporates the sweat as it forms on your body and a hot sun with rays that feel as if they're piercing one's body, any other beach in the world would be second place to this one. How lucky can we get?"

"Let's not get carried away," said Quirt. "It's a beach, with sand. Make yourself useful; go get some beer."

"C'mon Munson," said Capp. "Some cool ones for the body, then dive into the surf, and then some more cool ones."

"I hate salt water," said Munson. "It makes my skin itch. And when the nettles move in, those little jelly fish that sting, that's really gross. I'll lie on the beach, but screw going into the water."

"If the girls go in the water," said Capp. "I bet you go in. Ever made love in the water? It's great."

"You've got more ways to talk a person into doing something they don't want to do," answered Munson. "How do you do that?"

"Who knows," laughed Capp. "Let's get the beer."

They trudged through the deep white sand up to the bar and recreation building. It was one story, constructed of brick blocks painted white, long and rectangular, with widows all along the beach side so everyone in the building had a view of the ocean.

"This is a great place," said Capp. "If it wasn't so far from the base, I'd spend more time here. It's got a huge bar, tables, jukebox, a dance floor, burgers, hot dogs and a great view of the ocean, a big rectangular den of fun."

The families stayed at one end, away from the bar and the singles crowd. That allowed everyone to enjoy their day at the beach.

"Four beers to go barkeep," said Capp, "To quench a large thirst. We'll be back, can't stay in that sun too long."

"No bottles," answered the bartender who was about their age. "I'll put them in paper cups for you."

"Fair enough," said Capp. "Munson, grab a couple and we'll stumble back through the sand."

"Let's go," said Munson. "Need to get a few under my belt before the girls show up, my humor needs some priming."

"All beer does is make you hornier, if that's possible," said Capp, "But I must admit, you do get funnier."

They slogged back to the blankets where Quirt and Curtin were lying on their backs, absorbing a few sun rays. Capp looked at Munson, shook his head in mock disgust at the half asleep sweaty bodies, grinned, and then poured cold beer on their chests.

"You jerk-off," shouted Quirt as he and Curtin sprang to their feet, wiping the cold sticky beer off of their heaving chests. "What're you trying to do, give me a heart attack?"

"I couldn't resist that," laughed Capp along with Munson. "You guys lying there like a couple of blubbery walruses. That was funny. Here, have some beer."

"Funny to you," answered Quirt. "As your friend Pervis would say, I'll get even with you."

"Don't ruin my day by mentioning his name," said Capp. "However, I'll be watching you."

They both laughed and were taking a big swallow of beer when they heard squeals of laughter and shouting. The girls were here.

The four girls ran down the beach toward the blankets and to the cadets who were holding out their arms. Bodies collided, beer flew into the air, and eight laughing bodies fell onto the sand in a scramble of arms and legs.

"Party time," laughed Mary Jane as she tickled Quirt in his ribs.

"Swimming time," yelled Quirt as he picked her up, carried her down to the water, threw her into the surf as she squealed in mock protest, and dove in beside her.

The other six followed, ran into the water, each girl being dumped by each of the guys. The laughter and splashing of water was continuous for at least a half an hour.

"Time to dry out," said Capp. "Then some beer and dancing."

Mary Jane grabbed Quirt's hand, and pulled him toward the blankets,

"C'mon Jim, it's time to get a suntan."

Mary Jane was tall, slim, a brunette with hazel eyes that sparkled when she was happy, and she was happy being with Quirt. Quirt was indifferent to her, but enjoyed her vivacious personality. The others did not pair off; they were just a happy group of friends.

"O.K.," answered Quirt, "but I'm still too white, I'll burn like a lobster. I'll give it ten minutes, and then up to the bar for some dancing."

"So you burn," she said. "What difference does that make? Everyone gets sunburned once in awhile."

"You've never had shoulder harness straps dig into sunburned shoulders," answered Quirt, "It hurts. Besides, when your skin peels, you look like a dork."

They stood up to dry off, rubbing each other with large beach towels, and telling jokes that were somewhat off color, but nothing bad.

"I'm dry," said Capp. "Let's get some beer and get that jukebox jumping."

Everybody agreed and worked their way through the soft sand, to the Recreation/bar.

"Grab a table," said Capp. "I'll put some nickels in the juke box."

"I'll go with you and make sure you pick some good ones." said Rhonda, who liked Capp. "Let's have some slow ones that we can dance closely to, not always the fast songs."

Hmm, thought Capp, *Slow dancing with body contact. Maybe there's more to Rhonda than meets the eye.*

They all danced, laughed, drank some beer, and went back for more swimming, sunshine and dancing. Darkness was setting in, and the beach was nearly empty.

"The bar's closing and I'm all beached out," said Capp. "Anybody have any ideas how to finish off the evening?"

"Why doesn't everyone come over to my house," said Mary Jane. "My parents are gone for the evening. We can put on some records and just hang out. Anybody have anything better?

"Sounds good to me," answered Capp. "Let's do it."

Everyone agreed it was the way to finish off a fun day. As they were walking to the cars in the parking lot, Rhonda squeezed Capp's hand,

"Can we stay here for awhile? The moon on the water is beautiful. Besides, a house is so enclosed compared to the beach, O.K.? One of the guys can drive my car. We brought two, so there's plenty of room for everyone."

"Quirt," said Capp as he walked over to him. "Drive Rhonda's car back to the house, we're going to stay for a while. Here are her keys."

Quirt looked at him, smirked, and said, "You son-of-a-gun. I bet she's a Baptist."

"You've got a dirty mind," laughed Capp. "I'm an honorable officer and a gentleman."

"Right," answered Quirt. "And I'm the Admiral of the Fleet."

Capp walked backed to Rhonda.

"C'mon, we'll find a spot where the moon is just ours. This part of the main beach is good for now, but I've heard of a spot closer to the Fort Road that's private. Maybe we'll check that out. In fact, let's check that out now, sound interesting?"

"I like privacy," whispered Rhonda. "Lead on."

Capp looked at Rhonda as they were walking. A blonde with short hair, blue eyes, long legs, not especially pretty but very intelligent. She was quieter than Mary Jane, and had a good sense of humor. She didn't have the electricity that Capp liked in women, but she was fun to be with.

"Here's some small sand dunes, said Capp. "We can lay a blanket between them and have complete privacy. It's made just for us."

"Perfect," answered Rhonda in a quiet voice.

As Capp laid the blanket on the sand, he thought he felt something on his leg, but disregarded it as they sat down together.

"What a beautiful night," said Capp.

He brushed her hair back off of her forehead, slid his hand around her shoulders, pulled her toward him, she didn't resist, and they stretched out on the blanket. He kissed her forehead, then her nose, and slowly moved to her moist warm lips. Her body quivered with

JOHN SCHLETER

anticipation. Capp held her close, his hands moved down to her smooth flat stomach. Their breathing was deep and heavy, their legs intertwined.

Something bit him on the leg, then the other leg, and his arm.

"Ouch, what's going on?" exclaimed Capp.

"Something's biting me!" screamed Rhonda

"Sand fleas," yelled Capp. "They're all over the dunes."

They jumped to their feet, trying to brush off the fleas, which actually were small flies that clung to their bodies.

"Run," shouted Capp. "Give me your hand and follow me. We've got to get to out of here."

They ran up to a level area, away from any grass or dunes.

"Stop here," said Capp. "So we can brush these things off. I think I've got mine off. Here, let me help you, they're mostly around the ankles."

For a moment they stopped slapping fleas, looked at each other and burst out in hysterical laughter.

"I wish there was something deep and philosophical I could say," said Capp, tears running down his cheeks from laughing. "But I can't. Let's go hang out."

They hugged, then walked hand in hand back toward the main beach and laughed at each others jokes, but as they looked at each other, in the back of their minds was the warm memory of what had just occurred, and wondered what would the evening have produced if the maddening sand fleas had not interrupted what was an obvious movement toward a night of tender passion. Would there be another rendezvous, or did the humorous shock of this evening bring them to a realization, that friends should just be friends, and emotional physical involvements could ruin a beautiful, fun filled, friendly relationship? Only time would tell.

182

28

Capp walked into the ready room; fluorescent lights with their harsh glare lit the room. Cadets seated at the tables, drinking gallons of coffee and tons of donuts, filled the room.

It was 0800, Monday morning. Outside, the weather was hot and humid as usual, but bright and sunny, great for flying.

"Looks like a full house," said Capp, as he joined Jim Quirt, Dwight Munson, and Dick Price. "The sky should be full of yellow birds, and we'll be on our final leg. Eighteen hops of stage three acrobatics. What a blast. Everyone have their barf bags?"

"I've got two," answered Munson laughing, "Just in case."

"Can you imagine what it's going to feel like?" said Dick Price, "Coming down from the top of a loop? This is the fun part of getting those gold wings."

Price was from Milwaukee, Wisconsin. He was an athlete, solidly built, and always funny.

"You've got a standard to uphold," said Capp. "I understand your brother is a fighter pilot stationed at Atlantic Field near Norfolk, Virginia."

"Yeah," answered Price. "Good Ol' Norfolk. My brother says it's been rumored that there are signs on the lawns: 'Dogs and Sailors stay off the grass.' They don't go there much. Virginia Beach is actually the closest city, good party town, which is where everyone hangs out."

"Your family has a tradition of Navy pilots," said Capp. "Wouldn't it be great to be assigned to the same squadron?"

"I don't think so," answered Price. "Maybe a sister squadron, we're both too competitive. We never liked to lose to each other in any contest. Blood would be on the floor before either one of us gave up. Being together might not be a good thing for our safety. Who knows? I'm proud of him, and hope to follow in his footsteps, a fighter jock."

"Sounds good to me," said Capp. "By the way, on my precision check ride, Lieutenant Farr showed me a barrel roll. He is good. No, he's great. The barrel roll was perfect. All the maneuvers are great. I'll probably want to go through C stage twice, just for the kicks. By the way, did anyone hear if Pervis got his precision check ride Friday?"

"He got an Up," answered Quirt, "even though he had to fly with Captain Kranz. I would've loved to hear the briefing. 'None of this nose up and down crap, Pervis, or I'll beat you over the head with the control stick.'"

Everyone laughed. The practical joke Capp had played on Pervis during his solo flight was almost a legend, part of the cadet folk lore. It was a funny story that got funnier with each telling, especially during beer drinking contests.

"The little creep is back on schedule with us," said Capp. "Too bad, I would've liked to rub it in that he's behind us, just to get a reaction."

"He'd be upset," said Quirt. "Maybe for both your sakes, it's good he passed. However, it would've been fun to see."

"Hey," said Capp. "When we get to formation flying, we need a name for our flight. How does 'Cobra Flight' sound? Just a thought, it sounds sinister."

"Sounds good to me," each of them agreed. "But, first let's get there," said Quirt.

"It's my briefing time soon," said Capp. "I'm going over to meet Kranz. Fly safe, see you guys soon."

"Hello, Mr. Capp," said Captain Kranz as Capp strolled into the briefing room. "Ready for some fun flying?"

"Yes, Sir," answered Capp. "This is what I've been waiting for."

"This is the fun part for us too," said Kranz. "It breaks the monotony of stage one and two, which are very important, but every fighter jock wants to be inverted and pull G's. This is the stage where cadets that haven't made up their minds about choosing single engine or multi-engine aircraft will usually make a decision. Not everyone likes to be upside down, and that's O.K. The Navy's a team. All types of aircraft are needed to win a war, not just fighters. Are you ready?"

"Yes, Sir," answered Capp. "Let's go inverted."

"We'll do a normal roll and a loop today," said Kranz. "I'll demonstrate each one, and then it's your turn. As usual, if I want control of the plane, I'll waggle the stick left and right, and tell you, 'I've got it.' Then I want to see both your hands up in the air. Don't ever freeze on the stick, that's dangerous to both of us, O.K.?"

"Yes, Sir," answered Capp.

"Let's go," smiled Kranz as he pointed to the door and the flight line.

"It's your bird," said Kranz as they walked up to the SNJ. "Taxi out, take off, and fly to the acrobatic area at 5,000 feet. I'll take over when we arrive."

"Roger." answered Capp. *It's nice to know he has confidence in me,* thought Capp, *Makes me want to try harder.*

The taxi, run-up, and take off were normal, with no problems.

I still get a kick out of seeing a long line of SNJ's, fishtailing left and right, taxiing out for take-off, thought Capp. *It looks comical. Maybe I've got a warped sense of humor.*

"I've got it," said Kranz as they arrived at the restricted airspace. "Let's try a roll. It's simple, but basic. By the way, if you start feeling woozy, let me know. We'll stop. It's easy to feel bad when you're not flying the bird. As you know, the roll is the worst. It fouls up your inner ear fluid.'

'Pull the nose up 20 degrees; stick left, the nose falls while rolling, and ends up on the horizon, wings level. Magnetic heading should be the same as when you started, your turn."

"I got it," radioed Capp.

This is a piece of cake, thought Capp. *Pull the nose up, stick left and, whoa. The nose is way below the horizon. Pull it up. What happened?*

"Welcome to the world of simple maneuvers, but not that simple," radioed Kranz. "When you pulled your nose up, you didn't neutralize the stick. You kept back pressure. The nose got off center and you scooped out. Try it again."

How basic, thought Capp. *Keep the miserable stick neutral. Here goes. That's better. Not as good as Kranz, but practice, practice, practice.*

"You're getting the hang of it," radioed Kranz. "Do five more."

Jeez, I'm glad I didn't close the bar last night, thought Capp. *Hangovers and rolls don't go together, especially not this many.*

"O.K., enough of the barf maneuvers," radioed Kranz, "Time for a loop. Climb to Angels eight and level off."

"Yes, Sir," radioed Capp.

"I've got it," radioed Kranz. "The secret is at the top. Don't pull too hard or you might spin because your airspeed is low. Keep positive g's, you want just enough to keep you in the seat. No negative g's or it'll get exciting.'

'Add power, lower the nose, pick up airspeed, level the nose, and then pull back on the stick. As you go over the top, tilt your head back, and look behind you to get your bearings. Reduce power coming downhill, and slowly increase pressure on the stick as your speed increases. Finish on the same heading and altitude as you started, your turn."

Here we go, thought Capp. *Pull back on the stick. I'm at the top. What a weird feeling to be upside down. The stick feels mushy. The plane isn't responding. If I pull too hard, I'll spin.*

"I got it, I got it," radioed Kranz as he waggled the stick, and rolled the plane level.

"At the top," radioed Kranz, "you didn't keep enough pressure on the stick. You flattened out instead of completing a circle. Your airspeed was decreasing, and the plane would have stalled. That's why we practice. Try it again."

That's embarrassing, thought Capp. *Concentrate. Pull up. I'm at the top. Keep pressure. Look straight back. Is it going to make the curve? It's slowly coming through. Jeez, what a view going straight down. Pull back the power. Stick pressure is heavy at high speed. Don't overcorrect. The nose is coming up. Yeahh. Level with the horizon. Too bad I'm off thirty degrees and below the altitude that I started. What the heck, I didn't spin. It's a start.*

"That's good," radioed Kranz. "You handled the stick pressure O.K. There's a lot to remember; power, rudder, RPM, heading, and altitude to make it perfect. Let's do a few more and head home."

Capp landed at Warner. As they walked backed to the briefing room, Capp said to Kranz,

"This is only the first hop, and my body feels like I've just gone fifteen rounds in a boxing ring."

"Acrobatics is work," laughed Kranz, "both physical and mental. You'll find sore muscles you never knew you had."

They debriefed. Kranz was very specific. He knew what Capp did wrong and offered suggestions to correct the errors. Capp sucked it up like a vacuum cleaner.

"I'll study tonight," said Capp. "Tomorrow, I won't scare you at the top."

"Believe me, I've been in much worse situations," answered Kranz. "Shake it off. See you tomorrow morning."

Capp went to the ready room to see if any of the group was back. He saw Dick Price.

"Hey Price," said Capp. "How'd it go today? Want to swap sea stories?"

"Was it embarrassing," answered Price. "On my first loop, I went straight up, choked and forgot to pull back on the stick. The plane would have slid backwards on its tail, probably ripping it off. The instructor grabbed the controls and recovered. I guess I forgot to do the loop, and instead was in awe by the experience of going straight up. This isn't like the movies, it's work! How'd you do? Perfect?"

"Are you kidding," said Capp. "I lost it at the top of a loop, flattened out, and the instructor took over. So don't feel bad, even the best foul up."

Price laughed. "Isn't this great, I can hardly wait to get back in the air and try it again."

"Tomorrow comes fast," said Capp.

A voice from a few tables away was heard to say, "So you guys fouled up." It was Pervis. "Instructor had to rescue both of you, that's not surprising, especially for Capp. My hop was perfect. If there were a 5.0 grade, I would've received it. Stick around and I'll tell you how to do loops and rolls. I'm the best, you should know that."

"I may barf." said Capp. "Something that stinks has arrived."

"Nice try to be funny," said Pervis, "But reality has finally sunk in, right? I give lessons in my spare time. See you tomorrow, as I don't hang around with second class pilots."

"You're a jerk," said Capp. "There's a lot of flying to do. We'll see who's the best. And it won't be you!"

Pervis curled his lip in a sneer like a cat that'd just caught a bird, laughed at Capp, and left.

"You two really don't like each other, do you?" asked Price. "I thought it was just a rumor."

"What you see is what you see," said Capp. "I think he's dangerous, don't know why, but I really don't want to be near him. C'mon, let's head off to ground school, and then a cool beer."

"Other than a perfect loop," said Price, "That's what I want to hear. Not ground school, the beer, that is."

29

"Where's Munson and Curtin?" asked Capp to Jim Quirt. "We need some chow and get on the road to fabulous New Orleans. We're here in the parking lot, where are they? It's morning, and soon it'll be afternoon. I want to be in the French Quarter drinking Tornadoes at Tom O'Danbills bar for lunch."

"I don't know," answered Quirt. "Maybe they went to the galley without us."

"Let's check their rooms," said Capp. "Both are sack rats. They probably forgot about it."

"I don't think so," answered Quirt. "Last night when we all decided to go today, they were excited. Munson was drooling over the thought of great Cajun chow."

"C'mon," said Capp. "Follow me up the squeaky wooden steps and into the squeaky passageway. At least they'll hear us coming."

Capp walked into Munson's room. Curtin was there, propped against the wall with a bored look on his face. Munson's roommates were still in bed and not happy about the commotion Munson was creating.

Jake Field rolled over in his cot, with his blanket pulled up around his neck, and the pillow over his head. He peeked out from under the pillow.

"What's the problem? Can't a guy get some sleep? Munson, grab your bag and shove off. What are you waiting for?"

"I can't find my rubbers." answered Munson.

"What!" gasped Fields. "Rubbers! You're making a pest of yourself for rubbers? Are you nuts? New Orleans is sin city. You can buy a bushel of rubbers there. Besides, you're not going to find any women. Get out of here so I can sleep. Rubbers. Unbelievable."

Capp was laughing, and tried not to hurt Munson's feelings.

"We'll buy some in the Big Easy," said Capp. "You'll probably make out four or five times, Jake's just jealous."

"Oh yeah, right," said Jake. "Munson couldn't get some even if he paid for it. Just go."

Capp picked up Munson's bag and led him out of his room, down the squeaky passageways, and outdoors.

"Next time, keep one in your wallet," said Capp. "If you get caught during a room inspection with them nestled among your shorts, it'll be a demerit. Keep them in your locker at the U.S.O. in town."

"That's where they are," answered Munson cheerily, "I forgot all about that."

Capp, Quirt, and Curtin looked at each other and just shook their heads.

They walked down the sidewalk over the green lawn to the parking lot behind the barracks.

"Get in the car," said Capp. "I'll leave the top up. It's too windy on the highway. We'll grab some bacon and eggs, and motor over to the USO to change into civvies."

"Warner Field does have great chow," said Capp as they left the galley, "other than all that disgusting extra hamburger. Let's head into Pensacola. Then, we're off to drinking and debauchery."

The USO was a military social club in Pensacola for all servicemen. It was located in an older two-story building, with a dance floor and a grill for hamburgers. No alcoholic beverages were sold, and local bands played on weekends. It was bright and cheery. Hostesses would talk and dance with lonely sailors and soldiers, most of whom were young and homesick.

The biggest attractions to the cadets, however, were the lockers. They just wanted a place to change into their civilian clothes. Not wearing their uniforms was illegal, but they all did it. The Navy either didn't know, or looked the other way.

Capp led the group into the USO.

"Every chance I get, I always buy a beer for that senior cadet who clued me in on the USO and its lockers. Can you imagine going out of town in your uniform? They're uncomfortable and not good drinking clothes. I once loosened my uniform tie in a bar because I was hot, and an Air Force Colonel chewed me out. Can you imagine that, an Air Force puke trying to talk down to a hot Navy pilot?'

'Munson, you got your rubbers? We don't want you to turn down any loving tonight. Hey, what gives? Aren't you going to change into civvies?"

"Yes I found my rubbers," answered Munson. "And no, I'm not changing into civvies. Girls love a man in a uniform."

The other three groaned.

"You're going to foul us up with the co-eds in the French Quarter," said Capp. "They want college boys, not military types. At least, put your uniform on a hangar. If you wear it in the car for four hours, you'll be wrinkled and look like a slob. The Shore Patrol will pick you up, and we'll all be in trouble. You can change at NAS New Orleans, O.K.?"

"All right, all right, I agree under protest," answered Munson. "But I'm getting some tonight, in a uniform. You'll see."

"O.K.," sighed Capp. "Now let's get on the road. We've got to be back at the base by 1800 Sunday."

"Great weather, great food, and great booze," said Quirt. "What more could you ask? Two-block that gas pedal Capp, it's time to party."

"You know how to get there?" asked Curtin.

"Sure," answered Capp. "Just head 270 degrees until the sounds of Dixieland music are heard. Hold out your hand, and when someone puts a bowl of gumbo in it, you're there."

"And if you get bored by the drive," said Quirt, "We pass through Mobile and Biloxi, both party towns. We can always stop."

"Bullcrap," said Capp. "That's for other weekends. This time, it's New Orleans. Full power, we're off."

30

"Look at that sign," shouted Capp. "New Orleans-Crescent City and right down the road is the French Quarter, Bourbon Street, Dixieland, strip joints, women and booze. What a dream city. Let the parties begin."

Munson started stomping on the floor of the car, and shouted,

"Oh, I can smell the perfume of the women, feel the soft curve of their back, their undulating boobs, their long legs wrapped around my body, their red ruby lips on mine. I can hardly breathe."

"Avast, ye land lubbers," said Curtin laughing, slapping Munson on the side of his head, "We can't turn this loose. He's a sexual Frankenstein. No girl in the city is safe."

They all cheered.

"Munson," said Capp. "You're our leader tonight. If you can smell the women from here that want to get some, we're not leaving you out of our sight."

"I'm telling you," answered Munson. "It's a sixth sense. We're all going to score."

Again, they all cheered.

"C'mon," said Quirt. "Let's get to NAS New Orleans and find a place to crash. Free room and board leaves more money to spend on the fun things in life."

"Don't worry," answered Capp. "I called to reserve four bunks. They may be in the storage room for all I know, but they're ours."

"Wow," said Quirt, "The heat and humidity are really tough. It must be 100 degrees with a thousand percent humidity. Pensacola has humidity, but this is unreal. How can people live here? My shirt is stuck to my body, and I'm not even moving. Instead of Crescent city, it should be renamed Sweat city."

"Hey," said Munson. "Sweaty bodies make for better loving. Great food, and great loving, that's why people live here, nothing sterile about this place."

"I forgot about young Frankenstein," said Quirt. "Munson, I bet the only sex you'll get tonight is the five finger massage."

"You wait," replied Munson. "I'm on a quest."

They headed south across the Mississippi river toward the Naval air station and checked in with the duty officer. They were assigned four bunks in the enlisted barracks.

As they left the main gate back toward New Orleans, Capp said,

"First one to get carnal knowledge gets free beer for a week, honor systems in effect. Liars buy everyone beer, for two weeks."

"What if no one gets any?" answered Curtin.

"Are you kidding," said Capp. "We're going to get so much that we'll need extra vitamin pills for the energy we're going to use up."

"Who do you think has the record time for entering a bar, and getting action?" asked Munson.

"Rumor is, less than a minute," answered Capp, "One of the Blue Angels."

"Give me that uniform," said Munson. "What a leg spreader."

"The golden wings don't exactly hurt, replied Capp. "That's their nickname, you know, 'The Golden Leg Spreaders.'"

"Look at these bayous," said Curtin. Suppose there's an alligator in there, or a water moccasin? The water is so quiet and still, I wouldn't go in them for any kind of a boat ride. And the shanty shacks. Most don't have doors or window panes. What if it snowed?"

"Yeah, there are alligators and snakes in there, big enough to make a meal out of you," answered Capp. Wait until survival training, you'll find out all about them. And the chances of it snowing are about the same as Munson's chances of scoring tonight. Munson, your uniform is going to foul us up. I told you, co-eds like Joe-college types, not military guys. We're going to walk way behind you."

"The uniform shows power and virility," answered Munson. "You guys just don't get it."

As they entered the city, Capp said,

"Let's drive down Bourbon Street and scope out the hot spots. Then we'll park and hit them all, like mining for gold."

"It's crowded, people walking in the street holding drinks in their hands," said Munson. "Looks great! Hey, there's a strip club. Look at the body on the headliner. If she's for real, that's my first stop."

"Listen to the Dixieland music coming out of that corner bar, said Capp. "Now that's music, definitely a stop. Look! Most of the bars have Dixieland bands. This town could become a habit. The buildings sure look old and scruffy; guess they've been here awhile. Do you suppose the ones with the French balconies are cathouses?'

'We're parking right here, because around the corner is the infamous bar, Tom O'Danbills. That's where the co-eds hang out, along with music and large rum Tornadoes. It's always the first stop."

Capp parked. They hurried down the narrow street to Tom O'Danbills, which had two inside bars, and an open courtyard in the rear with lots of greenery. It was early afternoon and was already packed with multitudes of people. Patrons sang loudly in the large bar, accompanied by the piano player and a waitress standing beside him, who tapped on the bottom of a metal drink tray with coins inside of it that made a sound like a brass band while she kept time to the music. It was noisy and happy.

Over the noise, Capp shouted to the bartender, "Four Tornadoes, first rounds on me, is this great or what?"

The large frosted glass drinks of a rum mixture were served. They clinked them together in a toast,

"To women, to parties and more women," said Quirt.

"Hear, hear," they all cheered.

"There's a table of unattached girls over there," said Capp, "Let's see if they want to party."

"Go ahead," said Quirt. "I'll baby-sit Curtin and Munson. They're too horny to talk coherently. Wave if you want us to join up."

Capp walked over to the table and said, "Hi, I'm Chuck. Rumor has it that New Orleans is a party town. Anybody heard of a party, or can we start our own?"

The redhead with blue eyes that sparkled and perfect lips, tilted her head slightly, gazed at Capp and smiled.

"My, my, you are in a hurry. Is your Navy ship going to leave port or is there a more sinister plot?"

The other girls at the table giggled in a friendly way. All had great smiles.

"No ship, no plot," answered Capp with a smile. "Just trying to live life to the fullest, who knows what tomorrow will bring? By the way, how'd you know I was in the Navy?"

"I saw your group come in," answered the redhead. "It's elementary my dear Watson, one of you is wearing a cadet uniform. I've attended the annual dance balls at the Pensacola cadet club, so the uniform is familiar. And so is the hurry to party."

"How'd I ever miss you at the ball," said Capp. "You would've given me another reason to fight for our country, your honor, and of course the right to party. Can I call you by your first name?"

The redhead again gazed coolly at Capp. She whispered in the ear of her friend, "I like his personality, he's happy. And he's better looking than most of the men around here. "Yes, she said. "My name is Mary Ann, Mary Ann Beaumont. Tell you what. My father loves the military. He was in the big war-in Europe. He's the manager of a brewery, one block north of Bourbon Street. Tonight there's an open house for his friends, some Tulane students, and now, you and your friends. Tell the security guard at the door I invited you, he'll let you in. I'll be there. It's always a fun time. In the meantime, have a fun on Bourbon Street. The music is great. See you tonight."

"We'll be there," answered Capp. "For sure, I'll be there. Thanks for the invitation. I'll be looking forward to seeing you tonight."

Capp left the table and went back to his group, who were standing at the bar.

"What's up," said Munson. "Did you get shot down? It looked like you and the redhead were getting along. Should we all go over there?"

"Munson, you little fart," said Capp. "Your uniform got us invited to a free beer party tonight. I'll never doubt you again, well maybe. Jeez, is that redhead Mary Ann gorgeous. And her friends look good too, might be an interesting evening."

"Capp, you son-of-gun," said Munson. "I knew you could do it. You can have Mary Ann. The brunette's got great knockers. Oh, I love knockers."

"Remind me to keep my sister away from you," said Capp. I'm going to find a Dixieland bar. Drink up, let's get out of here."

"What do you mean," answered Munson. "Strip clubs are where I'm going. If I want Dixieland, I'll buy a record."

"That's why they make chocolate and vanilla ice cream," answered Capp. I like chocolate, you like vanilla. We're both happy."

"We'll hit them all," said Quirt. "Let's go."

They walked up Bourbon Street, crowded with people carrying drinks and laughing.

"Here's a good skin show, right on the corner." said Munson. "Let's go in and watch the action."

"O.K.," answered Capp. "But the problem with strip joints is that they're all look and no touch, that's Un-American."

It was dimly lit inside. The stale smell of cigar and cigarette smoke lingered in the air, along with the strong smell of an antiseptic cleaner that was used to clean the floors. The combination of the odors stunk, and made for an unpleasant experience to anyone that had even a minimal sense of smell. That however, was part of the strip club experience. On a small raised stage, a three-piece band played uninspired music. The musicians had a permanent bored expression on their faces, as if they really didn't want to be there. A scantily dressed dancer had just finished her act and was replaced by another dancer, fully clothed. She looked as bored as the band, and began to slowly discard items of clothing, until only one or two remained.

"Take it off, take it off." shouted Munson. He was excited. "Look at the boobs, look at the legs, what more could you want?"

"They look like underfed runaways," answered Capp. "I'm going to find some Dixieland music. Let's meet at the Court of Three Sisters about 1800. A quick chili dog from the vendor, and then we can motor over to the beer bash."

Capp and Quirt left, leaving Munson and Curtin trying to control their hormones. Two of the clubs waitresses had sat down with them; it might be a long night.

"The Duke's of Dixieland," said Capp. "It doesn't get any better than that. Now we're talking real music."

The Dixieland bar was crowded. Every musician played his happy music with enthusiasm. They laughed and talked to each other during, and between the sets.

"What a difference," said Capp. "These are pro's who like their job, just like us."

The afternoon passed quickly, as it always does when a good time was being had. At 6:00 P.M., everyone rendezvoused as agreed.

"Ah, smell those chili dogs, said Capp. "The aroma makes your mouth water, and your stomach growl, a true French Quarter experience."

"Four chili dogs with raw onions," Capp said to the cart vendor, who was stationed on the corner.

"Gentleman, never ask the vendor what's in the dog, or how old they are," said Capp. "You don't want to know. Enjoy, and keep your alka-seltzer close by."

The cart vendor served up the four chilidogs.

"Don't worry," he said. "They're always fresh, no matter how old they are." He laughed, "Would I lie to you?"

After they finished, the group headed over to the brewery. It had a solid tall wooden wall barring entrance from the street. No one could see inside. There was a door on the end of the wall, and Capp knocked loudly with the clapper on it. The door opened slightly, and a very large man peered out at them.

"Mary Ann Beaumont invited us to the open house, said Capp. "Can we come in?"

"Just a minute," said the large man, and closed the door. The door re-opened a short time later. "O.K., you can come on in."

They entered into a large courtyard, decorated with small trees and flowers. It was crowded with well-dressed guests, all who had a beer in hand. The brewery building was hidden behind all the greenery.

Mary Ann saw them come in, waved and walked over to them.

"Welcome," she said. "Emil told me you were here. I'm glad you decided to come."

"Thank you," answered Capp. "I never knew something like this existed in the French Quarter. What a pleasant surprise. And by the way, tell Emil we're the good guys."

"He really is intimidating, isn't he?" said Mary Ann laughing. "He was in Daddy's battalion at Normandy's Omaha Beach. Daddy saved his life. They both survived and Emil has been with him ever since, a gentle giant. Follow me and I'll serve the best beer you've ever tasted, freshly brewed, right out of the keg."

She served them each a large glass of frosty beer.

"Enjoy," she said. "There's plenty more where that came from, and there's no charge, an open bar. I've got to mingle with the guests; make yourself at home. She looked at Capp, "No, I'm not free for a late night cup of coffee, at least not tonight. Here's my number. Call me, and we can do the town at another time."

She smiled, turned, and walked over to a group of people.

"Jeez," said Capp. "I thought I was fast. Look at the way she walks, tall and straight, and is great looking. This could be the start of a beautiful relationship."

"Oh, Oh," said Munson. "Do I detect a chink in the armor of a confirmed bachelor? I'm going to mosey around and see if there are any possibilities. You know what I mean."

"Don't hold your breath," said Capp. "This looks like a sophisticated crowd. However, I see some co-eds over yonder, help yourself."

Munson was on his second beer, leaning against the bar, when he felt a presence next to him. He turned and saw the most beautiful woman he'd ever seen, looking at him. Her long brunette hair cascaded down on to her bare shoulders, a dark brown dress that fit her tanned full body like a glove, large velvet brown eyes set on top of high cheekbones, and perfume that made his brain swirl.

"Can I buy you a beer?" she breathed in a husky low voice.

"Sure," laughed Munson uneasily, "But actually, let me do the honors."

"You're a Naval flight cadet, aren't you?" she asked.

"Yes I am," answered Munson, trying to act cool. "The uniform gave me away again."

"I've heard you're all in spectacular physical condition," she said. "Do you do push-ups?"

"Push-ups are my specialty, especially one arm pushups," answered Munson. "In fact I set the record for our flight." Munson thought, *I'm lying, but as the old saying goes, tell them what they want to hear.*

Her warm hip pressed against Munson, "That's exciting, she answered. "This party is boring; would you like to see something else in the French Quarter? I'm sure you'll enjoy it."

Munson felt a fullness growing in his trousers, his heart pounded, and sweat formed on his brow.

"My God, thought Munson. *"This woman has turned me on. Careful, I don't want to be embarrassed.*

"You're every wish is my command," answered Munson.

"I was hoping you'd say that," she breathed. "Let's go for a pleasant tour." She smiled, tilted her head, "I'll be the teacher and you can be the student. I think we'll both get along just fine."

She turned and walked toward the gate. Munson followed her obediently, like a puppy dog. A smile was on his face, wide enough to split his ears.

As the evening wore on, and after much beer was consumed, Capp asked Quirt.

"Have you seen Munson?"

"Yeah," answered Quirt. "He left a few hours ago with a great looking broad. She was older than him, but very well preserved. He had that horny look on his face we all know so well."

"Great," said Capp. "I want to get back to Bourbon Street. How're we going to find him?"

"He's a big boy," answered Quirt. "That's his problem. He knows where we're staying, onward to Bourbon Street."

About two in the morning, the three of them were partied out. Their tongues thick, and speech slurred from too much alcohol.

"If we don't leave soon," Capp announced. "I'll never remember how to get back to the barracks. Where the hell is Munson?"

"Probably in seventh heaven," answered Quirt. "Can you believe that he may be getting some, and not us? That's disgusting. I'm ready for the sack. Off to the barracks."

Capp barely found his way back to the air station. They collapsed into their bunks, knowing that a painful hangover awaited them later in the morning.

"Where's Munson?" said Capp sitting up on the side of his bunk, "It's 0700 and his bunk's empty. We have to be back at Pensacola by 1800 today or get big demerits if we're late. Noon is the latest we can leave and still make it safely."

"If your stomach can handle it," said Quirt, "Let's grab some chow and then check with the duty officer. Munson may have left a message."

They ate and went over to the duty officer's desk.

"Are there any messages for Chuck Capp from a Munson?"

"You bet," said the Petty Officer of the watch. "Just came in a few minutes ago."

Capp read the note. It read,

"You owe me beer for a week. Pick me up in the French quarter in front of Tom O'Danbills at 1100, Munson."

At 1100, Capp drove by as instructed. There was Munson, with a lecherous grin on his face. He got in the car and announced,

"Guess what you losers, I like older women. What a night. What a morning."

"Tell us, what happened?" asked Curtin in a high pitched voice.

"It was unbelievable," answered Munson with a sigh. "She was so gentle. Her fingertips, they had electricity in them. Every time I thought

I could do no more, she aroused me. I must have set a record for one-arm pushups. I thought I'd died and gone to heaven."

"That enough," growled Capp. "We're all getting horny. Did you get her name?"

"Naw," answered Munson. "That was her deal, no names, no ties, just a one-time party."

"Who'd have thought," said Capp as he shook his head. "Munson, Munson with his uniform. I must be losing my mind. Hang on; we're on our way back to reality. Pensacola, here we come!"

31

"Time to practice those crazy acrobatics by ourselves," said Capp to Quirt. Are you ready?"

"We'll find out at the top of a loop," answered Quirt. "Hey, all we can do is die."

"I like your attitude," said Capp. "Be perfect, or die. Let's hope you're perfect. If you're not, I'll never speak to you again. The Navy gives us one flight with an instructor. Then let's us go solo a couple of times to see how bad we scare ourselves. Suppose that's their way to weed out those that are on the edge of DOR?"

"Look around," answered Quirt, "Got any hunches as to who's going to hang it up?"

They both looked around the ready room, which was full of coffee drinking cadets. Some stared off into space. Some were laughing and joking with each other. Some were involved in a card games.

"If I knew how to figure that out," answered Capp, "I'd be a millionaire. Remember all those tests they gave us in Pre-Flight? I bet the Navy was trying to figure out the same thing. They never tell us the results."

"Yeah," said Quirt. "The two I remember best were the "sweat test" and the "vertigo trainer.""

"I almost forgot about those," answered Capp. "What a joke. They gave each cadet a piece of litmus paper and were told to squeeze it. If you sweat, it changed color. None if us knew if that could wash us out, the rumor was that it could, but we didn't know. I was really nervous because my paper changed color. A few of the cadet's paper didn't change. I think they were too stupid to be scared, or didn't hear of that rumor. If you never get scared, how do you know when you're approaching trouble? That crawly feeling on the back of your neck when fear arrives goes back to the caveman days. That's what keeps a person alive."

"And the vertigo trainer," said Quirt. "Pilots who fly in clouds on instruments can get vertigo, and it can kill. You're flying right side up, but your brain tells you that you're in a bank, or even upside down. If you don't believe your instruments, and instead believe your senses, you roll to what you think is level flight, but now you are in a severe bank or even upside down. Then you're in real trouble. Pilots I've talked to say it's frightening. You sweat, hard; your arms are tight and tense as they want to instinctively follow your senses which are trying to over-ride your eyes that are on the instruments which of course are correct. The most lethal time is right after take-off in the clouds, especially at night. You move your head down to change radio channels, and when your head comes back to the front, bang, you've got vertigo. The fluid in your inner ear causes it, confusion. It takes discipline to ignore your senses and believe the instruments."

Quirt continued, "Remember, they put you in chair that revolves like a barbers chair? You close your eyes. They spin the chair slowly, and then faster, then abruptly stop it. At the same time, you are told to open your eyes. Every person jumped right out the chair onto the floor; I almost killed myself. I heard some cadets broke their arms when they hit the floor. The fluid in your inner ear gets all fouled up, and when you open your eyes, somehow your brain tells you that you should be somewhere else. Since we went through it, they've now put in a seat belt as they lost too many cadets to broken limbs and bruised bodies. It's a great training device to show the danger of vertigo, but I've no idea how the chair is a predictor of success in flying. It's probably not, because everybody jumped out of the chair."

"I know," answered Capp. "Sometimes I think we're guinea pigs for sadistic psychologists who like to see people suffer. Pervis should know about that. He's a psych major with a dark personality. He probably designed the tests."

"Speaking of Pervis," said Quirt, "He just walked in, and is sitting over at the far table."

"Hang tight," said Capp, "I'll be right back."

Capp strolled over to where Pervis was sitting, "Hey Pervis, I need your help, got a minute?"

"Now what?" answered Pervis warily? "Whatever it is, you know I don't trust you."

"Nothing, nothing," said Capp with a big smile. "Quirt and I were talking about those silly tests given to us in Pre-Flight to see if they could figure out who might flunk out of the flight program. We decided they're sadists and we're guinea pigs. What do you think?"

"What the hell brought that up?" answered Pervis. "You're about to fly. Don't you think a discussion about procedures would be better?"

"We did that," said Capp. "Now we need to know if that sweaty litmus paper is going to count against us if push comes to shove."

"You guys are weird," answered Pervis. "In my mind, that counts more against you than a piece of paper. No wonder you're never going to be number one. You worry about stupid things."

"Did you have a sweaty litmus paper?" said Capp.

"What difference does it make," answered Pervis. "It didn't mean crap."

"Oh," said Capp. "You got sweaty too. I bet you were sweatier than me."

"I bet not," answered Pervis. "Jeez, why am I talking to you? You really are irritating. Go back and babble with Quirt."

"Man, are you testy," said Capp. "I just thought you might want to have an intellectual discussion."

Pervis just groaned and rolled his eyes.

Capp left Pervis and sat down at the table with Quirt.

"Well," said Quirt. "Did you get an answer?"

"Naw," answered Capp. "Just needed to have my morning jollies, I like to irritate him, he's such a jerk."

"Hey guys," said Dick Price. "Mind if I sit down?"

"Pull up a chair," answered Capp. "We're about to head out for solo acrobatics, how about you?"

"Same thing," said Price. "What a blast. I love coming over the top of a loop, barely in control, and then piercing the sky back down the chute, listening to the increase in the wind roar across the canopy as the speed picks up."

"A true artist," said Capp. "One who can paint a pretty picture of what is generally considered to be sweaty boring maneuver. The French cadets like loops too. Are you sure of your heritage?"

"You've got to have some fun," answered Price. "That's my way to reduce stress."

"Good for you," said Capp. "It's time for my hop, see you guys later. Keep your eyes open. There's a lot of haze out there."

"I'll walk to the flight line with you," said Price. "My bird's ready too."

Capp took off for a one-hour flight. He flew over to the acrobatic area. The haze was forecast to exist up to six or seven thousand feet. Everyone was briefed to clear the area before commencing maneuvers, beware of other planes, and don't have your head up-and-locked. Look around.

Capp climbed to five thousand feet, leveled off, and commenced a few rolls.

I think I've got those down good, he thought. *Let's climb up and try some loops.*

At eight thousand feet, he again leveled off.

Here goes, he thought. *Hope I don't stall at the top. Push the nose over, 200 knots, level off, keep the power up, pull the nose up, keep pulling, now at the top, look back toward the tail and the horizon, keep pressure on the stick, and, I made it! Wow, first attempt. Am I hot or what? Back down the hill, reduce power and level off. Yeahh! Let's do that again.*

Capp completed five more loops. All were very good.

Enough of loops, thought Capp, *Let's go down and practice some crosswind landings, never can get enough of those.*

205

Dick Price climbed to six thousand feet.

I don't need to climb to eight thousand, he thought. *That's only a safety factor in the event the plane spins. I'm hot. I made nothing but perfect loops with the instructor. It's hazy. Don't see any other planes. Here we go. Up, over, and down. Perfect. Let's do a few more to use up the time. Then I'll head back to Warner.*

On the third loop, Price went over the top and started down the backside. He turned his gaze from behind, and looked out of the front of his windshield. To his shock and horror, he saw a yellow SNJ directly in his path, as his plane was pointed straight toward the ground.

"Where'd he come from?" shouted Price out loud. "He's right below me."

Price tried to turn, but it didn't work. Everything was happening too fast.

"Pull up," shouted Price to himself in a panic. He pulled back hard on the stick. His plane shuddered as it stalled, snapped into a spin, and smashed into the right wing of the lower plane. They both burst into flames.

With its wing severed from the fuselage, the lower plane flipped around, and around, in an uncontrollable spin.

Price died instantly. The two pilots in the lower plane were knocked unconscious. They died in the impact with the ground.

Capp was on final approach to the crosswind runway when he heard a transmission on Guard channel, which was only used in an emergency.

"Mayday, Mayday," transmitted a pilot. "Whiskey Charlie 444, ten miles southwest of Whiting. Midair collision, two planes, both on fire have impacted the ground, cannot see any survivors. I will circle until the rescue plane arrives, out."

Warner tower transmitted on its primary frequency and Guard channel, "All planes clear the area ten miles southwest of Warner. Warner Field is closed until the ready plane has cleared the airfield." The tower repeated the instructions several times.

What's going on, thought Capp. *Sounds bad, wonder who it is? Let's hope it's not anyone I know.*

After about five minutes, the tower transmitted,

"Warner Field is now open for takeoff and landings. Avoid the area ten miles southwest of Warner; emergency aircraft are in that area."

Capp added power and climbed to two thousand feet. *Think I'll circle here for a few minutes. The traffic pattern will be loaded due to the delay. This crummy haze, bet that was part of the problem.*

It's been ten minutes, thought Capp. *There should be room to get into the pattern.*

Capp landed and taxied into the flight line. As he got out of the plane, he asked the plane captain.

"What happened? Any details?"

"The scuttlebutt is that three pilots are dead. But that's only a rumor," answered the plane captain. "You guys sure have guts. All of us ground-pounders really respect what you're doing. You never know if tomorrow it's going to be you."

"Thanks," said Capp. "We know the risks. But we couldn't do anything without your support. Let's hope the scuttlebutt about the deaths is wrong. Thanks again."

Capp checked the plane in, and walked over to the ready room. It was packed with cadets.

"Any word?" said Capp to no one in particular.

"Not yet," answered Sam Herman, one of the dedicated bridge players. "The Duty Officer will brief us when there's something official. Want to learn to play bridge to pass the time? It could be awhile, might take your mind off the tension."

"No Thanks," answered Capp. "But I'll take a rain check on your offer."

Quirt walked in, saw Capp and sat down.

"I was in the air when I heard the Mayday. What do you suppose happened?"

"Nobody knows," answered Capp. "The tension in here is so thick you can cut it with a knife. Flight operations have been cancelled for the rest of the day. How about a coffee?"

"No cream or sugar," said Quirt, "Just black and hot."

The ready room was quiet. Everyone was staring at the door, waiting for the duty officer to report. A half hour passed with no word. The heat and humidity added to the drama. Sweat rolled down the cadet's backs.

"Attention on Deck," shouted one of the cadets.

Everyone stood up at attention.

"Carry on," said the duty officer.

A hushed murmur rolled through the room.

"It's my sad duty to inform you that two cadets and a flight instructor were killed this morning in a mid-air collision. Lieutenant Roger Anderson, Cadets Marvin Ostrum and Richard Price are the deceased. Further details will be available when more is known about the accident. My sincere condolences to those that knew them as friends and fellow pilots, they will be missed."

"Attention on Deck," was called. The Duty Officer turned, and departed from the ready room.

"What a crock," said Capp quietly to Quirt, "I'm sick to my stomach. Price was here just a few hours ago. We walked out to the flight line together. We talked and had some laughs. It's unreal, life here is an illusion. It can pass quickly my friend, so enjoy every minute of it. And you know what? All of us are going to crawl into an SNJ tomorrow and fly as if nothing happened, or could happen. It's a tough business."

32

The death of Dick Price and the other two pilots hung heavy over flight operations.

The Warner Operations and Safety departments met to review what facts they had. They speculated:

"If dangerous or sloppy tendencies in Price had been recognized and corrected by whatever method was necessary, would three pilots still be alive?"

Flight briefings were more intense, safety rules re-emphasized, procedures reviewed over and over. All cadets knew there'd be an over reaction from the instructors. That was normal after a fatal accident. Unsatisfactory, or Down flights would increase. There were to be no gray areas. Black or white was the order of the day. Marginal cadets were to be washed out. It was not a time to fly a poor flight.

Capp, Quirt, Munson and Curtin had finished morning chow. They walked slowly toward the hangar.

"The word is out," said Capp. "Fly just an average flight and a Down may be your gift. The pressure's really on. The Warner Base Skipper wants heads to roll. Scuttlebutt has it that Price fouled up, and caused the accident. The Skipper ordered all of Price's instructors into his office this morning. They've got to explain their grades they gave to Price that are in his flight jacket. Also, how they briefed and flew procedures with him. I wouldn't want to be in that room."

"Why do they think Price was at fault?" asked Munson.

"Because of the estimated altitude of the mid-air collision," answered Capp.

"Well don't stop," said Munson.

"Remember the briefing yesterday morning?" said Capp. "The haze layer went up to about angels six or seven. Acrobatics that take up a lot of airspace, such as loops, spins, and barrel rolls were to be at angels eight or higher. That allowed for clear visibility to see other planes. Also, recovery would be completed before entering the lower haze layer. It was a safety briefing; in effect, an order."

"I remember," said Munson. "Until I climbed above angels seven, it was murky."

"According to pilots in the area who saw the accident," continued Capp, "Just before impact they saw a plane dive into a second plane. There was a ball of flame when they collided at or slightly above their line of sight. They were at angels five, so the mid-air occurred close to angels five."

"Doesn't sound good," said Munson.

"No," answered Capp. "Price was on the same hop as me, loops and rolls. If he started a loop at angels eight, even if he got in trouble, he would have recovered by angels six. He told me his loops were perfect, so I assume he wasn't in trouble. My guess is that he started a loop in the haze, and didn't see the other plane before going vertical."

"And if he saw the other plane, close, while on the downhill," said Munson. "Even a Blue Angel would have had a mid-air. There probably was no room to maneuver."

"Who knows what really happened," said Capp. "It does prove one thing, however. Pilots and senior officers, who have a lot more experience than us, make the rules. They're for a reason. He paid the ultimate price for violating them. Hey, enough of the morbid crap. Flying is a ball. Just do it by the numbers. And my friends, that means all of you."

They all shook hands.

"The numbers," they said in unison.

"This is the next step," said Capp as they entered the hangar and walked into the ready room. "Acrobatics is the name of the game. Finish this stage and we're prepared to dogfight with anyone. Think about it, there are only so many maneuvers a plane can fly, and after today we'll know ninety nine percent of them. Kind of gives a person a feeling of power. What do you think?"

"You're on a roll again," answered Munson. "Let's go."

Capp walked into the briefing room, and waited for his instructor. He went over his procedures again, just to make sure he knew them cold. Through experience, he knew that once in the air, you couldn't refer to any book.

"Cadet Capp?" said a tall instructor.

"Yes, Sir," answered Capp.

"Captain Kranz has a cold and is grounded. I'm Lt. Bill Olson and we'll be flying together on this hop. Let's sit over here. You've got an impressive flight jacket, Capp. "I expect an outstanding performance."

"I'll give it my best," answered Capp.

He wondered if all of the students were to be assigned different instructors for the next flight in line, as kind of a mini check ride. Better be on my toes for this one, thought Capp.

They briefed on the barrel roll, the half Cuban eight, and the slow roll.

"The barrel roll is fun," said Olson. "The half Cuban eight is just a variation of the loop. The slow roll is the one that causes some students problems. It's work, and requires lots of concentration. Some pilots don't think it's fun. Think of a totally coordinated roll maneuver in slow motion. The problem point is when you're inverted and rolling back to a level position. If you don't hold the nose up with the stick, or confuse the rudder controls, you'll split-s straight down, inverted. The rudder pressure is the secret throughout the whole maneuver. However proper stick pressure is also necessary, any questions?"

"No, Sir," answered Capp.

The airfield was noisy as usual. Engines roaring, planes taxiing out for take off, and others landing.

As they completed their pre-flight inspection, Capp wanted to test the water of Olson's attitude toward procedures.

"What a tragedy about the mid-air," said Capp.

"You're right," answered Olson. "I've lost several friends in flight operations. Other than combat, all of their deaths were a result of pilot error. Either they or another pilot fouled up. Planes don't kill pilots, pilots do. Remember that. There may be exceptions, but not many. That's why in this stage of your training, if you can't or won't follow procedures; you're done. It's that simple, O.K.?"

"Yes Sir," answered Capp.

Wow! thought Capp, *The water has been tested. It's cold and unforgiving.*

They took off, headed southwest and leveled off at eight thousand feet.

"I'll do the first barrel roll, you do the rest," radioed Olson. Pull your nose up, 45-degree angle to the right. At the 90 degree bearing, you're inverted, and the wings need to be level with the horizon. Keep pulling through and end up where you started, piece of cake, your turn."

Olson makes it look so easy, thought Capp. *Here we go. Up, over, around and back to where I started. It was easy. What a beautiful maneuver.*

"Great," radioed Olson. "You have no problem. Do a few more and then we'll try a half Cuban eight."

Capp finished three, and Smith radioed.

"Next is the Half Cuban eight. Pull up into a loop. As you're forty-five degrees on the backside, roll out. Continue the dive and pull up into another one. It was designed to bomb the enemy on one heading, and then on a reciprocal heading. Once radar guided anti-aircraft guns became operational, the half Cuban eight was an invitation to be shot down, an easy target. Gunners drool when they see a plane in that maneuver, but it's one of many things you're trained to do. However, avoid it in combat, your turn."

Capp pulled up into the first half of a loop, continued over the top, and on the backside, rolled out, dove, got his speed up and did a second one.

"Between that and the barrel roll," radioed Capp. "I don't know which one I like best. Those are my two favorites."

"Roger," radioed Olson. "Do a few more and then we'll get to work."
Capp finished two more and Olson radioed, "I've got it."

"Roger," answered Capp and held up his hands so the instructor could see he was not on the stick.

"Follow me through on the controls during the slow roll," radioed Olson. "Don't push, just feel how they coordinate."

Every Navy pilot has done this, thought Capp. *It can't be that tough.*

"Pull the nose up twenty degrees, slowly roll to the right, and feed in left rudder to hold the nose up. When your wings are ninety degrees to the ground, full left rudder is needed or the nose will drop. Keep rolling. Slowly take out rudder.'

'When you're inverted, rudder is neutral; the stick is full forward to hold the nose up. Don't release pressure on the stick.'

'Continue the roll and feed in right rudder. At ninety degrees of bank, full right rudder is needed. Continue to roll, let off rudder pressure and you'll end up level, in a slightly nose down attitude. Give it a try."

This looks hard, thought Capp. *Pull up the nose, start to roll; Oh crap. At ninety degrees of bank I didn't have enough rudder and the nose fell through the horizon. How embarrassing.*

"Try it again," radioed Olson. "You have to use the full rudder travel."
Capp gritted his teeth and started again.

"Keep pushing rudder," radioed Olson. "O.K., you're past ninety degrees, start feeding in forward stick. Let out the rudder. Good. Keep rolling. Add right rudder, let off stick pressure. Keep rolling. Atta boy, you're doing well. Concentrate. And we're level. Terrific."

"My thighs are quivering," radioed Capp. "That's work."

"I told you so," answered Olson. "Try two more and we'll head back to Warner."

Capp finished. They landed and walked to the debriefing room.

"Great job," said Olson. "You should be proud you didn't spilt-s while inverted. That's always exciting. You're next two hops are solo; practice, practice and practice. That's all I have, any questions?"

"No, Sir," answered Capp. "However, a hot shower and some aspirin will be in order for my legs."

Olson laughed and departed the briefing room.

On the way out, Capp saw Pervis and his instructor de-briefing. The instructor was animated in the use of his hands, neither had a smile on their faces.

Pervis is always too serious, thought Capp. *He should lighten up.*

Capp entered the ready room to see if any of the guys were back from their flights. None were there. He was about to leave, when Pervis entered, looking downcast.

"You're chin is rubbing the deck," said Capp. "Cheer up. Smile, the day is young. The beer is cold."

"Get lost," growled Pervis. "I don't need any of your happy horsecrap funny jokes. I just need to think."

"What about?" said Capp. "Just ask me; girls, booze, parties, acrobatics, dull instructors? I've got experience with them all."

"You'll probably hear anyway, from your idiot friends," answered Pervis. "Somehow they get to know everything. I did a split-s out of the slow roll."

"So what?" answered Capp. "It's a tough maneuver."

"I did it every time," said Pervis. "It's like I have a mental block. My hand freezes on the stick, it won't go forward."

"Normally I'd laugh like crazy," said Capp, "because you're so paranoid about this number one thing. But I won't. I hope you can work it out. Just practice, practice and practice, it'll come."

"Did you split-s?" asked Pervis.

"Sorry to say, but no, my slow rolls all came out good," answered Capp. No split-s. But my thighs are suffering from all the pressure on the rudders."

"So you'll be listed ahead of me on the board," said Pervis. "You'll probably be laughing at me behind my back. That's not fair."

"Pervis," said Capp. "You need to get a life. This number one thing is going to destroy you. Fly because you like it, not because you want to beat me, or anyone else, O.K.?"

"We'll see," replied Pervis. "I'm still going to beat you."

"You won't," said Capp. "But try to smile. Your face may break, but give it a try. Good luck on your next hop, I'm leaving."

33

It was hot and humid at Warner Field. The evening air hung in a mist like a swamp, because of the saturated dew point.

Capp was in his bunk, and watched the solitary black wall fan. It was above the sink near the doorway and slowly moved left and right. He timed its movement. It took his mind off of the oppressive heat in the room.

"Damn, is it miserable," moaned Capp. I'm lying here with nothing on but my skivvies, sweat runs all over my body, that stupid wall fan oscillates one cycle every fifteen seconds and blows air on me for three seconds, which means I have no air on me for forty eight seconds of every minute. What crap. How can you rebels stand to live in this country?"

"Are you speaking to me sir?" asked Moose Redmond, who was across the room in his bunk, reading a procedures book. "We live here, because there's none of that funny little white cold stuff that falls from the sky in flakes; which results in extreme discomfort to normal human beings. Only Yankees and sub-humans would be dumb enough to put up with that."

"Up North," answered Capp, "I can put on a sweater or turn up the heat in the furnace to stay warm." Here, I can't take off my skin to get any cooler. Jeez, I can't wait until the fall season begins. Of course, then the hurricanes come aboard. You've got to admit, it could be better."

"Boy, are you a grouch tonight," said Redmond. "Go over to the ACRAC where it's air conditioned. Get a beer, and come back only when I can recognize the happy go lucky Capp I know so well. Right now, you're starting to sound like Pervis."

"O.K., O.K. you win," groaned Capp. "I don't ever want to be accused of being like that jerk. See you later."

Capp put on his uniform, and walked down to Quirt's room. Quirt was lying on his bunk; a cigarette dangled from his mouth, the smoke slowly rising and then disappeared, as wind from the fan tore through it. His legs were spread so as not to touch each other, his skivvies and undershirt were wet from sweat. He looked equally as miserable as Capp felt.

"C'mon hot shot," said Capp. "Let's go to the ACRAC and cool off. Redmond thinks I've lost it in this heat. He even accused me of acting as ornery as Pervis, can you believe that? You look like you could take a break too. C'mon."

"Tomorrow's our acrobatic C-18 check rides," answered Quirt, "Our final flight at Warner, and we've all got mixed emotions. This has been a fun base with good flying. Hold on until I get my scruffy uniform, with the wrinkles that are permanent because of this heat. It's probably a good idea to loosen up for awhile, and if nothing else, to get out of this steam bath."

Capp pulled open the front door of the ACRAC. The blare of the jukebox greeted them.

"It's just like our little home away from home," exclaimed Capp. "The noise, the music and the clink of the beer bottles, a different world, a little island away from the stress and heat of the mundane. Hey, there's Munson and Curtin. Let's join them."

"What do you say guys?" "Looks like all the Yankees are over here to stay cool."

"There's a lot of Rebels too," answered Curtin. "The barracks are like a sauna."

"Everyone ready for your check ride?" said Capp. "Assuming we'll get an Up, these may be our last few beers on these hallowed grounds. I'm going to miss this place, been lots of fun."

"What do you mean, assuming we'll get an Up?" answered Munson. "Of course we'll get an Up. We're hot, and I don't mean the temperature. And, for the record, I don't think there's a bar you don't like. Sampson Field's ACRAC will be just as great. And if it isn't, there's always the Gulf Breeze in Pensacola."

"Jeez," answered Capp. "My life's an open book. I'll get a couple of pitchers at the bar, be right back."

He wandered over to the bar, "Two pitchers, barkeep, and keep the change."

"Drinking before a check ride?" a voice from down the bar was heard. "That's not smart."

He looked to his right. There was Pervis, by himself, as usual.

Capp walked over and stood by Pervis.

"What are you tonight, the keeper of the kegs?"

"No," answered Pervis. "I just don't think it's smart to drink before an important hop, and the final check ride rates right up there as one of the toughest. I'm drinking pop."

"Well that's your idea," answered Capp. "If you can't party all night and fly a 4.0 hop the next day, you don't deserve to be a Navy pilot. Besides, we're not going to get crocked, just taking a break from the barracks heat. Hope I can sleep tonight."

"The heat agrees with me," said Pervis. "I'll sleep all night, wake up and fly a perfect check ride tomorrow. The final score for top cadet will be-Pervis number one, Capp way behind."

"We're tied for number one right now," answered Capp. "I'm the one that's going to fly a perfect hop. You need to be better than good, I don't plan to lose."

"I'll be good," said Pervis, "Better than you."

"I've heard your slow roll stinks," answered Capp. "Don't lose any sleep over that, I wouldn't want you to worry. Are your palms sweaty? Is your litmus paper turning color? Just think, you might get a lousy grade because of Slow Rolls, but don't dwell on that. Wow, come to think about it, I'm going to sleep real good tonight knowing that your slow roll is going to be your downfall. Excuse me while I quaff down a brew. Sleep tight, and don't let your nightmares bite."

"Your psychology stinks," said Pervis. "You're the one that's worried. False bravado doesn't impress me, it's so transparent. Go drink with your loser friends. I'm still going to whip your butt and end up number one. Tough."

"It's the bottom of the ninth, bases loaded," said Capp. "We'll see who strikes out, who chokes in the clutch? It won't be me. It never has. Remember that."

Capp grabbed the two pitchers of beer and left.

"What was that all about?" asked Quirt. "You and Pervis were nose to nose."

"Pervis is nervous about who's going to be the number one cadet at Whiting from our group," answered Capp. This last flight will determine the final standings at Warner."

"How do you know he's nervous?" said Quirt."

"He's not drinking booze or beer," answered Capp. "Pop to be exact, and that's not like him. It means he's uptight."

"Disgusting," said Quirt. "He should be kicked out of the program."

"Enough of Pervis," said Capp. "Let's have a toast. Raise your glasses, you with tiger blood in your veins. We don't have champagne, but beer will do. 'To our last flight at Warner, may it be our best.'"

"Hear, Hear," said everyone as they clinked their glasses together, laughed, and took a deep swig of cold beer.

"While we're reminiscing about our last day at Warner," said Munson, "Capp, I've often wondered how you came to choose the Navy instead of the Air Force. You know the Air Force is testing some hot fighters, and their budget is virtually unlimited."

"Give me three reasons why you chose the Navy," answered Capp. Then I'll tell you my story."

Munson thought for a minute,

"That's easy, aircraft carriers, dress white uniforms-the blue ones are also cool, and a feeling that Navy pilots have more class with better training."

"Well," said Capp, "You've almost told my story. I always wanted to fly so bad that I could taste it. When I was a kid, I used to arrange my bed cover so it had bumps which were used as mountains and valleys.

My parents bought me little metal airplanes which I used to strafe and bomb imaginary enemy soldiers in the blankets hills and valley's.'

'In college, I joined the Air Force ROTC. Our class was sent to take the flight physical. I was the only one who passed in a class of thirty. The eye exam blew most of them out. One of my classmates told me to sign up for the regular Air Force, now, while I still can pass the flight exam. "Go fly jets," he said. "College could always be completed, in or out of the Air Force."

"I took his advice," said Capp. "I called the Air Force recruiter, and was told to go down to the local Armory to sign up. It was a large gymnasium type building. About one hundred persons were there to join the Air Force. I wanted to be in the flight program, walked up to a large fat Sergeant and told him what I wanted. He yelled at me to get in line, which I did. After about a half hour, papers were given to me to be completed. A flight physical was to be taken the following day. I explained that I had passed all that the day before. The fat sergeant again yelled at me, accused me of bad hearing, and that he'll tell me what to do, and when to do it. It was degrading.'

'During a break I went downtown, and wondered if I was doing the right thing. About that time, down the street walked a Navy pilot in his dress white uniform, gold wings on his chest, blue shoulder boards with a gold stripe, oozing confidence, and on his arm was a great looking woman. It was the most impressive sight I ever saw.'

'I walked to a phone, called the recruiting office at the Naval air station, and inquired if I could have an appointment to get information on applying for Naval flight training. I was told to come out immediately, if that was possible, for a tour. Naturally I was curious, and said I'd be right out.'

'At the gate, I was met by a sharp looking Navy Lieutenant; imagine that an officer. Was I impressed, especially after dealing with the obnoxious Air Force Sergeant. After introductions, he took me to the flight line. We watched reserve pilots in F4U Corsair fighters practice take off and landings. What a beautiful airplane, with its gull shaped wings, deep blue navy color and white stars painted on the wings and fuselage. As you know, it's one of the fastest propeller aircraft in the world."

"Until jets were introduced," said the Lieutenant, "The Corsair was the premier fighter in the navy. The reserves fly them, and are ready to go into combat at a moments notice. They're scheduled to receive F9F Panther jets in the very near future."

"He then took me to the Officers club which was plush, just like a country club, and bought me lunch," continued Capp. "I was introduced to a Lieutenant Commander, an ace who had shot down six Japanese Zero's in World War II. The Lieutenant Commander, an intense type, said,

"Lots of pilots can fly fighters, but only navy pilots land on aircraft carriers. We're a cut above the Air Force. If you want the best, fly Navy."

"My head was swimming," said Capp. "The Navy's treatment of me had such class compared to the Air Force, the contrast so vivid, and it was obvious they wanted me. In my Air force experience, I was just a number. At that moment, my mind was made up. The rest is history. Here I am and glad of it. The Navy's exciting, fun, and the training is 4.0. End of story."

"Jeez," said Munson. "What a great story. Mine is boring compared to that. I graduated from college in physics; saw a recruiting poster with an aircraft carrier and a Navy officer in his dress whites. I signed up. That's it."

"As the old saying goes," said Capp. "There are many stories in the big city. However, the main thread that runs through all of us is… we want to fly. That's important. Without that desire, the flight program would fail. There isn't a bum in the group. Well, almost no bums."

The group laughed, again clinked glasses and took another swig of beer.

"Gentleman," said Capp. "Heat or no heat, it's back to the barracks. A big day tomorrow; we pass, pack, and part company with good old Warner Field. And then a new experience awaits us, formation flying, it's going to be great. Good luck to all of you. I'm out of here."

"Us too," said the other three.

The four of them walked to the barracks, each bragging how great they were compared to the others.

Confidence and arrogance was in the air.

34

It was Friday. It was hot. It was humid. It was acrobatic check-ride time.

Capp, Munson, Quirt, and Curtin were all seated in the briefing room, reviewing procedures for the check ride.

"I didn't sleep worth a crap last night," said Capp. "Hope I don't forget what to do at the top of a loop."

"Don't worry," answered Quirt. "None of us slept good. My mind kept going over procedures. I couldn't shake it off. The heat didn't help either. All of us could probably write the procedures book, don't know why we're all studying. Nervous habit I guess. You're good, Capp. Just fly your normal way."

They all knew the number one cadet spot was up for grabs. Just as in a baseball game where a pitcher was on the way to a no-hitter, no one mentioned it. Capp was a competitor. His adrenaline was roaring. His flight mates knew he'd have no trouble flying a good hop. Most of his nervousness was the desire to beat Pervis, to be number one. Other than Pervis, no one was close to first place except the two of them. This hop was it.

"Wouldn't it be a crock if the engine broke, and I couldn't get airborne?" asked Capp. "I'd have to wait until Monday to fly this hop."

"You know there are spares to cover that event," answered Quirt. "Relax. Just like you tell women, it's going to be great. Go out and fart into the wind. It'll clear your mind."

"You're right," laughed Capp. "This is the eighteenth hop in acrobatics. I can do the procedures in my sleep, or half in the bag. Either way, I'm ready."

"Atta boy," said Quirt. "Here come our instructors. Safe flight everyone."

"Good morning Lieutenant Robinson," said Capp. "I'm ready to brief."

"Let's sit over here," said Robinson. "As you know this is your final flight. I don't have fangs, but I do expect an above average hop. Average doesn't cut it anymore. Just follow procedures and you'll do fine."

I've heard this guy's a hard-ass, thought Capp, *He wants it by the book and that's what it's going to be.*

The pre-flight and run-up of the SNJ was good.

Everything works perfect, thought Capp, *Let's add some power and get on with the show.*

"Request permission for take-off," radioed Robinson. "We're next in line. Let's not keep everyone waiting."

So this is the way it's going to be, thought Capp. *He wants to shake me up. Sorry, my friend, I don't get shook.*

"Warner tower," radioed Capp. "Whiskey Charlie 222, ready for take-off."

"Roger Whiskey Charlie 222," answered the tower, "Cleared for take off. Turn left after airborne."

"Roger," answered Capp.

Capp took the runway, locked the tail wheel, added power, pulled the nose up into the air, raised the gear and flaps, reduced to climb power, and turned to the acrobatic area.

How was that for perfect, Robinson, thought Capp, *Now to climb to eight thousand feet and show this guy how a hot-dog flies.*

"Do the procedures in the order as we briefed," radioed Robinson. "Regular roll, barrel roll, loop, half Cuban eight, a slow roll, and if we have time, we'll do an engine out procedure."

That jerk, thought Capp, *We didn't brief for engine-out. However, today he's the boss, so hang loose. Here we go.*

Capp performed all of the maneuvers to perfection.

This is unbelievable, thought Capp. *It's as if I'm locked into a groove. Even the slow roll was great. Drank beer last night with hardly any sleep, guess I've learned to be a Navy pilot. What fun.*

"We're out of time," radioed Robinson, "I'm sure you know how to do an engine-out. Anyway, it wouldn't have counted, just something to fill out the period. I've never given a 4.0 grade on a check-ride. You're the first one. Congratulations, you have an Up. Take up a heading to Warner and let's go home."

"Yes, Sir," radioed Capp jubilantly. "It's my pleasure."

"Hooray," shouted Capp into the cockpit. "No one can hear me over the roar of the engine, but I'm done. Yeahh!"

Actually, Robinson did hear Capp.

*Nothing like a happy cadet, h*e laughed to himself. *He'll do fine in the fleet.*

Pervis was sweating profusely, even at the cooler high altitude. He had Split-S out of his first slow roll.

What's going on? thought Pervis in a panic. *I can't hold the nose up when inverted. Why's my hand shaking? C'mon, calm down. I can do it.*

"Try it again," radioed his instructor, Captain French.

I can't coach him, thought French. *This is his check ride, not an instruction hop. I know he's a good pilot. We'll try a few more, but there's a limit.*

Up with the nose, thought Pervis. *Pull the nose up, start a roll, I'm at the ninety degree position, Oh no, the nose is sliding toward the horizon, can't hold it up, not enough rudder, crap. What's wrong with me?*

"Try it again," Mr. Pervis, radioed Captain French.

Pervis pulled the nose up and started again.

This one's good, thought Pervis, *I'm inverted, nose is holding, start to roll out, right rudder, no left rudder, got confused, Oh no, the nose fell through. It'll never come back to the horizon. I may throw up.*

"Mr. Pervis," radioed Captain French. "I don't think today is your day. Let's head back to Warner. You can try this again next week."

Pervis had tears in his eyes. He couldn't believe it. He had a Down. *A Down!* His hand trembled. It radiated through the control stick. An image of his father laughing at him, passed in front of his eyes.

French felt it and knew that Pervis's mind was not on flying.

"I've got it," radioed French. "Relax."

They landed, taxied into the chocks, checked in the SNJ, and walked to the debriefing room. Pervis was silent the whole way.

"Care for a coffee?" said French.

"No thanks, Sir," answered Pervis.

French ordered a coffee with cream and sugar from the airman at the coffee mess.

"Tell me Mr. Pervis," he said, "Is there something personal bothering you? Something you want to share with me?"

"No, Sir," answered Pervis, his eyes looked down at the deck. "The harder I tried, the worse it got. Don't know why."

"It seemed as though you weren't able to hold enough rudder," said French. "The nose fell through and you lost control."

"My practice hops were the same way," answered Pervis. "I can't seem to solve the problem."

"Where were your rudder pedals?" said French, "All the way forward, back, or in the middle?"

"All the way back," answered Pervis, "To get the most throw."

"Sometimes, that's not always the best," said French. "Your knee is locked in a closed position. You may need to move the pedals forward a notch or two. It allows your leg to straighten out and apply more pressure. Try it next time. You fly the plane excellent, that's no problem. But you need to perform all the maneuvers. Good luck. You'll conquer the problem. Anything else before I leave?"

"No, Sir," replied Pervis. "I'll try your advice about the rudder position."

Captain French left. He had to record a Down in Pervis's flight jacket, and inform operations. Pervis would be scheduled for a solo flight followed by another check ride. In the present atmosphere resulting from the fatal accident, two downs would probably be grounds for washout.

Pervis stared at the ceiling, his mind blank. He tried to comprehend what just happened. He thought back to his childhood days, the beatings from his father when he wasn't number one, when he wasn't the best. His memories were painful and he didn't want to think about them, but they gnawed into his psyche, his head hurt.

"Peter," his father would say, "Did you get an 'A' in all your subjects?"

"No father," Pervis answered, "I got a 'B' in chemistry. All the rest were 'A's. "That's all right, isn't it?"

"Of course not," answered his father. "You never seem to make it to the top. There's a weakness in you, must be from your mother. Why do you always fail to make it to the top? You always fail at the last moment. You're a disgrace to me and my family."

"I'm your family; I'm your son," he cried out, "Why don't you love me? Why can't you accept me for what I am? One 'B' isn't bad. Did you get straight 'A's?"

"Why you impertinent little brat," shouted his father. "How dare you speak to me that way. I'll teach you to talk back to me."

"Pervis's father hit him across the face, hard, knocked him across the room and caused his nose to bleed.

His mother heard the commotion and ran into the room. She screamed when she saw Peter spread out on the floor, blood all over his shirt.

"Sam, Sam, stop it," she shouted, "you've been drinking. Leave Peter alone. He's a good boy."

"No he's not," shouted back his father, "Just once he's got to show me that he can be the best at something, anything."

Pervis snapped back to the present.

"I'm not going to be number one, he said to himself. *It's not my fault. It's Capp's fault. He psyched me out last night in the ACRAC. He told me I was going to fail on the slow roll. He said it over and over. It's implanted in my brain, that son-of-a-bitch, he's the cause.*

I've got to get even, he thought, *if it's the last thing I do. He's got to suffer. I'm in control, and terror's my option, at the right place and the right time. Revenge is mine, however long it takes.* His eyes had a look that would frighten the devil.

225

35

The word spread quickly through the barracks. Pervis got a Down on his acrobatic check ride. Everyone knew the intense competition between Capp and Pervis, and their extreme dislike for each other. The number one cadet at Warner Field was settled. Capp was the winner.

Capp was so excited, that he didn't stay around the ready room. He went straight to his room in the barracks, to pack, and say goodbye to friends.

As Capp entered his room, it was full of his flight-mates, other friends, cadets who knew the competition story and didn't know Capp personally, but wanted to shake his hand for his success.

"Bless my cotton-pickin butt," yelled Moose Redmond as Capp entered, "The winner and still champion, 'Cadet, make love to all the women,' Charles C. Capp. Let me slap your back, and give you a big kiss."

Redmond almost broke Capp's back with an over exuberant back slap, but backed off with fawned terror when Capp drew back his fist to avoid any type of kiss.

"You may be bigger than me Redmond," laughed Capp. "But only my mother and any available woman can kiss me. Thank God you're only congratulating me. I'd hate to be on the end of an angry back slap."

"Haw, Haw," laughed Redmond. "You Yankees are really tender."

Quirt, Curtin, Munson, and many other cadets gave Capp energetic slaps on his back, and offered their congratulations.

"The way my back is going to feel in the morning," said Capp, "I'll wish I'd gotten a Down. Well time to pack and check out of here."

"Bullcrap," said Redmond, "Tonight we party. All of us are done. We all got an Up, except Pervis. Beer, broads, music, and more broads, this will be a night to remember."

"You know, I really feel sorry for Pervis," said Capp, "His dauber must be dragging on the deck. Much as I think he's a jerk, I don't want him to think about D.O.R. He needs to be cheered up, any ideas?"

"You are an old softy," answered Redmond, "but you're right. Remember after the shower party with the French cadets, we were going to take Pervis to the raunchiest, most brawling, country bar in Pensacola and let him dance with the girl of the meanest redneck in the bar. It would be a fitting tribute to the end of an illustrious career.

"Jeez," said Capp. "I don't want him to die, just get some juices flowing."

"I'll take care of him," answered Redmond, "It'll be a blast."

"Redmond," said Capp. "After a few drinks, you're wilder than most hillbillies. Are you sure?"

"Hell yes," answered Redmond. "He couldn't be safer with a platoon of marines."

"O.K.," said Capp. "But if it starts to go out of control, get his skinny little butt out of there. Agreed?"

"I cross my heart on the memory of my daddy's mule," answered Redmond. "Pervis doesn't like you, especially now. I won't tell him you're coming. Meet us at the Corral at 2100. That's when the music starts."

Redmond went down to Pervis's room. He was sitting at his desk, holding his head in his hands.

Redmond pulled up a chair.

"Want to talk about it?" asked Redmond, "You've had a tough day."

"No I don't want to talk about it," answered Pervis. "It wasn't a tough day, it was a horseshit day."

"Right," said Redmond carefully. "Look, some of the guys are going out tonight for a brew, and we want you to come with us. You don't have to, but sitting here, thinking about it will drive you nuts. Some beer, music, and good-looking broads can't hurt. What do you say?"

Pervis looked at Redmond suspiciously, "Are you sure?"

"You know me." answered Redmond. "If I didn't want to, I wouldn't ask you. It'll be good for you."

"I don't want to go to the Gulf Breeze," said Pervis, "If you know what I mean."

"No problem," answered Redmond, "No cadets at this place. Then it's done. Sibley, Marino and I will be down at 2045. Get your dancing shoes on. It's party time. See you later."

"I hate to be patronized just because I'm upset, thought Pervis. *"Most rebels are Cretins, but going out with them could be fun. I've never told anyone, but not having any close friends is hard. I've never made the effort to make friends, I guess now may be the time, even with Cretins."*

The Corral was one of the rowdier country bars in town, but it always had a great band on weekends, and a large dance floor. Country folks like to dance. As with most bars, if you minded your own business, it was safe. What you don't do is sit at the bar and stare at the guy with the beard, torn shirt, and tattoos, or dance with his girl. That's not safe.

"C'mon, let's get a table by the dance floor," said Redmond. "It's closer to the action."

As they sat down, a waitress stopped at their table, "What'll you thirsty looking guys have?"

"Two pitchers and five glasses," Redmond answered. "I drink faster than these guys. I bet you like fast guys."

"No," she smiled, "I like guys that are long and slow. You look as though you qualify for long, but would have to be taught, slow. But don't hold your breath, I'm not available."

"Everybody's available," answered Redmond. "It's just a matter of timing."

"I'll get your beer speedy," she laughed,

"Damn, this is great," said Pervis, "Much better than sitting at the barracks."

"I told you so." said Redmond. "Hey, the music started. Find yourself a partner. There's a table of broads, let's see if they want to dance."

"I don't know how to dance," answered Pervis. "Think I'll just watch."

"Bullcrap," said Redmond. "This is a party. Everything's a three step. The girls will follow you. Don't worry, they're used to amateurs. When the music's fast, stand in front of her and stomp your feet to the beat of the music, mainly the bass drum, just follow its beat. She'll do all the work, just the opposite of making love. The funs out on the dance floor, not in your chair, follow me."

They asked the four girls to dance, and they all got up.

Pervis took the shortest one, not very good looking, but had nice shaped legs in tight jeans. It was a slow dance. He counted 1, 2, 3, and it worked. She followed him.

"I like men that are my size," she said. "With the tall guys, my nose is always in their chest, not very romantic. My name's Betty Lou, what's yours?"

"Pete, Pete Pervis, You dance nice, makes me feel like a pro."

"It's a long night," she said, "You'll just get better and better. She pulled him close and put her head on his shoulder. "Don't go too far away."

The music ended, and similar to homing pigeons, everyone went back to their tables.

"Wow," said Pervis, "I can't believe what I've been missing. This dance hall is great. How has this been kept a secret?"

"Well," answered Redmond. "You Yankees think us Reb's are stupid. This is our part of the world, and we know how to have a good time. Country music is the soul of the earth, and it's sexier than your silly-ass jazz, or whatever you call it. Enjoy yourself, I am. It looks as if you and the little blond might be a pair, the back seat of my car's at your disposal if you need it."

Pervis laughed a silly happy laugh, and then stopped cold.

Capp, Quirt, Munson and Curtin walked into the bar. They sat at a table across the room from Redmond's table.

"Who invited them?" demanded Pervis.

"Aw, don't worry about them," answered Redmond. "They probably got bored with the Gulf Breeze, and came to a real bar. Besides, they're not going to dance with you."

Pervis relaxed,

"You're right, probably just a coincidence."

After a few hours of beer and dances, Redmond pulled Pervis aside,

"See that redhead over there with the big knockers and long legs," said Redmond.

"Yeah," answered Pervis quizzically.

"She's the local dance hall Queen; beautiful, and seductive. When the music starts, ask her to dance. She'll play hard to get, but keep after her. She's worth it."

"She is beautiful," said Pervis, "Why don't you ask her to dance?"

"Not to brag," answered Redmond, "but tonight's your turn. She'll turn you every way but loose."

The music started and Pervis went over to ask her to dance.

"Jeez," said Sibley, "That's Roy Carter's girl. He's the meanest son-of-a-bitch in Pensacola, and jealous as horny toad. He'll tear Pervis apart."

"Let's just see what happens," laughed Redmond. "Maybe Carter has mellowed. Besides, she'll never say yes."

Pervis asked her to dance. She shook her head no. He kept asking; she kept shaking her head no. After about ten requests, she got up and danced with Pervis.

"Can you believe that?" gasped Redmond, "The little fart is dancing with her. Look around; see if you can spot Carter. Be alert, this could get scary."

The music ended, Pervis walked the redhead back to her seat, and came back to his table.

"She was really nice," said Pervis. "She asked me if I'd ever met her boyfriend. I said no. She said I will. Wonder what she meant by that."

It was quiet while the band took a break. The muffled talk of table conversation was in the background.

All of a sudden there arose a Rebel war cry from across the room that was so loud it sent chills up and down Redmond's spine.

"Oh crap," said Redmond to Pervis, "You're about to meet Mr. Carter."

"Who's Mr. Carter," asked Pervis.

"The redhead's boyfriend," answered Redmond. "It's time to go on defense."

From across the room, walking fast toward Redmond's table, was a large man with long black hair, scruffy beard, tattoo's, black cowboy boots, black cowboy hat, dressed in jeans, a tight black tee shirt cut off at the shoulders, and with a chair held over his head. He kept shouting the rebel war cry.

Capp saw what was happening and jumped out of his chair. He shouted to his friends,

"C'mon, this looks bad."

Carter reached the table and tried to smash the chair on Pervis's head. Pervis ducked, and the chair smashed to pieces on the table.

"I'm going to kill you," shouted Carter at Pervis. "No one dances with my girl!"

Pervis fell down, and Carter grabbed him. Pervis kicked him in the groin.

Carter screamed, and doubled over in pain.

"You little bastard, wait'll I get my hands on you. You're dead."

"C'mon, C'mon," shouted Pervis, as he stood defiant with his fists raised in a boxer's stance, "There's more where that came from."

Carter's friends started to get up from their tables, toward Pervis.

Capp ran over to Redmond,

"Get Pervis the hell out of here. We'll try to block the doorway."

Redmond grabbed Pervis around his waist, hoisted him over his shoulder, and ran toward the door. They reached Redmond's car, threw open the doors, and flung themselves inside. Redmond burned rubber all the way down the road. He hoped no redneck car was behind them.

They reached the bright lights of downtown Pensacola. Everyone relaxed. There were in the clear.

"Did you see what Pervis did to that animal," roared Redmond with laughter. "He kicked him right in the nuts. You're all right. I'll take you with me in a fight anytime."

"Was that great or what," laughed Pervis, "I've never had so much fun, damn, was that exciting. We've got to do that again."

"Not in that bar," laughed Redmond. "That redneck wants your hide. He's really pissed at you. By the way, no one I know of, other than you, has ever danced with his girl. You can put a notch in your gun handle. What a blast. That was one hell of a party."

"You knew that when you sent me over to his girl?" asked Pervis, "That I could have gotten my butt kicked, or worse yet, killed?"

"Hell yes," answered Redmond. "It was Capp's idea. He felt you needed an adrenaline rush to get back to reality. You and him don't like each other, but he doesn't want you to quit. Did you get a rush?"

Pervis couldn't believe it. Capp actually did something for him, and not against him.

"Damn, it was a rush," shouted Pervis. "My legs are still shaking."

Redmond let loose with a rebel war cry. Pervis laughed and joined him. It was a hell of a party.

In all of his life, Pervis never felt so good.

But deep inside, he hated Capp and wasn't going to let this one night, stop his quest for vengeance.

36

Chuck Capp walked out into the bright sunshine, stretched his arms toward the deep blue sky, and shouted to the heavens:

"New day, new airbase, new instructors, new hazards, new challenges-never a dull moment, a journey into the unknown. Can we hack it? Will we die? Will we live? Come on you jolly fellows, our destiny awaits us."

He walked toward the aircraft hangar where the flying action was about to commence.

Capp, Quirt, Munson, Cy Curtin, were among the cadets who milled around the assignment board. Instructors were assigned and listed on the board.

Sampson Field in Florida was the primary airbase for formation flight instruction. Formation flying is how a group of airplanes flies from point A to point B. If a military pilot can't fly airplanes from A to B, in formation, that pilot gets washed out.

As in Warner, there was an award for the top student pilot, and also the top flight.

In the flight training command, Sampson field had the highest wash-out and D.O.R. rate, due to the complexity and pressures of formation flying.

Ground school studies were intense. Procedures for formation flight were taught one step at a time. Many of the wash-outs were cadets who didn't do their homework studies. As was the case at Warner, the pre-flight briefing reviewed each flight's procedures. These were important for a safe, productive flight. Instructors were deadly serious. If a cadet did not appear to be motivated both in his studies and his willingness to accept constructive criticism, he could be a danger to everyone, a candidate for Wash-Out.

Munson and Curtin were standing next to each other, shuffling back and forth trying to overcome the tedium of waiting for their instructors.

"What do you think?" said Munson.

"About what?" answered Curtin.

"About what type of airplane you're going to sign up for in advanced training?" said Munson.

"I've got some ideas, what're you thinking?" questioned Curtin.

"Multi-engine." said Munson. "The more I think about it, the less I like fighters. Landing aboard an aircraft carrier, at night, in the middle of a storm with heavy seas, the less I want that kind of stress."

"I though I'd never say this," answered Curtin. "But I'm leaning the same way. Multi engine aircraft have a team of crewmen working together in one plane completing various tasks together. Instructor pilots I've talked to that flew multi-engine admit it's really rewarding and satisfying to have a crack team in one aircraft. Besides, fighter pilots have to do everything themselves, they're alone in the cockpit. If they get in trouble, there's no one to help.

"Can I tell you something if you never tell anyone else." said Munson.

"Boy Scout's oath." answered Curtin.

"I'm becoming nervous about flying." said Munson. "I'm not frightened, but my confidence isn't there anymore, and that can be dangerous. This occupation doesn't lend itself to carelessness, which makes for a short span of longevity. If a pilot makes a serious mistake, or a fatal error, tragedy is quick and violent. I don't want to take anyone with me. Death isn't an option I want to exercise.

Curtin gulped and stared at Munson.

"Have you read my mind?" said Curtin. "I wasn't about to tell anyone about my feelings, but you've got the guts to let it out for yourself. I've done some serious soul searching, and it's embarrassing to admit, but I'm not sure that this is the life for me either.

"Look at Capp," said Munson. "Damn how I envy him. That son-of-a-gun could care less who's assigned as his instructor. He knows he can hack it. What a lucky turd. He was born with an itch to fly."

"Yeah," answered Curtin, "I bet he gets fighters and carriers, just like he wants, a real fighter jock. Looks like our instructors are here, you take it easy, and be safe."

"You too." said Munson.

"Mr. Capp?" said a tall, skinny instructor.

"Yes Sir." answered Capp along with a salute.

I'm Lieutenant Jay Martin, welcome to Sampson Field." said Martin. "At ease. This will be the most intense flying you'll ever experience, but rewarding if you can cut it. Let's go brief."

This guy's all business, thought Capp. *He flew Panther jets in Korea while in a carrier squadron. His reputation is that of a steady intense instructor, serious, married, a good teacher and strictly by the book. I'll suck up everything he can teach me.*

They walked to the briefing room, found an empty spot at one of the long tables, and opened up their syllabus sheets that covered the procedures for each hop.

"Acrobatics and solo were merely an initiation to what'll go on here." said Martin. "At Warner, you were told to stay away from all other planes. Here, it's just the opposite. We want you close to other planes. It's a transition, but you'll get used to it.'

'As you learned in ground school, our first hops are the two of us, called a Section. We'll practice the procedures and maneuvers necessary to become a formation pilot. We'll also preach safety. Once you've mastered the section maneuvers, four plane or Division flight is next, any questions?"

"No, Sir, answered Capp. "I'm ready to go."

"Great," said Martin. "Let's check out and take off."

Capp lined up on the runway. Martin lined up slightly behind and to the right of him, a section take-off. Capp was impressed.

What a view, a huge yellow airplane just a few feet from me. It's almost scary. Finally, I'm starting to feel like a combat pilot, because this is how they get around. Martin stayed on his wing until they leveled off at six thousand feet.

"I'm going to move away," radioed Martin. "Work your way in behind my right wing, just as we briefed."

"Roger," radioed Capp.

Move in slowly and adjust the power, thought Capp. *Let's not have a mid-air. I was told to brace my forearm on my leg thigh if needed to eliminate the up and down bobbing, especially when tucked in close to the leader. Concentrate on the tip of his wing and line it up with his helmet. Keep it that way and you'll always be in perfect position.*

The student would fly Section beside the instructor, on one side, back at a forty five degree angle. Turns would be made left and right, the wingman staying in the same angle and position. That required power to be reduced or added. Reduced if you were on the inside of the bank, and added if you were on the outside or topside of the bank.

Next, Crossovers would be accomplished by moving from the right side to the left side. Power was reduced, the wingman moved below and behind, then over to the other side of the lead plane. Power was then added to get back into position. It was dangerous if the wingman didn't drop down and behind, as two objects can't be in the same place at the same time.

So far so good, thought Capp. *At least I didn't crash into my instructor.*

Next was Break up and Rendezvous, or how to join up on other aircraft. Capp had studied hard to make sure he understood the angles.

The Rendezvous was accomplished by turning inside of the leader at a 45 degree angle. It was just geometry. If a wingman got on too shallow of an angle, say 10 degrees, the plane would get too far back. Lots of power would have to added to get to the leader. Not efficient. That was called a Sucked position.

Too far ahead, say 60 degrees, an Acute position, and the wingman would close too fast, requiring him to reduce the angle quickly, or chop power with the result that the wingman's plane could end up in a sucked position if too much power was chopped. An acute position could be very dangerous at this stage of the training. Closing fast, and not knowing how, or being too slow in making adjustments could result in a mid-air collision.

And last, but not the least, came the Cruise position, the most complex of the maneuvers, it took the most practice. Sliding from the left side and/or the right side of the leader, without changing power, while the leader banked left and right, and finishing at that 45 degree angle when the leader rolled level, was difficult, it was tricky, moving your aircraft back and forth without changing power. However, pilots did use power if they got too far out of position. It was the first taste of combat maneuvering. When the leader was in a left bank, he wanted to see the student on his left side. If the instructor banked right, he wanted to see the student on his right side.

Formation flying was hard work and most cadets find every muscle in their body sore and aching from the tension and exertion of hauling around a powerful airplane that sometimes had its own mind. Gradually, it became easier, especially the mental part, which had contributed to the tension.

Capp was in great physical shape and took the abuse to his body in stride. He was always excited to get to the next phase. Physically and mentally he had an advantage over many of the other cadets.

Capp's instructor enjoyed flying with him and thought,

A real natural pilot, someday we may be in a fleet squadron together. Better him than some students I've flown with.

What a gas, thought Capp. *Imagine, there are people who'll never experience the exhilaration of having a powerful military plane strapped to their butt, and fly on the edge of danger with real pro's. Damn, this is great!*

Munson was not having such a good week. The maneuvers were O.K., but for some reason he couldn't get close to the lead plane. He didn't have the confidence to be aggressive and tuck it in as close as the instructor wanted. He tried, but when he got close, his hand would start squeezing the flight control stick, and the muscles in his arm would get tense. That resulted in his plane bobbing up and down, not a good feeling. Then he'd have to move out to become steady. A firm, but relaxed grip with small movements was necessary.

Some pilots never overcame the Super-Grip, and wouldn't be candidates for the Blue Angels flight demonstration team. If a student pilot couldn't control his extreme bobbing up and down, he wasn't going to get his wings. Wing mates couldn't fly smoothly next to an aircraft that had huge up and down attitude changes.

Section plane instruction was over. Next were four plane formations, called Divisions. Two, two plane sections, that moved in coordination with each other. It was also called a Finger Four formation, or Thatch's weave developed by a Navy pilot in World War II. It results in the sections protecting each other through independent maneuvering, as a team.

That night at the ACRAC, cadets told their flight stories to anyone who would listen. They all stretched the truth a little to each other, but that was expected. They laughed at each other's latest escapades and dirty jokes. Camaraderie happened. A trust in each other, knowing that their lives depended on each other, the intangible that makes for great morale, and a potent combat force.

"A toast to the hottest division of student pilots known to man," exclaimed Capp. "To 'Cobra Flight', the number one division in the Navy featuring Quirt, Curtin, Munson, and me. Let's hear it for the best-number one."

"Boo," shouted other cadets with laughter. "We're number one."

"O.K.," answered Capp. "We're all number one. Let's hear it for the Navy,"

"Yeahh," came the loud response, "The Navy."

Munson did not raise his glass.

"Hey Munson," laughed Capp. "C'mon. You're part of our team."

"Sorry my friends," answered Munson. "But I've got serious thoughts about quitting, I may D.O.R."

His statement caused a pall on the merry-making. All conversation and beer drinking stopped; the cadets stared at him incredulously. Munson was very popular among his fellow pilots.

"You know," said Munson quietly. "I'm afraid I'm going to die, or kill someone else. I have nightmares of crashing into another plane, and I wake up in a cold sweat."

Everyone was quiet while they mulled over his last words.

"No way," said Capp. "You've had too much to drink. You'll feel better in the morning."

"No," answered Munson, "The dreams won't go away. The beer has nothing to do with it. I'll give it a few more days, but the thought of Division flying really makes me nervous. I had trouble with two plane Section, and with four in the same airspace...I don't know...I just don't know. I haven't made a final decision one way or the other, but the problem is, my confidence is gone, and that could be dangerous to the other planes in the Division. It doesn't seem to make sense to stick around with the horrible possibility that my nightmares might become reality."

Capp, now knowing Munson was serious, lowered his voice, put his hand on Munson's shoulder, and looked him in the eye.

"Look," said Capp. "No one here that thinks you're an incompetent pilot, in fact we all know you're way above average. No one would think any less of you if you decide to D.O.R. In fact it takes more guts to bail out of something you like, but know you shouldn't continue in, than to play mental games and end up getting hurt or worse yet, buying the farm. Try Division, but don't push it. If you're not comfortable, we all understand."

"Thanks," said Munson. "I wasn't sure how you guys would take it." His voice started to tremble, "You're the best damn friends I've ever had."

Pervis was standing nearby. He overheard Munson's confession, and unfortunately decided to walk over and make his presence known.

"Well, well," said Pervis sarcastically. "I knew you were a coward the first day I met you. Real men don't quit. I guess you're not a real man."

Capp jumped up. He grabbed Pervis by the collar, tightly, and choked off his air.

"You miserable little pervert, if you ever say anything about this and

I hear of it, you'll be walking bowlegged with a high voice the rest of your life!"

Capp pushed Pervis away roughly and growled in a guttural voice, "Now get the hell out of here!"

Pervis gasped for breath, backed away, and luckily for him was smart enough not to say more to Munson.

He slinked away, but was overheard to say,

"That son-of-a-bitch Capp, somehow I'm going to hurt him, hurt him bad, and I'm going to enjoy every minute of it."

The following morning, two aircraft were involved in a mid-air collision during their first day of Division plane formation.

The initial news of the accident spread quickly. Capp went out on the hangar deck by the assignment board. The hangar became crowded as everyone wanted to know who was in the flight. Capp saw which flight was involved and who was in it. He didn't know the cadets personally, but knew they lived in the barracks next to his.

All flight operations were suspended while the facts of the accident were relayed to the Operations department. The report came through that two planes had a mid-air collision which resulted in fatalities to two pilots. Within a short period of time, facts of the mid-air were given to the Cadets.

From all reports, during a crossover, the number four plane got too close to the underside of number three. The propeller of number four chewed into the bottom of number three. It acted like a giant corkscrew, locked into the hard metal and screwed forward, ripped open its bottom, and into the soft tissue of the number three's pilots legs and torso, just like a meat grinder.

What a horrible way to die, thought Capp. *Damn, I hope it was fast!*

The number four pilot was crushed against the bottom of the number three *aircraft.*

I can't imagine the last few seconds of his life! thought Capp, *the terrible realization of what he'd done. Terrified, watching his cockpit windshield disintegrate in front of his face...helpless to stop it, as metal crushed his body.*

Munson was in the ready room waiting for his first division hop, when the crash siren went off. He walked over to the coffee cart, poured a cup of hot black coffee and sat down. His hands trembled so badly that he had to drink holding the cup with both hands.

When it became known that two cadets had been killed in the mid-air accident, Munson stared into space, and recalled his nightmares of last night. His stomach twisted into a knot, with waves of nausea that surged up into his chest. He didn't want to regurgitate, and fought the overwhelming gagging feeling in his throat. He looked at a cadet that was sitting nearby, and said in a quivering voice,

"It's time to come to reality."

Munson left the ready room and walked to the Administration building, up the stairs, and into the Operation offices.

"Hello", said the yeoman pleasantly who walked over to the counter where Munson stood. "Can I help you?"

Munson threw back his shoulders, took a deep breath to bolster his pride, and announced,

"I quit!"

"I want to D.O.R."

37

The word of Munson's D.O.R was met by shock and disbelief among the cadets at Sampson Field. The Navy braced themselves for additional D.O.R's from cadets who were also in that thought process, but needed something to push them toward that decision. It was psychological, and expected.

It happened in business's frequently when an employee quit, there usually followed a spate of resignations from other employees who had the same concerns, were job shopping, but needed a someone to light the fuse, to start the exodus.

Tomorrow, after turning in all of his cadet personal property, Munson would be assigned to the enlisted men's barracks after drawing his enlisted uniform, and await his orders, probably to an aircraft carrier in an administrative division which handled paperwork. He had to complete the remaining portion of two years on active duty. Then he'd join the active reserves to complete the remainder of six years according to his NavCad contract.

Capp had decided Munson needed a send-off party, a D.O.R party.

Munson was at the cadet barracks packing his personal belongings.

Capp burst into his room, followed by Quirt and Curtin. He grabbed Munson around the shoulders.

"We can't let you leave this way, without a proper Naval ceremony. We're going to make your greatest desire, your greatest wish come true. What is it?"

"Hey," answered Munson as he sat in a chair. "You don't have to do this, I feel like a traitor."

"Traitor, my burnished butt," said Capp. "You're moving on to another chapter in your life. You haven't done anything wrong, and we want to do something our last few hours together. What do you say? What is it that would be remembered by you when you're the president of some company, drinking martinis in a fancy corporate executive office?"

"Are you guys serious about this?" said Munson.

"Right on," answered Capp. "Put your wallet away. Tonight's your night. Isn't that right?" as he turned to Quirt and Curtin.

They all responded with a cheer,

"Cobra flight lives again."

"Well," said Munson with a leer and a smirk. "It's been rumored that there are many beautiful young ladies in Pensacola, inside *the* luxury hotel, the Palacio, that wish to make the acquaintance of healthy young men. I'm a healthy young man, and it would make my heart proud to do nothing better than to fulfill their wishes. In fact, it would be my patriotic duty to help them out."

"I should have guessed," laughed Capp. "You're the only man I know that walks around in a state of perpetual arousal. What do you think guys, think he can handle it?"

"Probably not," said Quirt. "But after New Orleans, I'll never bet against a horse with a proven track record. What about you Curtin?"

"Why not?" answered Curtin. "The worse that could happen is he'd die of a heart attack, with a smile on his face. Let's do it."

"Your patriotic duty, huh," said Capp. "Well nothing's more cherished than a patriot; you'll probably get a medal. C'mon hero, off to the Palacio. Heaven help those ladies."

They charged down to the parking lot, piled in Capp's car and roared off toward Pensacola for a night of laughter and camaraderie.

As they drove through some small towns and approached the outskirts of Pensacola, Capp had a thought.

"Munson, you need to check out of the USO and get your civvies out of your locker. In fact, that's a good idea. We'll all put on our civvies.

We don't want to be in uniform for the final soirée. What the hotel doesn't know won't hurt them.

"Yeah," answered Munson. "This is going to be tough. It's like saying good-bye to a friend."

"There's a USO in most towns with major military bases," said Quirt. "You can rent a locker there and pretend you're in Pensacola. Don't look back, you're moving on."

They parked next to the USO, went in, dressed in their civilian clothes, canceled Munson's locker and put his clothes in Capp's locker.

"Goodbye old friend," said Munson as he stood on the sidewalk looking at the USO. "You've been a life saver. But now for more important things, I can smell the perfume of those lovely ladies already. Yeahh."

They wheeled away from the curb, down the main boulevard, and toward the Palacio.

"There it is," shouted Munson. "Oh man, my legs are trembling. You really are some great friends."

"That's not your leg trembling," laughed Capp. "I've never been here before; let's hope the rumors are true. Let's hit the bar, and then I'll get a room."

They parked in the lot beside the hotel, walked over to the marble steps and entered the front door into the lobby.

"Wow," exclaimed Munson. "This is really classy, a bit different from good old Navy Splinterville where we live. Look at the marble floors, the chandeliers, the marble pillars; rich people must've built this in the early 1900's. Why do we spend our time at a scroungy bar like the Gulf Breeze, when this is here? I like it."

"The reason," laughed Capp as he tried to hold down Munson's excitement, "is that we get paid a NavCad's salary, not an executive's salary. Some day it'll be affordable, but not until we get our wings along with an Ensign's pay, OOP's, sorry, I mean when you own your own business. Let's hit the bar and get the party going."

"Now this is class," said Quirt as sat a table with large cushioned leather chairs. "The mahogany bar and its artwork on the wood trim is worth a tour, craftsman just don't make things like this anymore."

"Jeez," said Capp. "You guys act as if you're from the sticks and have never been in a nice hotel before."

"I have," said Quirt. "But it's just such a contrast to our present living conditions. You know, every few months we should stop here to get back to reality."

"Fair enough," answered Capp. "But for now what are we drinking? Beer is out, martini's everyone?"

The waitress had stopped beside Capp,

"Good evening, can I get you gentlemen something from the bar." She was brunette, middle aged, pretty, and dressed in a red Spanish blouse and dress.

"Yes," answered Capp. "We'll have dry martini's all around, and you might as well bring two extra for our rotund friend. He needs courage."

"Sounds like a big night," she laughed. "I'll be right back."

"Not bad for an older broad," said Munson. "Wonder if she's free tonight?"

"Forget it," answered Capp. "We've got other plans for you. Besides, she's got a ring on her finger, and her husband is probably a lot bigger and meaner than you are. I'm going to get a room for old 'Lech' and see if I can drum up some business. Don't drink my drink Quirt, O.K.?"

"Jeez," answered Quirt. "Have I ever done that to you before?"

"All the time," said Capp. "It's your trademark. Be right back."

Capp walked over to the main desk, the clerk an older man with a mustache came over and with a smile asked,

"May I help you?"

"Yes please," said Capp. "A single room for the night, my luggage is in the car, I'll bring it in later."

"Sign here," said the clerk. "Room 225 in the rear, that will be sixty five dollars."

Capp paid in cash, filled out the form using Peter Pervis's name, a fictitious address in Tallahassee Florida, and took the room key. He then walked over to the bell captains desk.

"Hi," said Capp to the bell captain, a wrinkle faced, short but wiry looking man about fifty years old. Capp assumed the bell captain, who obviously was in charge, must be experienced in the ways of the world. "I've got an embarrassing business problem, and was hoping you can help me."

"I'll try," answered the bell captain. "The customer is king at the Palacio."

"I'm trying to close a big business deal," said Capp, "and my client has some amorous demands. He wants the services of a young lady. He's lonely, and I would be very appreciative of your help. He's in room 225."

The bell captain looked at Capp and assumed he was for real, not a cop.

How come all these military guys come in here, he thought, *and try to fake a tired old story like that which he's heard a thousand times. He'd make the kid squirm a bit. Their short haircuts give them away every time.*

"I don't know to what you're referring," answered the bell captain. This is the Palacio, and we have a standard to maintain. Perhaps you should try one of the hotels down by the wharf."

Capp's eyes were turning an ice blue; he didn't like to play games.

"The wharf hotels are not up to my standards," said Capp. "This is where my friend needs assistance, and only you have the means to help him."

Capp put his hand on the desktop, and showed the corner of a twenty-dollar bill, just enough so the bell captain saw it.

"Wait here a moment," answered the bell captain as he turned and walked back into a small room behind the desk that held luggage.

Damn, thought Capp. *Maybe the rumors of this place are wrong. I really don't want to spend money on a seedy hotel room by the wharf, especially after I've paid here. What a bummer.*

The bell captain returned in about five minutes.

"You said that room number was 225?" he asked.

"225, that's correct." answered Capp.

"Have your client, your business client, right?" said the bell captain sarcastically to let Capp he knew what was happening, "be in room 225 at Eight O' Clock." He pulled the twenty-dollar bill out from Capp's fingers. "Understand?"

"You bet," answered Capp with a smile. He knew the bell captain didn't believe him. "My client, is very grateful."

Capp walked back to the table where the three were laughing and talking, obviously starting to feel no pain from the effects of the martinis, and sat down.

"Munson, you old fart," laughed Capp as he slid the room key over to Munson. "Do us proud. Do your patriotic duty to the best of your ability. However, with the martini's you've drunk, maybe you won't be able to earn a medal. Room 225, Eight O' Clock, it's seven thirty, better get going."

Munson downed the remainder of his martini.

"Yuck, these are really bad," said Munson with a sour look on his face. "I don't know why anyone drinks them, but they sure do the trick. Don't worry about me, I may not be awarded the Medal of Honor, but I sure as hell can do the Distinguished Flying Cross. You did it, Capp you son-of-a-gun, you did it. Oh, I can picture her now, young, blonde hair, blue eyes, huge globes, legs that start at her shoulders, and very friendly. I'll tell you all about it. You guys are great."

Munson pushed back his chair, leaped to his feet and walked shakily, through the lobby, over to the stairway. He had that lecherous smile that only Munson could create.

Quirt was laughing and slapping his thigh, watching Munson as he weaved through the lobby.

"Look at him, the original dirty old man. He'll probably fall asleep in the saddle. They broke the mold when they made him."

"I hope he finds the room," said Curtin. "He was really tossing down the drinks. He's smashed."

"He'll be all right," answered Capp. "He's on a quest. Thanks guys for doing this. He really felt embarrassed about quitting. This at least, will let him know he's got our support."

Capp lifted his glass to the others.

"Cheers," he said. "May we all be as good as him."

"Cheers", they answered and clinked their glasses together.

Munson stumbled up the carpeted stairs, stuck the key in the lock, turned it and opened the door. The room's décor was in red, a single bed, white fabric drapes over the window, a table with two chairs, standard bathroom with a shower, and a radio.

"This isn't the Presidential Suite," said Munson to himself. "But I'm not here to be Presidential. It's time; she should be here any minute."

He did a little tap dance, fell against the bed, and giggled out loud,

"Boy Oh Boy," he said excitedly. "I can hardly wait. Think I'll pull back the covers so the deck is cleared for action", which he proceeded to do.

A knock sounded on the door. Munson's heart rate sped up as he hurried to the door and opened it.

Munson gasped. There standing before him was an older middle aged, shop worn looking woman with too much makeup on her face, lipstick that made her lips appear to be twice as large as normal, hair that was combed but scraggly, and a blue dress that looked as though it had seen it's best days. She pushed opened the door, stepped into the room, and closed the door behind her.

"Hi," she said in a bored, tired sounding voice. "I'm Veronica. Why don't we sit on the bed?"

Munson backed away.

"What in the hell are you?" he stammered. "Go away and send up your daughter. You're as old as my mother."

"Experience is what counts," she said. "You'll be very satisfied. Now let's go over to the bed."

"Wait a minute, just wait a minute," answered Munson. "What's the cost?"

"For a beautiful woman," she said. "It's fifty dollars."

"Fifty dollars? Fifty dollars!" shouted Munson. "Then what does it cost for an ugly old hag like you?"

"Look buster," she said. "I made an appointment and you owe me fifty dollars whether you want action or not."

"Get lost," answered Munson. "I'm not paying you anything. Get the hell out of here."

Veronica turned and knocked three times on the door. It opened, and in walked the biggest, ugliest, unshaven, man Munson had ever seen, he seemed to fill up half of the room.

"Understand there's a problem here?" he growled. "Pay the lady, now, or I'll tear your bony head off."

Munson was scared and for a second, panicked. He didn't know what to do. He wasn't going to pay anyone fifty dollars, but he also didn't want his head torn off. His pilot training took over,

Control your panic he thought, *control your emotions, and control the situation.*

He knew he had to act fast, do the unexpected.

"Go screw yourself," he screamed.

Munson ran directly at the huge bulk of a man standing in his way, threw a shoulder into him which knocked the enforcer off balance, just enough for him to grab the doorknob, throw open the door and run into the hallway. His heart was pounding. He looked back and saw the monster running after him.

"*Oh crap,* thought Munson, *I'm going to die, got to get outside.*

He ran down the stairs, stumbling and falling, grabbing on to the railing so he could keep going, ran out into the lobby, looked over at the table where the guys were still sitting, waved his arms, and then ran out the front door toward the parking lot.

Capp had just ordered another drink, as he figured Munson would be tied up for awhile. Something caught his eye. He looked up and there was Munson waving his arms, looking terrified, and then he was gone, running toward the front door.

"Something's wrong," said Capp. "Munson just ran through the lobby looking like the face of death. Let's get the hell out of here and find him."

The three of them ran out to the lobby and out the front door. They didn't look up, or they would have seen a fierce, huge, ugly man staring out from the second floor balcony.

"He probably ran to the car," said Capp.

They reached the car, but couldn't see Munson.

"Munson," shouted Capp. "Where are you?"

"Over here, I'm coming." answered Munson, his voice trembling, "Start the car, let's get out of here before that killer finds me, he's really pissed. And he's bigger than all of us together. Cmon, C'mon!"

They all jumped in the car. Capp started it and as they made their way toward the exit, a huge figure dressed in black lunged at the car.

"That's him," shouted Munson in a panic. "Don't let him get us!"

"Jeez," said Capp. "What in the hell is that? A Dinosaur?"

He jerked the wheel to miss the huge figure, stomped on the gas pedal and burned rubber out of the lot. He didn't slow down until they entered the main street.

There was silence as they drove back toward the USO to change clothes.

Capp broke the silence.

"I suppose you're going to tell us you got laid."

The tension was breached, the laughter uncontrollable, the bond of friendship stronger than ever.

38

It was 0800, the day after the fatal accident, and the hangar deck was full of cadets and instructors. Young intense men in khaki flight suits murmured at a low volume, with none of the loud talk or laughter that generally occurs when men of this caliber gather. The fatal accident was the main conversation. A safety meeting was scheduled today to review procedures and clear the air of rumors.

"Attention on Deck!" ordered the Duty Officer.

Everyone stood and came to attention as the Operations Officer arrived.

"At ease," he said, "Please be seated."

Muffled noises of shoes being scuffed and chairs being scraped on the concrete deck could be heard.

"Gentlemen, we have had a tragedy that no one ever wants to have repeated. Lieutenant Parks, our base safety officer will take over the briefing. He will review the facts as we know them."

The Safety Officer reviewed the accident in all its gory details. He then turned the meeting back to the Operations Officer.

"Gentlemen, you joined the Navy flight program to become a Naval Aviator. It is our job to make sure you move forward and accomplish that goal. As you know, flying is unforgiving of errors in judgment and inattention as this accident so grossly demonstrates. We expect all of you to raise your standards. A repeat of this type accident will not, I repeat, will not occur because of recognizable mediocre flying. I expect all of you who want those Gold Wings will be wearing them in the near future. Be careful, be brave, but most of all, be professional. Now go fly. Dismissed."

Flight operations commenced. As was usual after a fatal accident, the instructors were told to raise the standards, which would probably result in a few more washouts than normal, not many, but the effect was that students raised their flying up a notch, and were more aware of proper procedures.

The day was bright and sunny. Temperatures were cool in the morning, hot and uncomfortable in the afternoon. One benefit of early morning flights was that airplanes performed better in cool temperatures, the air was denser. But no one complained of afternoon flights, it was better than sitting around the ready room with no flight.

Capp, Quirt, and Curtin flew together. They were a proud bunch of friends, which made them a tightly knit team. They were, Cobra Flight. The fourth cadet who replaced Munson was Bill Alexander, a Physical Education graduate of the University of Arkansas. He was intense, and would fit right into Cobra flight.

The student flight of four and the instructor were doing formation maneuvers at six thousand feet. The instructor was on the mike more than usual.

"Come on Curtin," he radioed, "Get in there, you're not close enough. How're you going to get into the Blue's with flying like that?"

Curtin was tense. He could not shake off the accident. It stuck in his mind. All pilots talked to themselves while flying. He shouted into the noisy cockpit, "How close do you want me to get? Any closer and I'll have a mid-air."

Even Capp noticed that Curtin's old aggressiveness was not there. He felt that Curtin would hang in there and get over what was bothering him.

For Curtin, it was the longest, most difficult hop he ever had. At the end of the hop, he landed the SNJ in a full-stall maneuver that made the tail wheel contact the runway first, the main gear then quickly thumped next, with a solid sound. It was preparation for landing on an aircraft carrier. Curtin breathed a sigh of relief and was very glad to hear those thumps as the tires made contact with the runway. It meant he was home alive.

The debriefing in the ready room was always a casual setting, as the pilots were tired and sweaty from horsing an airplane around the skies for over an hour. Hot coffee was poured, cigarettes lit, and Cobra flight sat down to hear what the instructor had to say about each of them.

Jay Martin started,

"Well fellows, we weren't too sharp today. By any chance did you try to run the Gulf Breeze out of beer last night? Never mind where you were, your eyes tell it all. Leave your partying for the weekend. You'll live longer. Let's hope this afternoon's performance will be better."

Curtin listened to Martin. He waited until there was a break in the debriefing and said,

"Sir, I really don't want to fly this afternoon. I don't want to fly at all. It just isn't working. I think I'm a detriment to Cobra flight, and probably a hazard to all of you. That accident really shook me up, and I can't shake if off, this isn't how I want to spend the next few years, worrying about dying, or worse yet, to cause someone else to die. I love the thrill of flying, and the great camaraderie, but it's time to bail out. Plan the afternoon flight without me."

It took a moment for the shock of Curtin's words to sink in. No one knew he'd felt that way.

"Are you sure?" Martin replied, "Do you want to take a few days off to think about it? That accident has shook up a lot of people, but think about it, fatal accidents are rare."

"Thanks for your concern and the gentleman-like way you have treated me," said Curtin, "But that's it. It's final. I'll finish out two years as a sailor on a carrier or a destroyer. At least I'll be able to sleep at night. Thanks again. Now, I should be on my way to the administration building."

Capp, still in shock and not sure what to say, broke his silence. "You're a hell of a friend, and a great pilot. I'll fly with you any day. Evidently you've thought about this. It's a tough decision and I respect that. Cy, I wish you all the best, wherever life takes you."

Capp and Quirt shook Curtin's hand, bear hugged him, eyes wet with tears, and said goodbye. There's just that something that happens in the military, when men share each other's pain, experiences, and the occasional loss of life. It creates a bond. It cements them together, a little more each day, and that stays with them for the remainder of their lives.

After Curtin had left, Jay Martin said,

"Well, this has been a tough week, first Munson and now Curtin. Cobra flight is short one plane for the division. I'll stop by Operations to see if there's a cadet that's looking around for the best flight at this airfield. See all of you at 1400."

Capp and Quirt looked at each other and Capp said, "First Munson and now Curtin. We're down to a team of two. Don't you D.O.R, Quirt. I don't want to be the Lone Ranger. Curtin and Munson left a big hole in Cobra flight. We were just starting to feel like a real tight team. Let's hope our new flyboy will be a tiger."

Quirt sighed,

"I've heard the D.O.R. and wash-out rate in the program runs about forty percent. Whatever it is, we've help set the average. The four of us had some great times, what a crock."

At 1330, Capp and Quirt were in the briefing room. Jay Martin walked up to them and said,

"Gentleman, meet your fourth Cobra flight member. I assume you know each other, but if you don't, let me introduce cadet Peter Pervis."

Capp's jaw dropped. There standing in front of him, was in his mind, that miserable excuse for a human being. Pervis was wearing that strange, demented, crooked smile of his. He looked like a cat that had just swallowed a bird.

Capp spoke; his tone was obligatory, expressionless. "Welcome to Cobra flight," and he muttered under his breath, "If you can hack it."

"Thanks for the warm welcome," sneered Pervis. "Now you'll find out who's really number one."

"How the hell did you catch up to me and Quirt?" asked Capp. "You were two hops behind us when we finished at Warner Field."

"I took my solo and acrobatic re-check ride on the same day," answered Pervis, "And guess what, I aced the hop." He sneered, "My slow rolls were perfect.'

'Then I got a break in the weather. I was one of the few morning hops to get airborne, the rest of the days hops were cancelled due to bad weather. That's all it took to catch up to you two jerk-offs. Besides, now I get to fly with the great Capp. Remember me?" he hissed. "The real number one pilot at Warner, and currently tied with you at this field, I plan to be number one here, regardless of what it takes."

"You always say that," said Capp, "But you never come through. You'll never be number one, at anything."

"You'll see," answered Pervis with a sneer. "All good things come to those who wait."

"We only fly 4.0 hops in Cobra flight," said Capp, "Get used to it or transfer out."

"You'll see," said Pervis. "I'm better than you or Quirt."

"Bullcrap," answered Capp. "Just don't foul us up."

Jay Martin noted the animosity, but shrugged it off. "Gentleman, I know you're all competitive, and want to be the best at Sampson. I feel fortunate to have probably the best cadet pilots on the base in my division. I'll expect the best out of each one of you because of your talent. It should be a great experience for all of us."

As Capp found out later, in Pervis's division, two cadets quit, and the other one washed out. He was assigned to the next open flight, which was Cobra.

Quirt pulled Capp over to the side of the briefing room.

"Watch that little psycho, he's up to something. He makes my skin crawl."

"Maybe he needs another visit from our friendly snake," laughed Capp. "I heard it did a world of good for his attitude at Warner."

"I'm serious," said Quirt. "I've never seen him so strange."

"Thanks," answered Capp. "You've got a sixth sense which I appreciate. I'll watch him, carefully."

The flight briefed and took off into the rarified air above the lush beautiful Florida countryside. Maneuvers were performed as briefed.

Pervis impressed Jay Martin and felt Cobra flight had never looked so good.

Capp was assigned as Pervis's wingman, since Martin knew that Capp could hold the flight together in the number-four spot. Number four spot was always the most demanding. Martin had not flown before with Pervis, and that was a correct decision.

Capp was on Pervis's wing. He thought. *I have to admit he's pretty good. He's smooth, hangs on to the angles and stays in the proper position. Why's he such a strange person on the ground? What a waste.*

After the flight landed, Capp and Quirt went over to the ACRAC to see if by any chance Curtin was there. They had earlier checked his room and he was nowhere to be found. They hoped he had not checked out and left the base. Curtin was there drinking a soft drink. They grabbed a table and made a vow to stick to non alcoholic beverages after last night's over-indulgence, at least until the next time they needed a new perspective. If they had known about the phone call taking place, they may have left.

39

After the flight landed, Pervis ate chow and decided to go the ACRAC. He didn't want to talk to the other pilots, just to stay by himself. After a few drinks, he thought,

I haven't heard from Sue Ann Crawford. I'd better call to find out when the marriage date is. I want Capp out of this Navy.

He walked over to the public phone booth in the corner, put in a dime and listened as the coin jingled down the inside and came to a stop. It rang and then a soft girl's voice answered, "Hello."

"Hi Sue Ann, this is Pete Pervis. How are you?"

"Just fine" she answered brightly. "Nice to talk to you, I was going to call you earlier, but knew you were busy flying and didn't want to bother you. You've been so great in helping me during my crisis."

"Oh, that's O.K.," said Pervis. "Just wondering how you were feeling, and if you and Capp have set the wedding date yet?"

"Oh Pete," answered Sue Ann. "That's the beautiful part, there is no date, and we don't need one."

"No date?" Pervis stammered. "What are you talking about?"

"I had a miscarriage," answered Sue Ann. "I'm no longer pregnant. I don't have to marry Capp, and you don't have to worry about me anymore, isn't that terrific. I've been given a new lease on life, and believe me, no more baby making except with a husband. And I want to thank you for giving me some peace of mind. That was really helpful."

"Have you told Capp?" asked Pervis, as his voice cracked up.

"Why, yes." answered Sue Ann. "Why wouldn't I? He's not the father. I told him right away. Even though he agreed to marry me, under protest of course, I knew it caused him a great deal of stress. In fact, I was going to let him out of our agreement anyway, it wasn't fair to him. He's so nice."

The alcohol, the stress of flying, the weariness in his mind and body, and disappointment overwhelmed Pervis.

"You had it made!" shouted Pervis at the phone receiver in his hand. He pounded his fist on the side of booth. "I had it made. You screwed it all up by telling him. You could've had a husband, and Capp would've been out of my hair. Why didn't you call me first? Capp didn't have to know. It was perfect. I had my chance to get rid of Capp, and you screwed it all up."

"What are you talking about?" gasped Sue Ann. "I thought you were his friend? I thought what you suggested, was for me. You sound as though you don't care about me, or Chuck?"

"Are you naïve, or what?" shouted Pervis. "You let some smooth talker get you pregnant, when all you would've had to do was say 'No'. Then you listen to me with a far-fetched plan, and all you had to do was keep your end of the bargain. All you had to do is marry Capp, whether you were pregnant or not. You let me down."

"Chuck mentioned there was some cadet out to get him," cried Sue Ann in a trembling voice, tears running down her cheeks. "It's you, isn't it? You're despicable. Oh my God, what have I done? What did I almost do?"

"Oh, don't get so pious with me," sneered Pervis. "You thought it was a great idea. The only difference between you and me is, I admit I had an ulterior motive. Now that you're no longer pregnant, you can go through your feel-good self deception that you would've let Capp off. What a bunch of crap. I know better. I saw the look in your eyes. Capp was trapped, and you knew it. It was a perfect plan, for both of us, with or without a baby."

Pervis slammed the phone receiver down, back into its cradle.

Sue Ann, with tears in her eyes, stared at the phone receiver in her hand. She couldn't believe what she had just heard. She cried out loud,

"Oh, what a fool I've been. How could I have been so naïve? Never again, no man will ever again touch me until our wedding night, if I ever get married."

She was so exhausted that she lay down on her bed; her body and throat were in convulsions from her moans and tears.

"Well at least I know," Pervis mumbled to himself as he stormed back to the bar. "It's time for plan B; I've got to get rid of Capp by myself."

After a few hours of laughter, shared memories, and a promise to keep in touch with other, Capp, Quirt and Curtin heard a loud, slurred voice, shouting, "Capp. Where are you?"

It was Pervis, and it was obvious he'd had too much to drink.

"There you are," Pervis stammered, "You arrogant pretty boy. You have everyone faked out that you're the best cadet pilot. Well we finally are in the same flight, and I'm going to show you a thing or two."

Capp stood up and said, "Look, I don't have any gripe with you. Cool down and let's not have any trouble. Actually, I have to admit, you're a pretty good pilot. Not as good as me, but you're right in there. There is no best pilot. Everyone has strengths and weaknesses. Just try to be the best you can with what you have."

Pervis was having none of that. He wanted to fight. "Come on Capp, you chicken. I can beat you in the air, and on the ground." He lunged at Capp.

Several of the other cadets saw what was going on and they grabbed Pervis before any blows landed. They got him away from Capp, but Pervis was still yelling and writhing in the cadets' grip on his body as they moved him far away.

"I'll get you if it's the last thing I do, watch your six Capp!"

"Let's get out of here," said Quirt, "No sense giving him a second shot at you."

Capp was never one to duck a fight, but this time, he knew Quirt was right.

"Be careful Chuck," Quirt said as they walked back to the barracks, "That guy is crazy. He wants to hurt you, and I'm afraid something bad is going to happen between you and him."

They walked in silence back to the barracks, each submerged in their own thoughts.

40

"Cobra Flight, man your planes!"

Pilots love to hear those words, thought Capp. *It sends chills of excitement up and down the spine. Today's the day, the final flight in formation flying. Get through this and the next stop is Bremer Field, bombing and gunnery. What a life.*

Jay Martin their instructor was already airborne on his way to the rendezvous point. His call sign while in formation practice, regardless of the side number of his plane, was Cobra Lead. The flight consisted of the instructor and four cadet students. The student's call signs were, Cobra One through Four.

Martin didn't know of the vicious confrontation Pervis had with Capp at the ACRAC. NavCads who were at the ACRAC viewed the tantrums against Capp as the rants of a jealous competitor. They should have paid more attention. The rant was a showdown threat by Pervis,

"Capp had better watch his Six."

The "Six" is the rear of an airplane, and is the kill zone when in a dogfight.

It was a cloudy, sultry day, temperature in the 90's. Thunderstorm cells were building in the flight areas, something to be watched, but for now, not enough to stop flight operations. Visibility was eight miles, good for formation flying. Thunderstorms and rain had cancelled some flight operations the past week. Cadets were behind in their flight schedules. All planes were in the air to catch up. Everyone was briefed to be especially alert.

An ominous apparition of foreboding was also in the air. The Angel of Death spread her wings, and swooped above the Pensacola countryside.

Cobra Lead circled the Adams Farm at 5,000 feet. He waited for his flock to rendezvous. The farm was one of many rendezvous points, easy to find on a day like today.

Capp saw Cobra Lead circling and set his plane inside the instructor's circle, to rendezvous. There were two other planes in the flight ahead of him, which had already joined up. Capp adjusted his throttle, stayed in the cone, and slid to the outside of Cobra Two's right wing. The fourth and last plane of Cobra flight arrived. Everyone was on board.

Capp recognized the fourth plane as Pervis and thought, *that was unusual.* Normally Pervis was early and in the number one student spot so he could be the first leader in the student's formation. *Odd,* thought Capp, but threw the thought aside. He had to concentrate on flying.

All four were on the right, on a line of forty-five degrees to the right rear of the lead aircraft, a right echelon. The instructor flew near the students and was constantly changing position to see how the flight was progressing. However, during rendezvous practice, the instructor was the first plane. He could then watch the angles as each student joined up on him.

Cobra flight was in position. Cobra Lead radioed,

"Commence Break up and Rendezvous. Let's not overshoot and waste time."

Cobra Lead gave the break up and rendezvous signal, a circular motion of his hand over his head, with the right forefinger extended. The flight passed it down the line, to the following plane.

Cobra Lead broke to the left. After five seconds, each following plane broke left to get inside of the leader. Cobra two was in front of Capp. Capp was Cobra three the section leader, and Pervis Cobra four. Cobra one and two closed slowly on the leader, joined and crossed over to the right side of Cobra Lead.

Capp kept on the same radial, joined, and crossed over to the right side of Cobra Two.

Capp looked to his left and saw that Pervis was joining at too sharp of an angle. He was coming in acute, fast, into the same airspace as Capp.

Damn, thought Capp. *What's he doing? If he doesn't pull off power, he's going to hit me!*

At the very last second, Pervis pulled off power, and crossed behind and out to the right of Capp. Instead of crossing out laterally, and work his way back in, he pulled up high, and went into a sharp ninety degree left bank, his plane filled the sky. Capp saw Pervis, above and to the right of him, coming down toward him, fast.

Pervis laughed.

"Put fear into Capp, thought Pervis. *It may screw him up for the rest of the flight, and he'll get a Down. I'll fly right up his butt. That'll shake him up.*

He slid in much too close to the rear of Capp's plane.

"Cobra four," radioed Cobra Lead. "Get control of your plane. That join-up was terrible!"

"Roger." radioed Pervis.

Screw him, thought Pervis. *It's my plane and I'll do what I want.*

I've never seen Pervis so bad, thought Capp. *What's his problem?*

Cobra flight went through the basic formation changes needed to show the proficiency of each pilot.

The final formation consisted of, two-two plane sections. Capp's section with Pervis was on the right side of the Cobra One and Two. His section was to crossover to the left side, and end up as a finger four division, on Cobra One's left side.

Now's the time to put some more fear into Capp, thought Pervis.

Cobra One gave the section crossover hand signal, a vertical pumping of his right fist.

Capp repeated the motion and moved his head backward twice, the signal to Cobra Four to reduce power and slow down. That gave separation between his section and the leader's section. He reduced power and banked slightly to move left, behind Cobra One and Two.

Pervis moved in too close on Capp's right side, and far enough forward so Capp could see him.

I'll keep moving into Capp while we're behind the instructor so we can't be seen, thought Pervis. *Capp will panic and blow the crossover, which Martin will see.*

Martin however had moved out to the right to view the crossover, and was out of Pervis's vision.

Out of the corner of his eye, Capp saw Pervis closing. He looked to his right and saw that crooked sneer on Pervis's face.

That psycho, thought Capp. *He's trying to scare me. Well screw him; I'm not going to move out of his way. That way he'll have to stop.*

Pervis saw that Capp was not moving. That enraged Pervis.

I'll ram that bastard, he thought. *I'll say it was his fault because he stopped his turn. This is war!*

He's closing too fast, thought Capp. *He's going to ram me if I don't get out of the way. What's the matter with him? Has he gone crazy? I've got to move out of here or we'll have a mid-air!*

"Cobra Lead, Cobra three." radioed Capp. "Cobra four is trying to ram me. I'm breaking formation."

Capp pulled the throttle back to idle, rolled inverted, pulled back hard on the stick and commenced a Split-S.

I'll rejoin the flight after I pull up and have shook Pervis off my tail. Capp's speed built up fast.

Don't hit the ground, thought Capp. *Need some more G's. Pull back harder on the stick. Don't go into a high-speed stall, and spin. Easy, easy, I'm at Redline max speed. Don't want the tail to come off. Get the nose up.*

The nose of the SNJ passed up through the horizon, and Capp roared up, back toward the formation.

What in the hell, thought Capp almost in shock. *That crazy nutcase is right behind me. I can see him in my rear view cockpit mirror. What's he doing?*

Pervis had followed Capp down through the Split-S.

He's scared, thought Pervis gleefully. *And I'm going to keep it up. I've got to get closer. Add some power.*

Capp saw Pervis close in on his right rear side.

I'll try a barrel roll, thought Capp almost in a panic. *Maybe I can shake him. He's crazy.*

And then all hell broke loose, beyond the reflexes of even the best pilot. Pervis's propeller smashed into the right elevator of Capp's aircraft. There was an enormous crunching sound as the propeller ground into the metal. Parts flew off of Capp's plane. The nose of Capp's plane pitched down violently and started into a spin, a type of spin he had never experienced.

Cobra Lead saw the mid-air collision. He screamed into the airwaves, "Cobra Three, Cobra Four, bail out, bail out!"

Capp was in a confused mess. Dirt was flying all over the cockpit. G-forces were holding his hands down, and then up. The ground and sky alternated in his view as the plane spun.

Got to get the canopy open or I'll die! thought Capp.

Capp used all of his strength to pull open the canopy. He pushed himself out the left side of the cockpit, aimed his body at the rear of the wing, and hoped he wouldn't hit the tail section. The windblast took his breath away. Strangely, everything seemed in slow motion.

Capp was free of the plane. He panicked when he could not find the rip-cord but got control of his senses and found it floating free. He pulled it, and the silk canopy blossomed above him. Capp was surprised at the force of the shock of his parachute opening, it hurt his thighs. He needed to get his brain and body working, for he was dizzy and needed to get his bearings.

Capp watched two yellow planes, as they spun toward the ground. The engine on one of them was missing, it spun tail down. Both planes impacted the ground in a ball of flame.

Capp looked around and could not see another chute.

Jeez, he thought, *what a friggin mess.*

The ground came up fast. He hit hard. It felt as if he had broken every bone in his body. He lie there for a few minutes, and then realized he had to release his parachute, or be dragged to death. With his remaining strength, he struggled to unhook the clips. His hands were getting weak, but with one last effort, the clips released. His body felt like a thousand pounds. He was totally exhausted.

Back at Warner field, the ready-alert pilot heard the Mayday from Cobra Lead. The Alert plane was always warmed up, and the alert pilot was at the hangar.

When the crash siren went off, all planes on the ground stopped.

Planes in the air hearing the Mayday, and the towers transmission, flew away from the area of Warner.

The Alert pilot was already in the cockpit with the engine running. The ambulance with siren blaring screeched to a stop beside the ready alert plane. The flight surgeon leaped into the rear cockpit. He was barely on board as the plane roared for takeoff, straight ahead across the field, without regard for a runway. Time was of the essence to save a life. It was an inspiring sight to see. The medivac chopper was already in the air. Another ambulance roared out of the main gate toward the crash area, in the event the ready plane or chopper could not land due to rough terrain.

Cobra Lead made low passes over Capp. Martin was relieved when Capp stood up, and waved his arms to signal he was alive. Martin waggled his wings to show he understood. He remained on station until the ready-alert plane arrived. It couldn't land due to the rough terrain, but guided the ambulance to the scene.

The Medivac chopper went to the sites of where the airplanes had crashed. It also carried a flight surgeon.

Capp was placed in the ambulance. Luckily he was not seriously injured, and was able to sit up on a cot. The ambulance bounced over ruts and bumps on a back road to the airfield. The siren blared. He tried to relive what just had happened. It was mind-boggling.

Capp asked the flight surgeon, Lt. Walsh,

"Doc, have you heard anything about the other pilot?"

"I can't say," said Walsh, "until the official announcement is made."

"Don't give me that crap." shouted Capp angrily. "You've got a radio. I'm part of this mess. Call someone!"

Walsh dropped his eyes from Capp's gaze, and then looked back up.

"I know the pain you're in, and I don't want to cause you anymore stress. You've been through a lot."

"Dammit, tell me," said Capp. "I've got to know."

The flight surgeon hesitated, and then said.

"The other pilot is dead. The Medivac chopper found his body in the planes wreckage."

Capp felt all of his remaining strength leave his body. He collapsed onto the cot. Tears came to his eyes.

"You O.K.?" asked Walsh.

"Yeah." answered Capp, "Thanks, I had to know."

He lie back onto the cot, his forearm over his eyes.

"Doc," said Capp quietly. "Ever kill anyone?"

"Nope," answered Walsh. "Why do you ask?"

"The other pilot, Pete Pervis," said Capp. "We had problems with each other. I think he rammed my plane because he hated me. I think I caused his hate. I killed him."

"Hate is a very complicated emotion," answered Walsh. "If that's indeed what drove him to cause a fatal mid-air collision, then there was more to his hate than just you. He's the one that had to control himself, not you. He could've backed off. You didn't kill him. You're not responsible. Now get some rest."

Capp relaxed; his breathing became deep and steady. Images of Pervis floated behind his closed eyelids, the sneer, the face, the voice, and then the images disappeared-into the darkness of his subconscious.

41

That evening, Capp sat in the ACRAC, surrounded by his friends and fellow cadets. The mood was somber.

"Should I have seen this coming?" asked Capp, his voice cracking and tears in his eyes. Could I have prevented this? Was I the cause? Should I quit flying? Damn, I don't know what to think."

"Don't hold yourself responsible for this." answered Quirt. "There was something terribly wrong with Pervis, something that was there from his childhood. We're all competitive. We all harass each other and try to be the best. That's our nature, or we shouldn't be here. But we don't try to kill our flight-mates if they're better than us; we kill the enemies of our country. Pervis in his sick mind got that mixed up. You're not the enemy."

Quirt continued, "Capp I know you understand, death is part of military flight operations. If a pilot doesn't realize, or can't accept that, then to quit is the best option. That'll be your decision. I hope you don't, but it's dangerous to you, and also your fellow pilots if you've lost your confidence. Don't make a rash, quick decision, you're probably still in shock."

"Hang in there Chuck," said many of the cadets. "It's not your fault."

"Thanks guys, for your support," answered Capp. "I don't understand why this happened, and hope none of you ever have to go through this.

I'm scheduled to fly first thing in the morning; the flight surgeon gave me an Up. Operations want a pilot back in the air right away. That's their morbid way to harden a pilot against death and disaster. You all should know, I still want those Gold Wings. See you tomorrow. I'm going to my room, relax, and get my head back together."

Capp left and went to the barracks. He wrote a touching letter of condolence to the parents of Pete Pervis. They should know that their son was an outstanding pilot, and to lose a son in the prime of his life was a terrible ordeal, something no parent should ever have to experience. He hoped his letter would help.

Capp set the alarm clock for 0600. His final flight at Sampson would be a formality to get him back in the saddle again, and to not dwell on his accident. He was being trained to be aware of death, but not let it cloud the professionalism needed to set a goal and complete it to the best of his ability, regardless of the obstacles. Combat and death often travel hand in hand, and the sword of dedication in Capp was being forged to fine, strong steel.

He turned out the lights, fell asleep, and dreamed of Bremer Field, bombing and gunnery.

Tomorrow, a new day would dawn.

Glossary
Check My Six

ACRAC:	Aviation Cadets Recreation Activity Club.
AFT:	Rear.
ANGELS:	Altitude in thousands of feet.
BUY THE FARM:	Die. To be killed.
DECK:	Floor.
DEMERIT:	Mark against a Navcad for breaking a rule.
Division:	Four aircraft consisting of two sections.
D.O.R.:	Drop on request. Quit.
DOWN:	Not a passing grade. Flunk.
DUTY OFFICER:	Officer that represents Commanding Officer.
FORE:	Front.
GROUND LOOP:	Uncontrolled circling ground maneuver.
HEAD:	Bathroom.
LADDER:	Stairway.
LANDING GEAR:	Main wheels on the SNJ.
OINC:	Officer in Charge.
M.P.:	Military Police.
NAVCAD:	Naval aviation cadet.
PASSAGEWAY:	Hallway.
PORT:	Left side.
SCUTTLEBUTT:	Rumor.

SECTION:	Two aircraft. A leader and his wingman.
SNJ:	Two seat training airplane.
STARBOARD:	Right side.
THROTTLE:	Lever the pilot moves to add or reduce power to the airplanes engine.
UP:	A passing grade.
WASHED OUT:	Terminated from the flight program.

Printed in the United States
52246LVS00004B/324